PENGUIN BOOKS

THE DRUNKEN FOREST

Gerald Durrell was born in Jamshedpur, India, in 1925. In 1928 his family returned to England and in 1933 they went to live on the Continent. Eventually they settled on the island of Corfu, where they lived until 1939. During this time he made a special study of zoology, and kept a large number of the local wild animals as pets. In 1945 he joined the staff of Whipsnade Park as a student keeper. In 1947 he financed, organized and led his first animal-collecting expedition to the Cameroons. Since then he has made expeditions to many other countries including Guyana, Paraguay, Sierra Leone and Argentina and more recently to Mexico and Madagascar. In 1963 he and his wife went to New Zealand, Australia and Malaya to film a TV series, *Two in the Bush*, in conjunction with the B.B.C. Natural History Film Unit. In 1958 he founded the Jersey Zoological Park, of which he is the director, and in 1964 he founded the Jersey Wildlife Preservation Trust. Gerald Durrell's other books include *A Zoo in my Luggage*, *The Whispering Land*, *Three Singles to Adventure*, *Menagerie Manor*, *The Bafut Beagles* and *My Family and Other Animals* (all published in Penguins). He is the author of *Catch Me a Colobus* (1972), *Beasts in My Belfry* (1973), *The Talking Parcel* (1974), *The Stationary Ark* (1976), *Golden Bats and Pink Pigeons* (1977), *The Mockery Bird* (1981), *The Amateur Naturalist* (1982), *How to Shoot an Amateur Naturalist* (1984) (with Lee Durrell) and *Durrell in Russia* (1986).

Gerald Durrell

THE DRUNKEN FOREST

WITH ILLUSTRATIONS BY
Ralph Thompson

PENGUIN BOOKS

PENGUIN BOOKS

Published by the Penguin Group
27 Wrights Lane, London W8 5TZ, England
Viking Penguin Inc., 40 West 23rd Street, New York, New York 10010, USA
Penguin Books Australia Ltd, Ringwood, Victoria, Australia
Penguin Books Canada Ltd, 2801 John Street, Markham, Ontario, Canada L3R 1B4
Penguin Books (NZ) Ltd, 182–190 Wairau Road, Auckland 10, New Zealand

Penguin Books Ltd, Registered Offices: Harmondsworth, Middlesex, England

First published by Rupert Hart-Davis 1956
Published in Penguin Books 1958
23 25 27 29 30 28 26 24

Made and printed in Great Britain by
Richard Clay Ltd, Bungay, Suffolk
Set in Monotype Times

CONTENTS

For my wife
JACQUIE
*in memory of Prairie Pigs
and other Bichos*

EXPLANATION

THIS IS an account of a six months' trip that my wife and I made to South America in 1954. Our plan was to make a collection of the strange animals and birds found in this part of the world and bring them back alive for zoos in this country. From our point of view the trip was a failure, for, owing to a number of unforeseen circumstances, all our plans were upset. Our trip was to be divided into two parts. First, we were to make our way down to the southernmost tip of the Continent, Tierra del Fuego, to collect ducks and geese for the Severn Wildfowl Trust. On arrival in Buenos Aires we found that it was the holiday season, and all the planes flying south to the Argentine lakes and thence to Tierra del Fuego were booked for months in advance. Shipping was equally difficult. It was impossible for us to reach our destination in time to capture the nestlings, as we had hoped to do, so very reluctantly we called that part of the trip off. Our second plan was to go to Paraguay, spend some weeks collecting there, and then work our way back to Buenos Aires in easy stages by the Parana and Paraguay Rivers. This plan was also thwarted, though in this case the reasons were political. So we returned from South America with only a handful of specimens in place of the large collection we had hoped for. However, even a failure has its lighter side, and this I have tried to portray in this book.

The failure of our trip was in no way due to lack of sympathy or support from people both here and in Argentina, and we owe a very great debt of gratitude to a vast number of individuals. Our thanks will be found in the acknowledgements at the end of the book.

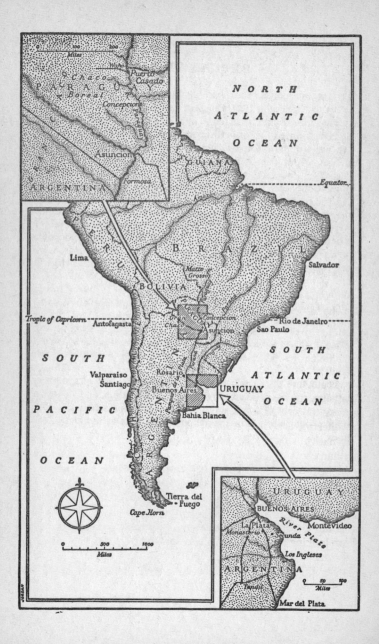

SALUDOS

As the ship nosed its way into port we leant on the rail and gazed at the panorama of Buenos Aires gradually curving around us. The sky-scrapers reared up under a vivid blue sky like multi-coloured stalagmites, their surfaces pitted with a million flashing windows. We were still staring raptly when the ship had tied up alongside the tree-lined docks, and the enormous buildings loomed over us, sending their shivering, Venetian-blind reflections across the rippling black water. Our meditations on modern architecture were interrupted by a man who looked so extra-ordinarily like Adolphe Menjou that for a moment I wondered if we had come to the right end of the American continent. Picking his way disdainfully through the gesticulating, yelling, garlic-breathing mob of immigrants that thronged the deck, he arrived in front of us, calm, unhurried, and looking so immaculate that one could hardly believe the temperature was ninety in the shade.

'I am Gibbs from the Embassy,' he announced, smiling. 'I've been looking all over First Class for you; no one told me you were travelling down here.'

'We didn't know we'd be travelling down here until we

9

got on board,' I explained, 'but by then it was too late.'

'It must have been a rather . . . er . . . unusual voyage for you,' said Mr Gibbs, glaring at a large Spanish peasant who had expectorated with enthusiasm within an inch of his foot, 'and rather on the moist side, I should have thought.'

I began to like Mr Gibbs tremendously.

'This is nothing,' I said airily; 'you should have been here when the weather was rough; it was positively damp then.'

Mr Gibbs shuddered delicately.

'I should imagine you will be rather glad to get ashore,' he said. 'Everything's in order, and we should have you through the Customs in next to no time.'

My liking for Mr Gibbs was reinforced with considerable respect when he sauntered carelessly into the Customs shed, smiling and exchanging a word or two here and there with the officials, suave and unruffled. From his pockets he produced gigantic forms covered in a rash of red seals that whisked our eccentric luggage through the shed and out the other side into a brace of taxis within ten minutes. Then we were whirled through streets that appeared to be as broad as the Amazon, lined with sky-scrapers, trees, and beautifully laid out parks. Within an hour of our arrival we were installed, six floors up, in a lovely flat overlooking the harbour. Mr Gibbs had drifted off to the Embassy, presumably to perform a few more miracles before lunch, and we were left to recover from our voyage. After half an hour's training in the intricate art of using the Argentine telephone, we spent a merry hour ringing up all the people we had introductions to and telling them that we had arrived. There were quite a number of these, for my brother had spent some time in Argentina and, displaying a rather cold-blooded indifference to the fate of his friends, had supplied me with their names and addresses. A few days before we had left England a postcard had arrived from him on which was scribbled the cryptic message: 'In B.A. don't forget to contact Bebita Ferreyra, Calle Posadas 1503, our best friend in Argentina. She is a sweetie.' I frequently receive this sort of information from my brother. So, acting on instructions, we phoned Bebita Ferreyra. When she came on the line my first impression was that she had a voice like the coo of a wood-pigeon. Then I decided it was something much more attractive than this: it was the coo of a wood-pigeon with a sense of humour.

'Mrs Ferreyra? My name is Gerald Durrell.'

'Ah, you are Larry's b-b-brother? B-b-ut where are you? Twice I phoned the Customs to find if you had arrived. Can you come to lunch?'

'We'd love to ... Can we get to your place by taxi?'

'But naturally. Come about one. Good-bye.'

'She sounds an extraordinary sort of woman,' I said to Jacquie as I put down the phone. I had no idea then that I was making the understatement of the century.

At one o'clock we were ushered into a large flat in a quiet street. On the tables were strewn a multitude of books on a variety of subjects – painting, music, ballet – and among them novels and magazines in three languages. The piano was similarly decorated with music ranging from opera to Chopin, and the radiogram was surrounded by records which included Beethoven, Nat King Cole, Sibelius, and Spike Jones. Even Sherlock Holmes, I felt, would have been unable to make a lightning diagnosis of character from these clues. On one wall hung a portrait of an exceptionally lovely woman in a large hat. On the beautiful face was an expression which was at once humorous and calm. It was, in fact, the sort of face that exactly fitted the voice I had heard on the telephone.

'D'you think that's her?' asked Jacquie.

'Very likely. But I expect that was painted years ago. I shouldn't think she looks a bit like that now.'

At that moment there were quick, firm footsteps in the hall, and Bebita entered. I took one look at her and decided that, in comparison to the portrait, the portrait definitely came a very poor second. She was the nearest approach to a Greek goddess that I have ever seen.

'I am B-B-Bebita Ferreyra,' she said, and appeared to understand our astonishment, for the amused expression in her blue eyes deepened.

'I hope you didn't mind us phoning you?' I said; 'only Larry told me I must contact you.'

'B-b-but naturally. I should have b-b-been insulted if you had not.'

'Larry said to give you his love.'

'And how is Larry? Ahh, he is an angel, that man; you have no idea what an angel he is,' she said.

It was only later that I discovered Bebita described everyone thus, however charming or malignant. At the time I found it a trifle astonishing to hear this term used to describe my brother. Of all the descriptions I could have thought of, this one seemed the least appropriate. We fell under Bebita's unique spell during that first meeting, and from then on we practically lived at her flat, eating tremendous and beautifully constructed meals, listening to music, talking nonsense, and enjoying ourselves. Very soon we came to rely on her for nearly everything. The most fantastic requests never ruffled her, and she always managed to accomplish something.

The first blow to our plans for the trip fell within three days of arriving in Buenos Aires. We discovered that the chances of our being able to get down to Tierra del Fuego were, to say the least, remote. The airline company were polite but depressing. If we cared to wait ten days or so it was possible that they might have a cancellation, but they could not promise. Gloomily we said that we would wait and see. It was Ian who suggested that, instead of mooching round Buenos Aires for ten days in a depressed and irritated frame of mind, we make a trip into the country-side near the city. Ian is an old friend of mine whom I had met in England during the war. In a moment of rash enthusiasm he said that I should really come out to Argentina on a collecting trip. If I did, he would do all he could to help; now he was stuck with us. He went to see his cousins, the Boote family, who owned a large *estancia* near the coast, some hundred odd miles from the capital. They, with a generosity that is typical of Argentina and all who live there, said they would be delighted to have us.

So early one morning the Bootes' car collected us. Ian hoisted his lugubrious and lanky frame from the depths and introduced us to a beautiful blonde sitting in the front seat, who turned out to be Elizabeth Boote, daughter of the house. Apart from her loveliness, we soon discovered that she had a remarkable ability to sleep; anywhere, at any time, you would find her sleeping peacefully and deeply, ignoring any minor uproar that happened to be taking place around her. This remarkable gift made us nickname her Dormouse, a name that she took grave exception to, but which nevertheless stuck.

CHAPTER ONE

OVEN-BIRDS AND BURROWING OWLS

ARGENTINA is one of the few countries in the world where you can go on a journey, and when half-way there see both your starting point and your destination. Flat as a billiard table, the pampa stretches around you, continuing, apparently, to the very edge of the earth. Here and there it is blurred with purple where the thistle grows, and here and there lies a dark rib of trees, but otherwise nothing breaks the smooth expanse of grass.

After we had left the outskirts of Buenos Aires behind, the blond and ivory sky-scrapers dwindling and shimmering in the haze like some curious crystal formation on the horizon, the road lay straight as a lance through the grassland. In places the road-side was crowded with rather fragile-looking bushes covered with pale green leaves and minute golden flowers. These flowers were so tiny, but grew in such profusion, that from a distance they could not be seen as individual blooms, giving instead a curious golden radiance to the bushes, as though each plant were wearing

14

a misty halo around it. From among these bushes flew scissor-tails as we passed, small black-and-white birds with immensely elongated tail-feathers. They have a curious dipping flight, and with each dip the tail-feathers would open and close like the blades of a pair of scissors. Occasionally a chimango hawk would fly across the road on heavy, blunt wings, looking clean and portly in its chocolate-brown-and-caramel plumage.

After an hour or so of driving, we turned off the main road on to a country track, deeply rutted and dusty, its edge lined with neat fencing. I noticed on each fence-pole strange lumps of what appeared to be dried mud; they reminded me of the termites' nests I had seen in Africa, but I thought it unlikely that termites would be found this far south in the world. I was puzzling over these curious protuberances when suddenly a bird flew out of one, a bird resembling the English robin in shape, with a plump breast and a pert tail. It was about the size of a thrush, with a pale fawn breast and rich rusty red upper parts. It was an oven-bird, and immediately I saw it I realized that all those peculiar hummocks of mud decorating the fence-posts were the extraordinary nests of which this bird was the architect and chief mason. Later I found that the oven-bird is one of the commonest, as well as one of the most endearing, of the Argentine birds, and its nests are as much a feature of the landscape as the giant thistles.

Now that our route curved towards the sea, we entered the swampy lands, and the edges of the roads were lined with wide, water-filled ditches, while vivid green patches on the golden grass of the pampa denoted the presence of wider stretches of water, thickly fringed with reed. The place of the oven-birds, scissor-tails, and chimangos was taken by waders and waterfowl. Screamers – great ash-grey birds the size of turkeys – rose from the roadside in strong but ungainly flight, giving their broken, flute-like cries of 'Wheeup ... wheeup ... wheeup' as they circled round. On the still, gleaming expanses of water, flocks of ducks swam, looking like plump, sleek business men hurrying to catch a train. There were grey teal, tiny and neat with their steel-blue beaks and black caps; red shovellers, heavy birds with vacant expressions behind the long spade-shaped beaks; rosy-bills, immaculate in their gleaming black-and-grey plumage, their beaks looking as though they had been freshly dipped in blood; drab little black-headed ducks, that swam among the others in a self-effacing way that was almost hypocritical, for this bird has emulated the habits of the cuckoo, laying its eggs in others' nests, so that they are adopted and the hard work of hatching and rearing is done by some other and easily hoodwinked species. On the mud flats were a scattering of herons; great jostling crowds of glossy ibis, whose long, curved beaks and deep mourning plumage contrasted strangely with their exuberant spirits as they pecked each other, pirouetted and flapped in the shallows. Here and there among them were smaller groups of scarlet ibis, vivid as shreds of a sunset against the darker plumage of their cousins. On the more open and extensive patches of water swam royal squadrons of black-necked swans, beautiful and unhurried, their foam-white plumage contrasting with the deep black of the head and delicately arched neck. Like courtiers among the proud flocks of black-necks were swimming a few coscoroba swans, dumpy, plain white, and definitely barnyard-looking. Also on these larger sheets of water were small skeins of flamingos, feeding in the shallows against the tall reeds. From a distance they were like moving heaps of pink and scarlet roses against the green. Each paced slowly and methodically in the dark waters, head down, neck curved in the shape of a large pink 'S', each bird attached by its sealing-wax pink legs to a blurred, shimmering reflection of itself. Drugged with such a gorgeous banquet of bird life, I sat in the car in a sort of ornithological stupor, noticing nothing but the glittering of feathered bodies, the splash and wrinkle of smooth water, and the flash of wing.

The car swerved suddenly off the track, bounced down a narrow lane shining with puddles, through a copse of giant eucalyptus trees, and drew up outside a long, low, white building that might have been an English farmhouse. In the front seat Dormouse Boote awoke from a sleep that had lasted unbroken since we left the capital, and surveyed us with dreamy blue eyes.

'Welcome to Los Ingleses,' she said, and yawned delicately.

The house inside had a delightfully Victorian flavour, with its dark and massive furniture, its animal heads and faded prints on the walls, its stone-flagged passages, and everywhere the faint and pleasantly astringent smell of paraffin from the tall, gleaming, mosque-like lamps. The room Jacquie and I occupied, though large, was dwarfed by an immense feather bed which was obviously straight out of Hans Andersen's story of 'The Princess and the Pea'. It was a bed to end all beds, almost as big as a tennis-court and as thick as a bale of hay. It enveloped you, when you lay on it, in a voluptuous embrace; you sank fathoms deep into its thistle-down-soft depths, and were lulled immediately into a sleep so complete and so relaxed that your rage on being awoken was almost homicidal. The window of the room, looking out on to the smooth lawn and rows of diminutive fruit trees, was fringed with eyelashes of blue-flowered creeper. Hung among the flowers, in such a position that I could see it from where I lay in bed, was a humming-bird's nest, a tiny cup the size of half a walnut shell, containing two pea-size white eggs. The morning after our arrival, as I lay in the warm depths of the gargantuan bed, sipping my tea, I watched the female humming-bird sitting quietly on her eggs, while her mate hovered and flipped among the blue flowers, like a microscopic, glittering comet. Bird-watching in these circumstances had a very great deal to be said for it, but at length Jacquie refused to believe that, under those conditions, I was adding greatly to ornithological knowledge of the Family *trochilidae*, so I was dragged reluctantly from the octopus-like embrace of the bed and forced to dress. Having done so, I was revolted at the thought that Ian might still be asleep, and strode across the passage to his room, determined to rout him out. I found him clad in pyjamas and a *poncho*, that useful Argentine garment that resembles a blanket with a hole in the middle through which you stick your head. He was squatting on the floor, sucking at a slender, silver pipe that was immersed in a small, round, silver pot which contained a dark and rather revolting-looking liquid with what appeared to be bits of grass floating on the top.

'Hullo, Gerry! You up?' he said, faintly surprised, and sucked vigorously at the little pipe, which responded with a musical gurgle like a miniature bath emptying.

'What are you doing?' I asked austerely.

'Having my morning *mate*,' he answered, giving another liquid gurgle on the pipe. 'Like to try it?'

'Isn't that the herb tea?' I inquired.

'Yes. Drink it out here as frequently, if not more frequently, than tea in England. Try some; you might like it,' he suggested, and handed me the little silver pot and pipe.

I sniffed suspiciously at the dark brown liquid with its crust of floating herbage. The scent was rich and pleasant, like a hay-field under a hot sun. I put my lips to the little pipe and sucked. There was a fruity wheeze, and a stream of boiling liquid gushed into my mouth and scalded my tongue. Wiping my streaming eyes, I handed the pot back to Ian.

'Thanks,' I said. 'I've no doubt it's an acquired taste to drink it at that temperature, but I'm afraid my taste-buds wouldn't stand it.'

'Well, you can drink it cooler than this,' said Ian doubtfully, 'but I think it loses its flavour.'

Later I tried drinking *mate* at a more humane temperature, and I found it pleasantly soothing, with its aroma of new-mown hay and faintly bitter, astringent taste that was quite refreshing. But I could never cultivate the ability to drink it at the heat of molten metal, as I presume a connoisseur would like it.

We meandered through an excellent breakfast, and then wandered out into the brilliant day to examine the surrounding country-side. Hardly had we left the copse of eucalyptus that ringed the *estancia* like a giant fence, when we came upon a tree-stump in the long grass, and perched on top of it was an oven-bird's nest. I was amazed, when I examined it closely, that a bird of this size could produce such a large and complicated structure. The nest was globe-shaped, roughly twice the size of a football, strongly made of mud combined with roots and fibres, so that it formed a sort of avian reinforced concrete. Looked at from the front, where there was an arched entrance, the whole thing resembled a miniature version of an old-fashioned bread-oven. I was interested to see what the inside of the nest was like, so, being assured by Ian that it was an old one, I prised it off the tree-stump and cut carefully through the brick-like top of the dome with a sharp knife. When the top was removed, the whole thing

18

looked like the inside of a snail shell: a passage-way ran in to the left for some six inches from the arched door, following the curve of the outside wall, but bent in at the right of the door so as to form the passage-way. Where the passage ended, the natural shape of the nest formed a circular room, which was neatly lined with grass and a few feathers. While the outside of the whole structure was rough and uneven, the inside of the little room and the passage-way was smooth and almost polished. The more I examined the nest, the more astonished I became that a bird, using only its beak as a tool, could have achieved such a building triumph. No wonder the people of Argentina look with affection upon this sprightly bird that paces so pompously about their gardens and makes the air shiver with its cheerful, ringing cries. Hudson relates a charming story about a pair which had built a nest on the roof of a ranch-house. One day the female unfortunately got caught in a rat trap, which broke both her legs. Struggling free, she managed to fly up into her nest, and there eventually died. Her mate flew about for several days, calling incessantly, and finally disappeared. Within two days he was back again, accompanied by another hen. The two birds promptly set to work and plastered up the entrance of the old nest, containing the first wife's remains. This done, they constructed a second nest on top of this crypt, and here they successfully reared their brood.

Certainly, as birds go, the oven-bird appears to have more than his fair share of personality and charm, for he has a strange power over even the most hardened cynics. Later on during our stay an elderly peon, who had no sentimentality in his make-up and suffered no qualms at killing anything from men to insects, solemnly told me that he would never harm an *hornero*. Once, he said, when out riding in the pampa, he came upon an oven-bird's nest on a stump. The nest was half completed and the mud still damp. Dangling from one side of it was the owner, caught round the feet by a long thread of grass it had obviously been using as reinforcement. The bird must have been hanging there for some time, fluttering vainly in an attempt to free itself, and it was nearly exhausted. Moved by a sudden impulse, the peon rode up to the nest, took out his knife and carefully cut away the entangling grass and placed the exhausted bird carefully on top of its nest to recover. Then an extraordinary thing happened.

'I swear that this is true, señor,' said the peon. 'There was I, not more than a couple of feet away from the bird, and yet it showed no fear. Weak as it was, it struggled to its feet, and then put its beak up and started to sing. For nearly two minutes it sang to me, señor – a beautiful song – and I sat on my horse listening. Then it flew off across the grass. That bird was thanking me for saving its life. A bird that can show gratitude in that manner, señor, deserves respect from a man.'

A hundred yards or so from the oven-bird's nest, Jacquie, who was some distance away to my right, started to make inarticulate crooning noises and to beckon me frantically. Joining her, I found she was gazing rapturously at the mouth of a small burrow, half hidden among the grass tussocks. At the mouth of the burrow squatted a small owl, stiff as a guardsman, watching us with round eyes. Suddenly he bowed up and down two or three times, very rapidly, and then froze once more into his military stance. This was such a ludicrous performance that both Jacquie and I giggled, and the owl, after giving us a withering glare, launched himself on silent wings and glided away across the wind-rippled grass.

'We must catch some of those,' said Jacquie firmly. 'I think they're delightful.'

I agreed, for owls of any sort have always appealed to me, and I have never been able to make any collection without a sprinkling of these attractive birds finding their way into it. I turned towards where Ian was pacing through the grass, like a solitary and depressed-looking crane.

'Ian,' I shouted, 'come over here. I think we've found a burrowing owl's nest.'

He came loping over, and together we examined the entrance of the hole where the owl had been sitting. There was a patch of bare earth from the excavations, and this was liberally sprinkled with the gleaming chitinous shells of various beetles and round castings composed of tiny bones, fluff and feathers. It certainly looked as though the burrow was used for more than just roosting in. Ian gazed down, pulling his nose reflectively.

'D'you think there's anything in there?' I asked.

'Hard to say,' he replied. 'It's the right season, of course – in fact the youngsters should be fully fledged by now. Trouble is these owls make several burrows, and they only use one for nesting in. The peons say that the male uses the others as sort of bachelor apartments, but I don't know. It means we may have to dig out any number of these holes before we strike lucky; but, if you don't mind a good many disappointments, we can have a try.'

'You can disappoint me as much as you like, as long as we get some owls in the end,' I said firmly.

'Right. Well, we'll need spades, and a stick of some sort to see which way the tunnels lie.'

So we retraced our steps to the *estancia*, and there Mrs Boote, delighted that we were hot on the trail of specimens so soon after our arrival, unearthed a fascinating array of gardening tools, and told a peon to stop whatever he was doing and to go with us in case we needed help. As we trailed across the garden, looking like a gravedigger's convention, we stumbled upon Dormouse Boote, slumbering peacefully on a rug. She awoke as we passed and asked sleepily where we were off to. On being informed that we were off to capture burrowing owls, her blue eyes opened wide and she suggested that she should drive us out in the car to the owl's nest.

'But you can't drive the car across the pampa ... it's not a jeep,' I protested.

'And your father's just had the springs renewed,' Ian reminded her.

She gave us a ravishing smile.

'I'll drive very slowly,' she promised, and then, seeing that we were still doubtful, she cunningly added, 'and think how much more ground you'll be able to cover in a car.'

So we lurched out across the pampa to the first owl-hole, the springs of the car twanging melodiously, and causing everyone except Dormouse twinges of conscience.

The hole we had found turned out to be some eight feet in length, curving slightly like the letter 'C', and about two feet at the greatest depths below the surface. We discovered all this by

21

probing gently with a long and slender bamboo. Having marked out with sticks a rough plan of how the burrow lay, we proceeded to dig down, sinking a shaft into the tunnel at intervals of about two feet. Then each section of tunnel between the shafts was carefully searched to make sure nothing was hiding in it, and blocked off with clods of earth. At length we came to the final shaft, which, if our primitive reckoning was correct, should lead us down into the nesting chamber. We worked in excited silence, gently chipping away the hard-baked soil. At intervals during our excavations we had pressed our ears to the turf, but there had been no sound from inside, and I was half convinced that the burrow would prove empty. Then the last crust of earth gave way, and cascaded into the nesting chamber, and glaring up out of the gloomy hole were two little ash-grey faces, with great dandelion-golden eyes. We all gave a whoop of triumph, and the owls blinked very rapidly and clicked their beaks like castanets. They looked so fluffy and adorable that I completely forgot all about owls' habits, and reached into the ruins of the nest-chamber and tried to pick one up. Immediately they transformed themselves from bewildered bundles consisting of soft plumage and great eyes, to swollen, belligerent furies. Puffing out the feathers on their backs, so that they looked twice their real size, they opened their wings on each side of their bodies like feathered shields, and, with clutching talons and snapping beaks, swooped at my hand, I sat back and sucked my bloodstained fingers.

'Have we got a thick cloth of some sort?' I asked – 'something thicker than a handkerchief, with which to handle these innocent little dears?'

Dormouse sped off to the car and returned with an ancient and oil-stained towel. I doubled this over my hand and made a fresh attempt. This time I succeeded in grabbing one of the babies round the body, and although the towel kept off the attacks of his beak, I was still pricked by his clutching talons. Having got a good grip on the towel, he then refused to let go, and it took some time to disentangle his feet and pop him into a bag. His brother, now facing the enemy alone, seemed to lose a lot of his nerve, and he was much less trouble to catch and put in a bag. Hot, earth-stained, but feeling very pleased with ourselves, we re-entered the car. For the rest of the day we zig-zagged across the pampa, waiting for pairs of burrowing owls to fly out of the grass. Then we would wander about the spot until we had located the hole and proceed to dig it out. We met with more disappointments than successes, as Ian had predicted we would, but at the end of the day (having dug up what appeared to be several miles of tunnel), we returned to the *estancia* with a very satisfying bag of eight baby burrowing owls, who promptly proceeded to consume meat and beetles in such vast quantities that we began to wonder if their harassed parents would really miss them, or whether they would look upon the capture of their offspring as a merciful release.

Having now got our first specimens from Los Ingleses, others followed rapidly. The day after the capture of the burrowing owls, a peon came to the house holding a box which contained two fledgling guira cuckoos. These birds are quite common in Argentina, and even more so in Paraguay. In shape and size they look like an English starling, but there the resemblance ends, for guira cuckoos are clad in pale fawny-cream plumage, streaked with greenish black, with a tattered gingery crest on the head, and long, magpie-like tails. They travel together through the bushes and woods in little companies of between ten and twenty, and they look very handsome as they glide from bush to bush *en masse*, like flights of brown-paper darts. Apart from admiring these flocks of cuckoos in flight, I had not really given the species any serious thought, until we received these two babies. I discovered immediately I undid the box in which they were confined that guira cuckoos are not like other birds at all. To begin with, I am convinced that they are mentally defective from the moment of hatching, and nothing will make me alter my opinion. As I lifted the lid from the box, it disclosed the two guiras squatting straddle-legged in the bottom of the box, long tails spread out, and ginger crests erect. They surveyed me calmly with pale yellow eyes that had a glazed, dreamy, far-away expression in them, as though they were listening to distant and heavenly music too faint for mere mammals like myself to hear. Then, like a perfectly trained harmony team, they raised their uneven crests still farther, opened their yellow beaks and let forth a loud, hysterical series of sounds like a machine-gun. This done, they lowered their crests and flew heavily out of the box, one landing on my wrist and one on my head. The one on my wrist uttered a pleased, chuckling sound and sidled up to the buttons on my coat sleeve, which he proceeded to attack with raised crest and every symptom of ferocity. The one on my head grasped a large quantity of hair in his beak, straddled his legs and proceeded to pull at it with all his might.

'How long has this man had them?' I asked Ian, astonished at the birds' impudence and tameness.

Ian and the peon had a rapid exchange of Spanish, and then Ian turned to me.

'He says he caught them half an hour ago,' said Ian.

'But that's impossible,' I protested; 'these birds are tame. They must be someone's pets who've escaped.'

'Oh, no,' said Ian; 'guiras are always like that.'

'What, as tame as this?'

'Yes. They seem to have no fear at all when they're young. They're not quite so silly when they are adult, but almost.'

The one on my head, discovering that the idea of scalping me was impossible, now descended to my shoulder and tried to see how much of his beak would fit into my ear without getting stuck. I removed him hurriedly and placed him on my wrist with his brother. They both immediately carried on as though they had not seen each other for years, raising their crests, gazing lovingly into each other's eyes, and trilling with the speed of a couple of road drills. When I opened the door of a cage and placed my wrist near it, both birds hopped inside and up on to the perch as if they had been born in captivity. Intrigued by this display of avian nonchalance, I went in search of Jacquie.

'Come and see the new arrivals,' I said, when I found her, '– the answer to a collector's dream.'

'What are they?'

'A pair of those guira cuckoos.'

'Oh, you mean those gingery things,' she said disparagingly. 'I don't call them very exciting.'

'Well, come and see them,' I urged; 'they're certainly the weirdest pair of birds I've come across.'

The cuckoos were sitting on the perch, preening themselves. They paused briefly in their toilet to fix us with a glittering eye and rattle a brief greeting before continuing.

'They're a bit more attractive when you see them close to,' Jacquie admitted; 'but I don't see what you're making a fuss about.'

'Don't you notice anything about them ... anything unusual?'

'No,' she said, surveying them critically. 'It's a good thing they're tame. Saves a lot of trouble.'

'But they're not tame,' I said triumphantly; 'they were only caught half an hour ago.'

'Nonsense!' said Jacquie firmly. 'Why, just look at them. You can see they're quite used to being in a cage.'

'No, they're not. According to Ian, at this age they're quite stupid, and they're very easy to catch, and as tame as anything. When they get older they develop a little more sense, but apparently not very much.'

'I must say they are rather peculiar-looking birds,' said Jacquie, peering at them closely.

'They look mentally defective to me,' I said.

Jacquie inserted a finger through the wire and waggled it at the nearest cuckoo. Without hesitation he sidled up to the bars and lowered his head to be scratched. His brother, enthusiasm gleaming in his eyes, immediately climbed on his brother's back to receive his share of the treat. Quite unconcernedly they sat like

that, one perched precariously on the other, both swaying to and fro on the perch, while Jacquie scratched their necks. Gradually, soothed by the massage, their crests came up, their heads tilted until their beaks pointed heavenwards, their eyes closed in ecstasy, and the feathers on the neck stood out straight, while the neck itself was stretched upwards and outwards until they looked more like feathered giraffes than birds.

'Quite definitely mental,' I repeated, as the top cuckoo stretched his neck too far, overbalanced, and fell to the bottom of the cage, where he sat blinking and chuckling testily to himself.

Later we got more of these fatuous birds, and they all proved equally simple. One pair was caught later on, in Paraguay, by our companion in the most amazing fashion. Walking along a path, he passed within a yard of a pair of guiras feeding in the grass. Thinking it strange that they had not flown away at his approach, he retraced his steps and again passed them. They just sat and stared at him foolishly. The third time he jumped at them and returned triumphantly to camp, carrying one in each hand. Owing to the ease with which even an unprepared person could capture these birds, it was not long before we had several pairs, and they afforded us endless amusement. In each of their cages there was an inch gap left for cleaning purposes. The cuckoos could have asked for nothing better, as by squatting on the floor and sticking their heads out, they could keep an eye on everything that went on in camp, and discuss it together in loud trills and chuckles. When they peered out of their cages like this, tattered crests erect, eyes bright with curiosity, their shrill voices screeching comments, they reminded me of groups of frowsty old charladies peering out of some attic window at a street-fight below.

The guiras had a passion for sun-bathing that was almost an obsession. The slightest gleam of sunshine in their cage would excite them beyond all measure. Trilling happily, they would crowd on to the perch and prepare for their sun-bath, which they considered a serious matter and one not to be undertaken lightly. To begin with, it was very important that the posture should be exactly right. They had to be seated comfortably on the perch, balanced so skilfully that they could remain sitting there even if they released their grip on the wood. Then they would puff out their feathers and shake them vigorously, like an old feather duster. After this they would puff out the feathers of their breasts, raise the feathers on the rump, lower their long tails, close their eyes, and gradually sink down until their breast-bones rested against the perch, breast-feathers drooping one side, the tail drooping the other. Then, very slowly and carefully, they would unclench their feet, and sit there, swaying delicately. When sun-bathing like this, with their feathers stuck out at odd and completely un-bird-like angles, they looked as though they were completely egg-bound; in that unprotected condition they also looked as if they had been severely attacked by clothes-moth. But, in spite of their crazy ways, the cuckoos were endearing birds, and even if we had only left them for half an hour they would greet our return with such joyful trills of greeting that you could not help feeling affectionate towards them.

The first pair we got – the ones from Los Ingleses – always remained our favourites, and underwent a lot of spoiling from Jacquie. At the end of the trip, when we had handed them over to London Zoo, we were not able to go and see them for nearly two months. Thinking that such brainless birds would by now have completely forgotten us, we approached their cage in the bird-house with mixed feelings. It was a week-end, and there were a number of other visitors clustered round the guiras' cage. But no sooner had we joined the spectators than the cuckoos, who a moment before had been preening themselves on their perch, stared at us with bright, mad eyes, erected their crests in astonishment, and flew down to the wire with loud rattles of excitement and pleasure. As we scratched their necks and watched them stretch out like rubber, we decided that perhaps they were not quite so unintelligent as we had supposed them to be.

CHAPTER TWO

EGGBERT AND THE TERRIBLE TWINS

THE great screamers were one of the commonest birds round Los Ingleses; within a radius of a mile or so one could see ten or twelve pairs of these stately creatures, pacing side by side through the grass, or wheeling through the sky on wide wings, making the air ring with their melodious trumpet-calls. How to catch the eight I wanted was a problem, for, as well as being the commonest of the pampa birds, they were also the most wary. Their goose-like habit of grazing in huge flocks, completely devastating enormous fields of alfalfa in the winter, has earned the wrath of the Argentine farmers, and they are hunted and killed whenever possible. So, while you could approach fairly close to most of the bird-life on the pampa, you were extremely lucky if you got within a hundred and fifty yards of a pair of screamers. We knew they were nesting all about us, but the nests were well concealed; and though we realized that several times we had been close to finding one, by the way the parents flew low over us with loud cries, we had never been successful.

One evening we were out at a small lake, thickly fringed with reed, setting up flight-nets to try to obtain some ducks. Having fixed my side of the net, I hauled myself out of the brackish water and wandered through the reed-beds. I stopped to examine a small nest, rather like a reed-warbler's, which was cunningly suspended between two leaves, and which proved to be empty, when my attention was attracted to a pile of grey clay which winked at me. Just as I was becoming convinced that there must be something wrong with me, the pile of clay winked again. Then, as the patch of ground at which I had been staring came into focus, I saw that I was not looking at a patch of clay, but at an almost fully grown baby screamer, crouched among the reeds, still as a stone, with only the lids flicking over its dark eyes to give it away. I went forward slowly and squatted down near it. Still it did not move. I reached forward and touched its head, but it lay quite quietly, ignoring me. I picked it up and put it under my arm like a domestic fowl, carrying it back to the car. It made no effort to struggle and displayed no symptoms of panic. Just as I reached the car, however, a pair of adult screamers flew over quite low, and, on seeing us, gave a series of wild cries. Immediately the bird in my arms turned from a placid and well-behaved creature into a flapping, panic-stricken beast that took me all my time to subdue and place in a box.

When we returned to the *estancia*, Dormouse's brother John came out to see how we had fared. With considerable pride I showed him my screamer.

'One of those damn things,' he said in disgust. 'I didn't know you wanted *them*.'

'Of course I do,' I said indignantly; 'they're a most attractive show in any zoo.'

'How many do you want?' asked John.

'Well, I need eight, really, though judging by the difficulty we had in getting this one I doubt whether I'll get that many,' I said gloomily.

'Oh, don't worry about that; I'll get eight for you,' said John airily. 'When d'you want them?... Tomorrow?'

'I don't want to be greedy,' I said sarcastically, 'so suppose you just bring me four tomorrow, and four the next day?'

'O.K.,' said John laconically, and wandered off.

Beyond reflecting that John had a peculiar sense of humour if he could joke about such a sacred subject as screamer-catching, I thought no more about it until the following morning I saw him mounting his horse. A peon, already mounted, waited nearby.

'Oh, Gerry,' he called, as his horse waltzed round and round impatiently, 'did you say eight or a dozen?'

'Eight or a dozen what?'

'*Chajás*, of course,' he said in mild surprise.

I glared at him.

'I want eight,' I said, 'and then you can get me a dozen or so tomorrow.'

'O.K.,' said John, and, turning his horse, cantered off through the eucalyptus trees.

At lunch-time I was in the small hut in which we housed the animals, attempting to make a cage. Three pieces of wood had split, and I had hit myself twice on the hand with the hammer, and nearly taken the top off my thumb with the saw. Altogether I was not in the most jovial of moods, and Jacquie and Ian had long since left me to my own devices. I was making another frenzied assault on the cage, when there was the clop of hooves, and John's voice hailed me cheerfully from outside.

'Hola, Gerry,' he called. 'Here are your *chajás*.'

This was the last straw. Clutching a hammer murderously, I strode out to explain to John, in no uncertain terms, that I was in no mood for practical jokes. He was leaning against the sweating flanks of his horse, a smile on his face. But what brought me up short and made my irritation evaporate was the sight of two large sacks lying at his feet, sacks that bulged, sacks that heaved and quivered. The peon was getting off another horse and also lowering a couple of sacks to the ground, sacks that seemed heavy, and that gave forth a rustling sound.

'Are you serious?' I asked faintly. 'Are those sacks really full of screamers?'

'But of course,' said John surprised. 'What did you think?'

'I thought you were joking,' I said meekly. 'How many have you got?'

'Eight, like you asked for,' said John.

'Eight?' I squawked hoarsely.

'Yes, only eight. I'm sorry I couldn't get a dozen, but I'll try and get you eight more tomorrow.'

'No, no, don't ... Let me get these established first.'

'But you said ...' began John, bewildered.

'Never mind what I said,' I interjected hastily; 'just don't get me any more until I tell you.'

'Right,' he said cheerfully; 'you know best. By the way, there's a very young one in one of the sacks. I had to put him in there. I hope he's all right. You'd better have a look.'

Feeling that the age of miracles was not past, I staggered into the hut with the heavy, heaving sacks, and then went in search of Jacquie and Ian to tell them the good news and get them to help me unpack the birds. Most of the screamers that we hauled out, tousled and indignant, from inside the sacks, were about the same size as the one I had caught the day before. But right at the very bottom of the last sack we emptied we discovered the young one that John had mentioned. He was quite the most pathetic, the most ridiculous-looking and the most charming baby bird I had ever seen.

He could not have been much more than a week old. His body was about the size of a coconut, and completely circular. At the end of a long neck was a high, domed head, with a tiny beak and a pair of friendly brown eyes. His legs and feet, which were greyish-pink, appeared to be four times too big for him, and not completely under control. On his back were two small, flaccid bits of skin, like a couple of cast-off glove fingers which had become attached there by accident, which did duty as wings. He was clad entirely in what appeared to be a badly knitted bright yellow suit of cotton wool. He rolled out of the sack, fell on his back, struggled manfully on to his enormous flat feet, and stood there, his ridiculous wings slightly raised, surveying us with interest. Then he opened his beak and shyly said 'Wheep'. As we were too enchanted to respond to this greeting, he very slowly and carefully picked up one huge foot, swayed forward, put it down and then brought the other one up alongside it. He stood and beamed at us with evident delight at having accomplished such a complicated manoeuvre. He had a short rest, said 'wheep' again, and then proceeded to take another step, in order to show us that the first one had been no fluke, but a solid achievement. Unfortunately, when he had taken the first step, he had not watched what he was doing, and so his left foot was resting on the toes of his right foot. The results were disastrous. He struggled wildly to extricate his right foot from underneath his left, swaying dangerously. Then, with a mighty heave, he succeeded in lifting both feet from the ground, and promptly fell flat on his face. At our burst of laughter, he looked up into our faces from his recumbent posture, and gave another deprecating 'wheep'.

At first, owing to his shape and the colouring of his suit, we called this baby, Egg. But later, as he grew older, it was changed to a more sedate Eggbert. Now, I have met a lot of amusing birds at one time and another, but they generally appeared funny because their appearance was ridiculous, and so even the most commonplace action took on some element of humour. But I have never met a bird like Eggbert, who not only *looked* funny without doing anything, but also acted in a riotously comical manner whenever he moved. I have never met a bird, before or since, that could make me literally laugh until I cried. Very few human comedians can do that to me. Yet Eggbert had only to stand there on his outsize feet, cock his head on one side and say 'wheep!' in a slyly interrogative way, and I would feel unconquerable laughter bubbling up inside me. Every afternoon we would take Eggbert out of his cage and allow him an hour's constitutional on the lawn. We looked forward to these walks as eagerly as he did, but an hour was enough. At the end of that time we would be forced to return him to his cage, in sheer self-defence.

Eggbert's feet were the bane of his life. There was so much of them, and they would get tangled together when he walked. Then there was the danger that he would tread on his own toes and fall down and make an exhibition of himself, as he had done on the first day. So he kept a very close watch on his feet for any signs of insubordination. He would sometimes stand for as long as ten minutes with bent head, gravely staring at his toes as they wiggled gently in the grass, spread out like the arms of a starfish. Eggbert's whole desire, obviously, was to be dissociated from these outsize feet. He felt irritated by them. Without them, he was sure, he could gambol about the lawn with the airy grace of a dried thistle-head. Occasionally, having watched his feet for some time, he would decide that he had lulled them into a sense of false security. Then, when they least suspected it, he would launch his body forward in an effort to speed across the lawn and leave these hateful extremities behind. But although he tried this trick many times, it never succeeded. The feet were always too quick for him, and as soon as he moved they would deliberately and maliciously twist themselves into a knot, and Eggbert would fall head first into the daisies.

His feet were continually letting him down, in more ways than one. Eggbert had a deep ambition to capture a butterfly. Why this was we could not find out, for Eggbert could not tell us. All we knew was that screamers were supposed to be entirely vegetarian, but whenever a butterfly hovered within six feet of Eggbert his whole being seemed to be filled with blood-lust, his eyes would take on a fanatical and most unvegetarian-like gleam, and he would endeavour to stalk it. However, in order to stalk a butterfly with any hope of success one has to keep one's eyes firmly fixed on it. This Eggbert knew, but the trouble was that as soon as he watched the butterfly with quivering concentration, his feet, left to their own devices, would start to play up, treading on each other's toes, crossing over each other, and sometimes even trying to walk in the wrong direction. As soon as Eggbert dragged his eyes away from the quarry, his feet would start to behave, but by the time he looked back again the butterfly would have disappeared. Then came the never-to-be-forgotten day when Eggbert was standing in the sun, feet turned out, dreaming to himself, and a large, ill-mannered, and obviously working-class butterfly of the worst type flew rapidly across the lawn, flapped down, and settled on Eggbert's beak, made what can only be described as a rude gesture with its antennae, and soared up into the air again. Eggbert, quivering with justifiable rage, pecked at it as it swooped over his domed forehead. Unfortunately, he leaned too far back, and for one awful moment he swayed and then he crashed on his back, his feet waving helplessly in the air. As he lay there, demoralized and helpless, the cowardly butterfly took the opportunity to land on his protuberant, fluff-covered tummy, have a quick wash-and-brush-up before flying off again. This painful episode naturally only made Eggbert feel even more belligerently inclined towards the lepidoptera, but in spite of all his efforts he never caught one.

At first, Eggbert gave us some concern over his food. He rejected with disdain such commonplace vegetation as cabbage, lettuce, clover, and alfalfa. We tried him on biscuit with hard-boiled egg, and he regarded us with horror for trying to force him into cannibalism. Fruit, bran, maize, and a variety of other things were inspected briefly and then ignored. In desperation I suggested that the only thing to do was to let him out in the kitchen garden in the faint hope that he would, young as he was, give us some indication of the sort of menu he desired. By this time Eggbert's food problem was worrying practically the whole *estancia*, so there was quite a crowd of anxious people assembled in the kitchen garden when we carried Eggbert out for the experiment. He greeted the assembled company with a friendly 'wheep', stood on his own foot and fell down, regained his equilibrium with an effort, and started off on his tour, while we followed in a hushed and expectant group. He passed through the rows of cabbages without a glance, and seemed mainly concerned with gaining control over his feet. At the tomatoes he started to look about him with interest, but just as it seemed he was coming to some sort of decision, his attention was distracted by a large locust. Among the potatoes he was overcome with fatigue, so he had a short nap while we stood patiently and waited. He awoke, apparently much refreshed, greeted us with surprise, yawned, and then ambled drunkenly on his journey. The carrots were passed with scorn. Among the peas he obviously felt that a little relaxation would be in order, and he tried to inveigle us into playing hide-and-seek among the plants. He reluctantly gave up this idea and moved on to the beans when he discovered that we refused to be side-tracked from the matter in hand. The bean-flowers seemed to fascinate him, but the interest was apparently aesthetic rather than gastronomic. Among the parsley and mint he was seized with a tickling sensation in the sole of his left foot, and his attempts to stand on one leg to search for the cause of the irritation made

him fall back heavily into a pool of rainwater. When he had been picked up, dried, and comforted, he staggered off and entered the neat rows of spinach. Here he came to a sudden halt and examined the plants minutely and suspiciously. Then he edged forward and glared at them from close range with his head on one side. The suspense was terrific. Just as he leant forward to peck at a leaf, he tripped and fell head first into a large spinach plant. He extricated himself with difficulty and tried again. This time he managed to seize the tip of a leaf in his beak. He tugged at it, but the leaf was a tough one and would not give way. He leant back, legs wide apart, and tugged frantically. The end of the leaf broke, and Eggbert was once more on his back, but this time looking distinctly triumphant with a tiny fragment of spinach in his beak. Amid much applause, he was carried back to his cage, and a large plate of chopped spinach was prepared for him. But then a new difficulty made its appearance. Even finely chopped spinach was too coarse for him, for having gulped it down he would straight away proceed to be sick.

'It's far too coarse, even when we chop it up finely,' I said; 'I'm afraid we'll have to prepare it in much the same way as his mother used to.'

'How's that?' asked Jacquie with interest.

'Well, they regurgitate a mass of semi-digested leaf for the young, so that it's soft and pulp-like.'

'Are you suggesting that we should try *that?*' inquired Jacquie suspiciously.

'No, no. Only I think that the nearest we can get to it is to offer him *chewed* spinach.'

'Oh, well, rather you than me,' said my wife gaily.

'But that's just the trouble,' I explained; 'I smoke, and I don't think he'd care to have a mixture of spinach and nicotine.'

'In other words, as I don't smoke, I suppose you want me to chew it?'

'That's the general idea.'

'If anyone had told me,' said Jacquie, plaintively, 'that when I married you I should have to spend my spare time chewing spinach for birds, I would never have believed them.'

'It's for the good of the cause,' I pointed out.

'In fact,' she continued darkly, ignoring my remark, 'if anyone *had* told me that, and I'd *believed* them, I don't think I would have married you.'

She picked up a large plate of spinach, gave me a cold look, and took it off to a quiet corner to chew. During the time we had Eggbert he got through a lot of spinach, all of which Jacquie chewed for him with monotonous persistence of one of the larger ungulates. At the end she calculated she had masticated something in the region of a hundredweight or so of leaves. Even today, spinach is not among her favourite vegetables.

Shortly after the arrival of Eggbert and his brethren we received a pair of animals which soon became known as the Terrible Twins. They were a pair of large and very corpulent hairy armadillos. Both of them were nearly identical in size and girth and, we soon discovered, in habits. As they were both female, one could quite easily have supposed that they were sisters from the same litter, except for the fact that while one was caught a stone's throw away from Los Ingleses, the other was sent over from a neighbouring *estancia* several miles away. The Twins were housed in a cage with a special sleeping compartment. It had originally been designed to accommodate one large armadillo, but owing to a housing shortage when they arrived, we were forced to put them both in the one cage. As it happened, since they were not quite fully grown, they fitted in very snugly. Their two pleasures in life were food and sleep, neither of which they could apparently get enough of. In their sleeping compartment they would lie on their backs, head to tail, their great pink and wrinkled tummies bulging and deflating as they breathed stertorously, their paws twitching and quivering. Once they were asleep, it seemed that nothing on earth would wake them. You could bang on the box, shout through the bars, open the bedroom door, and, holding your breath (for the Twins had a powerful scent all their own), poke these obese stomachs, pinch their paws, or flick their tails, but still they slumbered as though they were both in a deep hypnotic trance. Then, under the impression that nothing short of a world catastrophe would shake them into consciousness, you would fill a tin tray high with the revolting mixture they liked, and proceed

to insert it into the outside portion of the cage. However delicately you performed this operation, however careful you were to make sure the silence was not broken by the slightest sound, no sooner had you got the dish and your hand inside the door than from the bedroom would come a noise like a sea-serpent demolishing a woodshed with its tail. This was the Twins tumbling and struggling to get upright – to get to action stations, as it were. That was the warning to drop the plate and remove your hand with all speed, for within a split second the armadillos would burst from their bedroom door, like cannon-balls, skid wildly across the cage, shoulder to shoulder, in the manner of a couple of Rugby players fighting for the ball, grunting with the effort. They would hit the tin (and your hand if it was still there) amidships, and the armadillos and tin would end in the far corner in a tangled heap, and a tidal wave of chopped banana, milk, raw egg and minced meat would splash against the wall, and then rebound to settle like a glutinous shawl over the Twins' grey

40

backs. They would stand there, giving satisfied squeaks and grunts, licking the food as it trickled down their shells, occasionally going into a scrum in the corner over some choice bit of fruit or meat which had just given up the unequal contest with gravity and descended suddenly from the ceiling. Watching them standing knee-deep in that tide of food, you might think that it was impossible for two animals to get through such a quantity of vitamin and protein. Yet within half an hour the cage would be spotless, licked clean even to the least splashes on the ceiling, which they had to stand on their hind legs to reach. And the Twins themselves would be in their odoriferous boudoir, on their backs, head to tail, deeply and noisily asleep. Eventually, owing to this health-giving diet, the Twins increased their girth to such an extent that they could only just manage to get through the bedroom door, leaving about a millimetre's clearance all round. I was contemplating some drastic structural alterations when I found that one of the Twins had discovered the way to utilize this middle-age spread to her advantage. Instead of sleeping lengthwise in the bedroom, as she used to do, she now started to sleep across it, the right way up, with her head pointing towards the door. As soon as the first faint sound or smell of food reached her, she would shoot across the intervening space, before her companion could even get the right way up, and then, when halfway through the door, she would hunch her back and become wedged there as firmly as a cork in a bottle. Then, taking her time, she would reach out a claw, hook the food-pan into position, and proceed to browse dreamily, if not altogether quietly, in the depths, while in the bedroom, her frantic relative squealed and snorted and scrabbled ineffectually at the well-corseted and impervious behind.

The hairy armadillo is the vulture of the Argentine pampa. Low-slung, armoured against most forms of attack, he trots through the moonlit grass like a miniature tank, and nearly everything is grist to his mill. He will eat fruit and vegetables, but failing those he is quite happy with a bird's nest containing eggs or young; a light snack of young mice; or even a snake, should he happen to meet one. But what attracts the armadillo, as a magnet attracts steel filings, is a nice juicy rotten carcase. In Argentina,

where distances and herds are so great, it often happens that a
sick or elderly cow will die, and its body will lie out in the grass-
lands unnoticed, the sun ripening it until its scent is wafted far and
wide, and the humming of flies sounds like a swarm of bees. When
this smell reaches the nose of a foraging armadillo it is an
invitation to a banquet. Leaving his burrow, he scuttles along
until he reaches the delectable feast: the vast, maggot-ridden dish
lying in the grass. Then, having filled himself on a mixture of
rotten meat and maggots, he cannot bring himself to leave the
carcase when there is still so much nourishment left on it, so he
proceeds to burrow under it. Here he ponders and sleeps his first
course off until the pangs of hunger assail him once again. Then
all he has to do is to scramble to the top of his burrow, stick out
his head and there he is, so to speak, right in the middle of dinner.
An armadillo will very rarely leave a carcase until the last shreds
of meat have been stripped from the already bleaching bones.
Then, sighing the happy sigh of an animal that is replete, he will
return home, to wait hopefully for the next fatality among the
cattle or sheep. Yet, despite its depraved tastes, the armadillo is
considered excellent eating, the flesh tasting mid-way between
veal and sucking pig. He is frequently caught by the peons
on the *estancia* and kept in a barrelful of mud, being fattened
up until he is ready for the pot. Now, it may be considered
rather disgusting that anyone should eat a creature with such
a low taste in carrion, but, on the other hand, pigs have some
pretty revolting feeding habits, while the feeding habits of
plaice and dabs would, I've no doubt, leave most ghouls feeling
queasy.

There was another inhabitant of the pampa, with habits as
charming as the armadillos' were revolting, but I was never
privileged to meet it. This was the viscacha, a rodent about the
size of a cairn terrier, and with the same sort of low-slung body.
They have rather rabbit-like faces, decorated with a band of
black fur running from the nose along the cheek under the eyes.
Beneath this band is another one, in greyish-white, and beneath
this again is another black one, so the viscacha gives the impression that he had once decided to disguise himself as a zebra, but
had tired of the idea when half-way through the alterations. They

live in colonies of up to forty, in vast subterranean warrens known as *vizcacheras*.

Viscachas are the Bohemian artists of the pampa. They are very free and easy in their ways, and their massive underground community warrens are generally filled with an assortment of friends who have moved in. Burrowing owls dig small flatlets in the side of the viscacha's hallway. Snakes sometimes take up residence in the disused portions of the nest – presumably the viscacha's equivalent of the attic. If the viscachas enlarge their residence and several tunnels fall into disuse, a species of swallow immediately moves in. So many a *vizcachera* contained an odder assortment of types than most Bloomsbury boarding-houses. Providing these lodgers behave themselves, the viscachas do not seem to worry in the slightest how crowded the warren gets. The viscachas' artistic inclinations are, I feel sure, more than slightly influenced by surrealism. The area immediately around the mouth of the warren is cleared of every vestige of green stuff, so the front doors of the colony are surrounded by a ballroom-like expanse of earth, packed hard by the passing of many small feet. This bald patch in the middle of the pampa acts as their studio, for it is here that the viscachas arrange their artistic displays. The long, dry, hollow stems of the thistles are piled carefully into heaps, interspersed with stones, twigs, and roots. Anything else that catches the viscacha's eye is added to this still-life to make it more attractive. Outside one *vizcachera* I examined the usual pile of twigs, stones, and thistle stems which was tastefully intermixed with several oil tin cans, three bits of silver paper, eight scarlet cigarette packets, and a cow's horn. Somehow this whimsical display, arranged so carefully and lovingly out in the vast and empty pampa, made me feel a tremendous desire to meet a viscacha on his own ground. I could imagine the portly little animal, with its sad, striped face, squatting in the moonlight at the mouth of its burrow, absorbed in the task of arranging its exhibition of dried plants and other inanimate objects. At one time the viscacha used to be one of the commonest of the pampa animals, but his vegetarian habits and his insistence on clearing large areas of grass for holding his artistic displays got him into trouble with the agriculturists. So the farmers went to war, and the viscacha has been harried and slaughtered and driven away from most of his old haunts.

We never caught a viscacha, nor, as I say, even saw one. It was the one member of the Argentine fauna that I most regretted not having met.

INTERLUDE

WE had been assured by the air company that once we had got our specimens to Buenos Aires we would be able to send them off to London within twenty-four hours. So, when our lorry reached the outskirts of the capital, I phoned the freight department to tell them we had arrived, and to ask them which was the best place at the airfield in which to house the animals for the night. With exquisite courtesy, they informed me that we would not be able to send the animals off for a week, and that there was nowhere on the airport to keep them. To be stranded in the middle of Buenos Aires with a lorry-load of animals and nowhere to keep them was, to say the least, a trifle disconcerting.

Appreciating our predicament, the kindly lorry driver said that we might leave the animals in the lorry overnight, but that they would have to be removed first thing in the morning, as he had a job. Gratefully we accepted this offer, and, having parked our vehicle in the yard near his house, we set about the job of feeding the animals. Half-way through this operation Jacquie had an idea.

'I know!' she exclaimed triumphantly; 'let's phone the Embassy.'

'You can't phone an Embassy and ask them to put up your animals for a week,' I pointed out. 'Embassies aren't provided for that sort of thing.'

'If you phone Mr Gibbs he might be able to help,' she persisted. 'I think it's worth trying, anyway.'

Reluctantly, and much against my better judgement, I phoned the Embassy.

'Hullo! You back?' said Mr Gibbs jovially. 'Did you have a good time?'

'Yes, we had a wonderful time, thanks.'

'Good. Did you catch much of the local fauna?'

'Well, a fair amount. As a matter of fact that's why I phoned you; I was wondering if you could help us.'

'Certainly. What's the trouble?' asked Mr Gibbs unsuspectingly.

'We want a place to put our animals in for a week.'

There was a short silence at the other end, during which I presumed that Mr Gibbs was fighting a wild desire to slam down his receiver. But I had under-estimated his self-control, for when he answered, his voice was suave and even, unruffled by the slightest trace of hysteria.

'That's a bit of problem. You mean you want a garden or something like that?'

'Yes, preferably with a garage. Do you know of one?'

'I don't, off-hand. I'm not often asked to find ... er ... hotel accommodation for livestock, so my experience is limited,' he pointed out. 'However, if you come round and see me in the morning I may have thought of something.'

'Thanks very much,' I said gratefully. 'What time d'you get to the Embassy?'

'Don't come as early as that,' said Mr Gibbs hastily. 'Come round about ten-thirty. It'll give me a chance to contact a few people.'

I went back and related the conversation to Jacquie and Ian.

'Ten-thirty is no good,' said Jacquie. 'The lorry driver's just told us that his first job's at six.'

We sat in gloomy silence for some time, wracking our brains.

'I know!' said Jacquie suddenly.

'No,' I said firmly. 'I am *not* going to phone the Ambassador.'

'No, let's phone Bebita.'

'Good Lord, yes! Why didn't we think of it before?'

'She's sure to be able to find a place,' said Jacquie, who seemed to be under the impression that everyone in Buenos Aires was adept at finding accommodation for wild animals at a moment's notice. For the third time I went to the phone. The conversation that ensued was Bebita at her best.

'Hullo, Bebita. How are you?'

'Gerry? Ah, child, I was just talking about you. Where are you?'

'Somewhere in the wilder outskirts of the city, that's all I know.'

'Well, find out where you are and come and have dinner.'

'We'd love to, if we may.'

'B-b-but of course you may.'

'Bebita, I really phoned to ask you if you could help us.'

'Of course, child. What is it?'

'Well, we're stranded here with all our animals. Could you find somewhere for us to put them for a week?'

Bebita chuckled.

'Ahh!' she sighed, in mock resignation, 'what a man! You phone me at this hour to ask for shelter for your animals. Do you never think of anything else b-b-but animals?'

'I know it's an awful hour,' I said contritely, 'but we'll be in a devil of a mess if we don't find somewhere soon.'

'Don't despair, child. I will find somewhere for you. Ring me b-b-back in half an hour.'

'Wonderful!' I said, my spirits rising. 'I'm sorry to worry you with all this, but there's no one else I can ask.'

'Silly, silly, silly,' said Bebita; 'b-b-but naturally you must ask me. Good-bye.'

Half an hour crept by, and then I phoned again.

'Gerry? Well, I have found you a place. A friend of mine will let you keep them in his garden. He has a sort of garage.'

'Bebita, you're marvellous!' I said enthusiastically.

'B-b-but naturally,' she said, chuckling. 'Now, write down the address, take your animals round there, and then come here for dinner.'

In high spirits we rattled through the twilit streets to the address Bebita had given us. Ten minutes later the lorry stopped, and peering out of the back I saw a pair of wrought-iron gates some twenty feet high, and behind them a wide gravel pathway stretched up to a house that looked like an offspring of Windsor Castle. I was just about to inform the lorry driver that he had brought us to the wrong house, when the gates were flung open by a beaming porter, who bowed our dilapidated vehicle in as though it had been a Rolls. Along one side of the house was a sort of covered veranda which, the porter informed us, was where we were to put our things. Feeling slightly dazed, we unloaded the animals. I still had a strong suspicion that it might prove to be the wrong house, but at least the animals were accommodated, so we hurried down the gravel path and out through the wrought-iron gates as quickly as possible, before the owner could turn up and start protesting. At her flat Bebita greeted us, calm, beautiful, and looking slightly amused.

'Ah, children, did you arrange your animals comfortably?'

'Yes, they're all fixed up. It's a wonderful place for them. It's very generous of your friend, Bebita.'

'Ahh!' she sighed, 'b-b-but he is like that ... so sweet ... so generous ... and such charm ... ahh! you've no idea what charm that man has.'

'How long did it take you to persuade him?' I asked sceptically.

'B-b-but he offered; I did not persuade,' said Bebita innocently. 'I rang him up and told him that we wanted to put a few small animals in his garden, and he agreed straight away. He is my friend, so naturally he will say yes.'

She smiled at us brilliantly.

'I don't see how he could have refused,' I said; 'but seriously, we're terribly grateful to you. You're rapidly becoming our Fairy Godmother.'

'Silly, silly, silly,' said Bebita. 'Come and have dinner.'

Though we appreciated Bebita's legerdemain in producing a place for our animals, we did not realize quite what an extraordinary piece of magic it was until the following day, when we called on Mr Gibbs.

'I'm sorry,' he said apologetically as we entered his office. 'I've tried several places, but I haven't had any success.'

'Oh, don't worry about that. A friend of ours found us a place,' I said.

'I am glad,' said Mr Gibbs; 'it must have been very worrying for you. Where have you got them?'

'In a house in Avenida Alvear.'

'*Where?*'

'A house in Avenida Alvear.'

'Avenida Alvear?' asked Mr Gibbs faintly.

'Yes; what's wrong with that?'

'Nothing ... nothing at all,' said Mr Gibbs, staring at us blankly – 'except that Avenida Alvear is to Buenos Aires what Park Lane is to London.'

Some time later, when our captures had eventually gone off by air, we found that we definitely could not go South. The problem was, where to go? Then, one day, Bebita phoned.

'Listen, child,' she commanded. 'Would you like to go to Paraguay for a trip?'

'I should love to go to Paraguay,' I said fervently.

'Well, I think I can arrange it. You will have to fly to Asunción, and then my friend's plane will pick you up there and fly you to this place ... it is called Puerto Casada.'

'I suppose you arranged all this with one of your friends?'

'B-b-but naturally. With who else would I arrange it, silly?'

'The only snag I can see is our primitive Spanish.'

'I have also thought of that. You remember Rafael?'

'Yes, I remember him.'

'Well, he is on holiday from school, and he would like to go with you as interpreter. His mother thinks that the trip would do him good, on condition that you do not let him catch any snakes.'

'What an extraordinarily intelligent mother. I think the idea's excellent, and I love you and all your friends.'

'Silly, silly, silly,' said Bebita, and rang off.

So it was that Jacquie and I flew up to Asunción, the capital of Paraguay, and with us travelled Rafael de Soto Acebal, bubbling over with such enthusiasm for the whole trip that by the end of the flight he was making me feel like a cynical and jaded old globe-trotter.

CHAPTER THREE

FIELDS OF FLYING FLOWERS

THE sky was pale blue and full of morning light when the lorry bumped on to the small airfield outside Asunción. Still half-drugged with sleep, we descended stiffly and unloaded our equipment. Then we stood around, yawning and stretching, while the lorry driver and the pilot disappeared into a dilapidated hangar that stood on the edge of the field. Presently, to the accompaniment of loud grunts of exertion, they reappeared, pushing a small four-seater monoplane tastefully painted in silver and red. As the two men edged it out of the hangar into the sunlight, they looked extraordinarily like a pair of corpulent brown ants manoeuvring an extremely small moth. Rafael had seated himself on a suitcase, his head drooping languidly, his eyes half closed.

'Look, Rafael,' I said cheerfully; 'our aeroplane.'

He jerked upright and looked at the tiny plane being pushed towards us. His eyes widened behind his spectacles.

'No!' he exclaimed incredulously. '*This* our plane?'

'Yes, I'm afraid so.'

'Oh, migosh!'

'What's the matter with it?' inquired Jacquie; 'it's a dear little plane.'

'Yes,' said Rafael, 'that is what the matter ... it is *little*.'

'It looks strong enough,' I said soothingly, and at that moment one of the wheels went over a small tussock of grass and the whole structure wobbled and twanged melodiously.

'Oh, migosh, no!' came from Rafael aghast. 'Gerry, *ce n'est pas* possible we fly in this ... she is too small ...'

'It's quite all right, Rafael, really,' said Jacquie, with the cheerful optimism of one who had never travelled in a small plane; 'this kind is very good.'

'Sure?' asked our friend, his spectacles glittering anxiously.

'Yes, quite sure ... they use this kind a lot in America.'

'Yes, but Jacquie, America is not this Chaco ... See, she has only one wing, *n'est-ce pas?* That wing break, we go ... brrr ... bang ... into the forest,' and he sat back and surveyed us like a dejected owl.

Meanwhile the plane had been wheeled into position, and the pilot approached us, his gold teeth flashing in a smile.

'*Bueno, vamos,*' he said, and started to pick up the luggage.

Rafael got to his feet and picked up his suitcase.

'Gerry, I no like this,' he said plaintively, as he started to-wards our aerial transport.

When all our equipment was loaded, we found there was very little room left for us, but we managed to squeeze in, I and the pilot in the front, Rafael and Jacquie behind. I climbed in last and slammed the incredibly fragile-looking door, and it immediately flew open again. The pilot leaned across me and glared at the door.

'*No bueno,*' he explained, grabbing it with one powerful hand and slamming it so hard that the whole plane rocked.

'Oh, migosh!' came from Rafael faintly.

The pilot fiddled with the controls, whistling merrily between his teeth, the engine roared, and the plane began to shudder and vibrate. Then we lurched forward, the plane bouncing over the uneven ground, the green grass became a blur, and we were airborne. As we circled round, we could see the country-side below, rich tropical green, with the red-earth roads running like veins across it. We flew over Asunción, its pink houses gleaming in the sunlight, and then, in front of the blunt nose and the glittering circle of propeller, I could see the River Paraguay ahead.

Flying at that height, we could see that the river formed a fiery, flickering barrier between two types of country: below us was the rich red earth, the green forests and farmlands that surrounded Asunción and made up the eastern half of Paraguay; across the sprawling river lay the Chaco, a vast level plain stretching away to the horizon. Slightly blurred by the morning mist, this plain seemed to be covered with silver-bronze grass, marked here and there with vivid green patches of undergrowth. It looked as though a pair of shears had been taken to it and it had been clipped like the flank of an enormous poodle, leaving the green patches of wool decorating the tawny skin of grass. It was a curious, lifeless landscape, the only moving thing being the river, which glittered and twinkled as it moved over the plain, split now into three or four channels, now into fifty or sixty, each coiling and interweaving in an intricate pattern like the shining viscera of some monstrous silver dragon disembowelled across the plain.

When we crossed the river and flew lower, I could see that what I had first thought to be a dry plain of grass was in reality marshland, for now and then the water gleamed, as the sun's reflection caught it. The poodle wool turned out to be thorn-scrub, tightly packed, with occasional palm trees bursting up through it. In places the palms grew in serried ranks, almost as if planted: green feather dusters stuck in the bronze grass. Everywhere you could see the sudden, brilliant sparkle of water: an explosion of white light as the sun caught it; yet everywhere the undergrowth looked dusty and parched, its roots in water, but its leaves withered by the sun. It was weird, desolate, but strangely fascinating country. After a while, though, the landscape became monotonous, for there were no shadows except those of the shock-headed palms.

From somewhere under his seat the pilot produced a bottle, uncorked it with the aid of his teeth and handed it to me. It was iced coffee, bitter but refreshing. I drank, handed it to Jacquie and Rafael and returned the remains to the pilot. As he stuck the neck of the bottle between his teeth and tipped back his head to drink, the nose of the plane dipped sickeningly towards the silver curve of the river, two thousand feet below. Having drunk, he wiped his mouth with the back of his hand, and then leant over and shouted in my ear:

'Puerto Casado,' and pointed ahead.

Dimly through the heat-haze I could see that we were flying towards the black shape of a hill that had appeared suddenly and surprisingly in the flatness below.

'*Una hora, más o menos,*' yelled the pilot, pointing and holding up one finger – '*una hora* . . . Puerto Casado . . . *comprende*?'

For an hour I dozed intermittently, while the dark bulk of the hill grew closer and closer. The nose of the plane dipped as we glided down towards the earth, and the warm upward currents of air caught the tiny machine and shook and buffeted it until it swayed and dipped drunkenly like a flake of wood-ash over a bonfire. Then we banked sharply, and for one miraculous second the Chaco tilted up like a wall, the river hung over one wing and the horizon appeared above us. We straightened out and dropped steadily down to a strip of grass-field which would have been indistinguishable from any other part of the scenery if it had not been for a yellow wind-sock hanging limply on a pole. We bumped on to the grass and taxied to a standstill. The pilot grinned at me, switched off the engine, and waved his hand in an all-embracing gesture.

'Chaco!' he explained.

As we opened the door of the plane and got out, the heat hit us with an almost physical blow, and it felt as though the air had suddenly been sucked out of our lungs. The golden grass underfoot was as crisp and dry as wood shavings, patched here and there with clumps of yellow and flame-coloured flowers. We had just got the last of the equipment out of the plane when a lorry appeared in the distance, bumping over the grass towards us. It was driven by a short, fat Paraguayan with a twinkling smile, who seemed vastly amused at our arrival. He helped us pile the stuff into the back of the truck, and then we jolted off

across the air-strip and along a dusty, deeply rutted road through the forest. There was so much dust from our progress, and we were so busily engaged in holding on to the bucking sides of the vehicle, that I did not have a chance to see much of the passing country-side, and within ten minutes we roared into the village of Casado. It was the usual conglomeration of tumble-down shacks, separated by earth roads worn into furrows. We swept past a large mango tree which was obviously the centre of the village, for everyone seemed to be congregated in its shade, either sleeping, gossiping, or bargaining for the odd assortment of pumpkins, sugar-cane, eggs, bananas, and other produce lying there in the dust.

The little house in which we were to live was at one end of the village, and it was half hidden behind a screen of grapefruit and orange trees and shaggy bushes of hibiscus splashed with enormous scarlet flowers. The house and its cloak of foliage was surrounded by a network of narrow, shallow irrigation ditches, half choked with grass and water-plants. Round these a choir of mosquitoes hummed melodiously, and they were joined at night by a great variety of tree-frogs, toads, and cicadas. The tree-frogs would pipe and trill excitedly, the toads would belch in a ponderous and thoughtful sort of manner, and the cicadas would produce at intervals a sound like that of a soprano electric saw cutting through a sheet of tin. The house was adequate, without being luxurious. It consisted of three rooms, all inter-communicating in the Spanish fashion, and all of which leaked. Some distance away was the kitchen and the bathroom, connected to the house by a covered way. Ten minutes after our arrival I discovered we were expected to share our bathroom with quite a varied assortment of the local fauna: there were several hundred mosquitoes in there, together with a number of large, glittering, and agile cockroaches and several depressed-looking spiders that occupied the floor. The lavatory cistern had been taken over by some wide-eyed and anaemic-looking tree-frogs and a small vampire bat, which hung there chittering ferociously, and looking, as all bats do, rather like an umbrella that has seen better days.

It was rather unfortunate that I should have kept these zoological discoveries to myself, for Jacquie was the next one to enter the bathroom, and she reappeared at startling speed leaving a trail of soap, towels, and tooth-brushes behind her. Apparently, when she had entered, the bat had decided he was getting a bit bored with these constant interruptions, and he had swooped down from the cistern and hung, fluttering, in front of her face. She pointed out, rather acidly, that she had not hitherto considered bats essential to clean living. Eventually I managed to persuade her that the creature was harmless, in spite of his anti-social attitude; but afterwards, whenever she used the bathroom, she kept a very wary eye on the bat as he hung aloft, regarding her with an inimical stare.

We had just finished unpacking our things when we were greeted by another member of the local fauna in the shape of our housekeeper, a dark-skinned, dark-eyed Paraguayan woman, whose name, she assured us, was Paula. At one time she must have been a handsome woman, but now she had run slightly to seed. Her body bulged in all directions, but, even so, she still possessed an extraordinary grace and lightness of movement. She would drift through the house like a chocolate cumulus-cloud on its way to a storm, humming some love-song to herself, her eyes misty, indulging in her own peculiar

brand of dusting, which consisted of sweeping everything off
tables and chairs on to the floor, and then bending down with
great grunts of exertion to pick up the remains. It was not long
before we discovered that Paula occupied a high and honoured
position in the local community: she was nothing less than the
local Madam, and she had all the young unmarried females of
the village in her care. As their manager, trainer, and protector
she took her job seriously. Once a fortnight, when the river-
steamer arrived, she would take her girls down to the river-
bank and keep a motherly eye on them while they argued and
bargained with the steamer's crew and passengers. The steamer
always hooted when it was about three-quarters of a mile down
the river, to give warning of its arrival, and this was Paula's
signal to rush into her hut and dress. She would force her
enormous breasts into a minute brassière, leaving out those
portions which it could not accommodate, clad herself in a dress,
the design of which was almost as startling as its colour scheme,
push her feet into shoes with six-inch heels, pour about a cupful
of asphyxiating scent over the ensemble and then set off down
the road to the jetty, driving a chattering and giggling selection
of her wares before her. She looked rather like an amiable and
elderly schoolmistress, as she herded them along in this untidy,
shrill crocodile. Owing to the importance of Paula's position,
she had everyone, including the local constabulary, eating out
of her hand. No task was too difficult for her. Ask her for something – whether it was some smuggled Brazilian cigarettes or a
bowl of delicious *Dulce de Leche* – and she would immediately
marshal her girls and set them to scour the village for it. Woe
betide the man who refused to help Paula. His position in the
village (biologically speaking) became impossible. She was
definitely an ally worth having, as we soon found out.

Although I was eager to get out and see something of the
country, I had to restrain my impatience. The rest of the day
was spent in unpacking and checking our equipment and
getting the house more or less organized. Rafael, at my in-
stigation, questioned Paula about methods of getting into the
interior. She said there were three ways of doing this: on horse-
back, by ox-cart, or on an *autovía*. Further questioning revealed

the fact that the *autovía* was the form of transport which we came to call the Chaco railway, although the term railway was really a euphemism. It consisted of very narrow-gauge rails, on which were mounted dilapidated Ford 8s. This railway went some two hundred kilometres into the Chaco, and so from our point of view seemed a godsend. Paula said that if we went through the village to the line, we would find the *autovías* parked there, and a driver was sure to be around who could tell us when the next one was due to leave. So Rafael and I trotted off to investigate the possibilities of the Chaco railway.

Sure enough, on the other side of the village we came on the line, though it took a bit of finding, for it was so overgrown with weeds it was almost indistinguishable from the surrounding terrain. The line itself was so fantastic that I could only stare at it in mute, horror-stricken silence. It was approximately two and a half feet wide, each rail worn down and glossy with use, so buckled that they looked like a couple of silver snakes wriggling away through the grass. How any vehicle managed to stay on them was more than I would understand. Later, when I discovered the speed at which the *autovías* were driven along these lines, it seemed to me a miracle that we managed to survive our trips on them at all.

Some distance away we discovered a siding in which were parked several battered and inscrutable *autovías*, and under a tree nearby we found an equally battered and inscrutable driver, asleep in the long grass. On being awoken, he admitted that there was an *autovía* travelling some twenty kilometres up the line on the following morning, and, if we wished, we could travel in it. Endeavouring to forget the buckled lines, I said that this was what we would do; it would give us some sort of picture of the country, and we could find out what kind of bird-life was the commonest. We thanked the driver, who mumbled '*Nada, nada* ... it's nothing,' before falling back and dropping into a deep sleep again. Rafael and I went back to the house and told Jacquie the good news, carefully omitting any reference to the state of the railway.

The next morning, just before dawn, we were awakened by Paula, who undulated into the room, carrying tea, and beamed

at us with grisly cheerfulness that some people seem to reserve
for the very early morning. She waddled into Rafael's room,
and we heard him groan unintelligible replies to her sprightly
questions. Outside, it was still dark, but the whine of the cicadas
was punctuated by an occasional sleepy cockcrow. Rafael appeared, clad in a pair of underpants and his glasses.

'That woman,' he complained; 'she so glad when she wake
me ... I no like.'

'It's good for you to get up early,' I said; 'you spend half
your life in a somnambulistic condition, like a hibernating bear.'

'Early morning rising makes you fit,' said Jacquie unctuously,
stifling a yawn.

'Are you coming like that?' I asked our puzzled interpreter,
'or are you going to put some clothes on?'

Rafael's brow was furrowed as he tried to work out these
remarks.

'I should come like that,' I continued facetiously; 'it's a
very fetching outfit ... and if you leave your glasses behind, you
won't be able to see the mosquitoes.'

'I no understand, Gerry,' said Rafael at length. His English
was not at its best in the early morning.

'Never mind. Get some clothes on ... the *autovía* won't wait,
you know.'

Half an hour later we clattered down the line in the *autovía*,
through the banks of river-mist, opalescent in the early morning light. As we left the outskirts of the village, and the last
village dog dropped panting behind, the sun rose with sudden
brilliance from behind the trees and washed all the colour from
the rim of the eastern horizon, and we rocked and swayed along
the line, deeper and deeper into the Chaco forests.

The trees were not tall, but they grew so closely together
that their branches interlinked; beneath them the ground was
waterlogged and overgrown with a profusion of plants, thorny
bushes, and, incredibly enough, cacti. There were cacti that
looked like a series of green plates stuck together by their
edges, and covered with bunches of yellow spikes and pale
mauve flowers; others were like octopuses, their long arms
spread out across the ground, or curling round the tree-trunks

in a spiky embrace; others again looked like plump green busbies covered with a haze of black spines. Some of these cacti were growing and flowering with their fleshy bodies half covered in water. In between the *autovía* lines there grew a small plant in great profusion; it was only a few inches high, and topped with a delicate cup-shaped flower of magenta red. So thickly had it spread in places along the track that I had the impression of travelling along an endless flower-bed.

Occasionally the forest would be broken by a great grass-field, studded with tall, flame-coloured flowers that covered several acres, and neatly bisected by rows of palms, their curving fronds making them look like green rockets bursting against the sky. These grass-fields were sprinkled with dozens of widow tyrants – birds about the size of a sparrow but with jet-black upper parts and their breasts and throats as white as ermine. They perched on convenient sticks and dead trees, and now and again one would flip off, catch a passing insect, and return to its perch, its breast gleaming and twinkling against the grass like a shooting star. They were known locally as *flor blanca* – the white flower – a beautiful name for them. Here, then, was a whole field of flying flowers, fluttering and swooping, their breasts shining with the pure whiteness of the sun's reflection on water.

Probably the most astonishing tree in this landscape was one with a trunk which bulged out suddenly at the base, making it look like a wine-jar; it had short, twisted branches decorated half-heartedly with small pale-green leaves. These trees stood around in small groups, looking as though they had sucked up so much from the ground that their trunks had swollen in obesity.

'What are those trees called, Rafael?' I called above the clatter of the *autovía*'s wheels.

'*Palo borracho*,' he answered; 'you see how they are, Gerry – very fat no? They say they have drunk too much, so they call them the stick that is drunk.'

'The drunken stick ... that's a lovely name for them. Most appropriate place for them to live, too ... the whole forest looks drunken.'

And, indeed, the whole landscape did look as though nature had organized an enormous bottle party, inviting the weird mixture of temperate, sub-tropical, and tropical plants to it. Everywhere the palms leaned tiredly, the professional bar loungers with their too long heads of hair; the thornbushes grappled in an inebriated brawl; the well-dressed flowers and the unshaven cacti side by side; and everywhere, the *palo borrachos* stood with their bulging, beer-drinkers' stomachs, tilted at unbalanced angles; and everywhere among this floral throng hurried the widow tyrants, like small, slick waiters with incredibly immaculate shirt-fronts.

One of the disadvantages of this country-side was made very apparent when we rounded a bend and saw before us a beautiful stretch of marsh, ringed with palms, in which were feeding four enormous jabiru storks. They moved through the grassy areas and the lanes of bright water with a slow and stately step, reminding me irresistibly of a procession I had once seen of Negro preachers in white surplices. Their bodies were spotless white, and the heads and beaks, sunk meditatively into the hunched shoulders, were coal-black; they moved slowly and thoughtfully through the water, pausing occasionally to stand on one leg and shrug their wings gently. Wanting to watch them for a few minutes, I called out to the driver to stop, and he, looking rather surprised, brought the *autovía* to a screeching halt on the line, some fifty feet away from the storks, who took not the slightest notice. I had just settled comfortably back on the wooden seat and reached for the binoculars when a zebra-striped mosquito of incredible dimensions rose from the marsh, zoomed into the *autovía* and settled on my arm. I swatted him carelessly, and raised the binoculars to my eyes, only to lower them almost immediately to swat at my legs, on which another four mosquitoes had materialized. Looking about, I saw to my

horror that what I had taken to be a slight mist drifting over the grass was in reality a cloud of these insects which was descending on the *autovía* with shrill whines of excitement. Within seconds, the cloud had enveloped us: mosquitoes clung to our faces, necks, and arms, and even settled on our trouser legs and proceeded to bite right

through the cloth with undiminished ability. Slapping and cursing, I told the driver to start up, for bird-watching under those conditions was impossible, however enthusiastic one might be. As the *autovia* rattled off, most of the mosquitoes were left behind, but a few of the tougher ones managed to keep up with us for half a mile or so down the track. Being attacked every time you stopped rather detracted from the ride, for it was really quite impossible to halt in a place for more than ten minutes at a time without being driven nearly mad by the mosquitoes. This made any hunting, and particularly filming, a painful and irritating job; when fiddling about with lens and exposure meters I found it essential to have someone stand over me with a hat, to keep at least some of the insects at bay, otherwise it was impossible to concentrate and my temper frayed rapidly. By the time we had reached Puerto Casado again that afternoon I had exposed about twenty feet of film, and all three of us were scarlet and swollen with bites. But that first ride, however unpleasant, had given me some idea of the type of country we had to operate in, and the snags that were likely to be encountered. Now we had to settle down to the real job of extracting the fauna from the mosquito-infested depths of the Drunken Forests.

CHAPTER FOUR

THE ORANGE ARMADILLOS

THE first specimen caught by the local inhabitants of Puerto Casado turned up at our house forty-eight hours after our arrival. I was awakened at some dark and deadly hour in the morning, when the cicadas and tree-frogs were vying with the local cockerels for vocal supremacy, by a scream so loud and indignant that it completely drowned all other sounds. I sat bolt upright in bed and stared at Jacquie, who peered back at me, equally astonished. Before we had time to speak there came another ear-splitting cry, which I placed this time as emanating from the kitchen; it was followed by a shrill and incomprehensible burst of Guarani.

'Good heavens!' said Jacquie; 'that sounds like Paula ... whatever *is* happening out there?'

I crawled out of bed and felt for my slippers.

'It sounds as though she's being raped,' I said.

'It can't be that,' said my wife sleepily; 'she wouldn't scream about *that*.'

I eyed her disapprovingly and made my way out on to the

mist-shrouded back veranda. I was just in time to witness an extraordinary scene in the kitchen. The door stood wide open, and framed against the rosy glow of the fire stood our housekeeper, arms akimbo, her magnificent chest heaving with the effort of having produced that flood of Guarani. In front of her stood a short, thin little Indian, clad in tattered vest and pants, clutching in one hand a very battered straw hat, and in the other what appeared to be a football. As I watched, he spoke softly and soothingly to Paula, and then held out his hand with the football in it; Paula recoiled, and let out another scream of indignation so powerful that a large toad, who had been sitting near the kitchen door, leapt wildly into the dark safety of the hibiscus bushes. The Indian, who was made of sterner stuff, put his straw hat on the floor, placed the football in it, and proceeded to wave his arms and chatter; Paula drew a deep breath and started to wither him with a blast of invective. Two people, at five o'clock in the morning, preparing to shout each other down in the series of catarrhal honks which constitute the Guarani language, was more than I could stand.

'Oi!' I yelled loudly, '*buenos días.*'

The effect was immediate. The Indian scooped up his hat containing the football, and, clutching it to his gaping shirt-front, bowed and backed into the shadows. Paula hitched up her bosom, gave a minute but graceful curtsy, and then drifted towards me, quivering with emotion. '*Ah, señor,*' she said, panting a little and clasping her hands together fervently. '*Ah, señor, que hombre . . . buenos días, señor . . . yo lo siento . . .*'

I frowned at her, and broke into my most fluent Spanish.

'*Hombre,*' I said, pointing at the Indian, who was giving a wonderful display of adaptive coloration in the shadows, '*hombre . . . porqué usted argumentos?*'

Paula rushed into the shadows and dragged the unwilling Indian out. She pushed him in front of me, where he stood with hanging head, and then stood back and with a magnificent gesture pointed a fat brown finger at him.

'*Hombre,*' she said, her voice vibrating with passion, '*mal hombre.*'

'Why?' I asked. I was rather sorry for the Indian.

Paula gazed at me as though I was mad.

'*Por qué*,' she repeated. '*Por qué?*'

'*Por qué*,' I nodded, beginnnng to feel like something out of a Gilbert and Sullivan chorus.

'*Mire, señor*,' she said, 'look!' and she seized the hat that the Indian had crushed to his breast and displayed the football nestling inside. Now it was at close quarters, but in the shadow, I could see that the offending object was smaller than a football, but much the same shape. We all three gazed at it in silence for a minute; then Paula refilled her lungs and paralysed me with a machine-gun fire of rapid Spanish, the only word of which I could understand was the oft-repeated one of *hombre*. I began to feel in need of some assistance.

'*Momento!*' I said, holding up my hand, and then I turned and stalked back into the house.

'What on earth's going on out there?' asked Jacquie, as I reappeared.

'I haven't the faintest idea. Paula seems to be mortally wounded by the fact that an Indian is trying to sell her a plum pudding.'

'A plum pudding?'

'Well, a plum pudding or a football. It looks like a hybrid of the two. I'm just going to get Rafael to find out what it's all about.'

'It can't be a plum pudding.'

'Aha!' I said, 'this is the Chaco ... anything can happen in the Chaco.'

In Rafael's room I found him, as usual, curled into a tight knot underneath a pile of bed-clothes, vibrating gently with snores. I stripped the clothes off him and slapped his rump. He groaned loudly. I slapped him again, and he sat up and peered at me, his mouth drooping open.

'Rafael, wake up. I want you to come and translate.'

'Oh, no, Gerry, not now,' he wailed, peering myopically at his watch. 'Look, she is only five-thirty ... I cannot.'

'Come on,' I said relentlessly, 'out of bed. You're supposed to be the translator of this party.'

Rafael put on his glasses and glared at me with tousled dignity.

'I am translate, yes,' he said, 'but I am not translate at five in the morning.'

'Look, stop talking and get some clothes on. Paula's got an Indian out there and they're arguing over something that looks like a football ... I can't understand what it's all about, so you've got to come out and translate.'

'How I love this Chaco!' said Rafael bitterly, as he pulled on his shoes and followed me, groaning and yawning, to the kitchen. Paula and the Indian were still standing there, and the football still reposed in the Indian's hat.

'*Buenos días,*' said Rafael, blinking sleepily at them, '*qué pasa?*'

Paula's bosom swelled, and she proceeded to tell the whole story to Rafael, dancing about the veranda in a wonderful, flesh-undulating pantomime, breaking off now and then to point at the silent culprit with his plum pudding. Eventually she came to a breathless halt, and leaned exhausted against the wall, holding a fat hand to her heaving torso.

'Well?' I asked Rafael, who was looking bewildered, 'what's it all about?'

Rafael scratched his head.

'I no understand very well, Gerry,' he said. 'She say this man bring a bad thing ... er ... how you say? a dirty thing, no? Then he tell her lie and say you buy this.'

'Well, what is the blasted thing, for Heaven's sake?'

Rafael rapped a question at the plum-pudding owner, who looked up and smiled shyly.

'*Bicho,*' said the Indian, holding out the hat.

Now, the first and, to my mind, most important word I had learned on arriving in South America was '*bicho*'. It meant, literally, an animal. Any and every living creature was classified under this all-embracing term, and so it was naturally one of the first that I had committed to memory. So, hearing the Indian use the magic word, I suddenly realized that what I had mistaken for a plum pudding was a living creature. With a cry of delight I pushed past Rafael and pulled the straw hat from the little

Indian's grasp and rushed into the kitchen, so that I could see its contents by the light of the oil lamp. Inside the hat, curled into a tight ball, lay a creature I had long wanted to meet. It was a three-banded armadillo.

'Rafael,' I called excitedly, 'just come and look at this.'

He came into the kitchen and stared at the creature in my cupped hands.

'What is it, Gerry?' he asked curiously.

'It's an armadillo ... you know, a *peludo*, the small kind that rolls into a ball ... I showed you pictures of it.'

'Ah, yes,' said Rafael, light dawning, 'here she is called the *tatu naranja*.'

'What does *naranja* mean?' I asked curiously.

'*Naranja* mean orange, Gerry – you know, the fruit.'

'Oh, yes, of course. It does look rather like a big orange rolled up.'

'You want this?' Rafael inquired, prodding it with a cautious finger.

'Good Lord, yes; I want lots of them. Look, Rafael, ask him where he caught it, how much he wants for it, and can he get me some more.'

Rafael turned to the Indian, who was standing beaming in the doorway, and asked him.

The little man nodded his head vigorously, and then broke into halting Spanish.

Rafael listened and then turned to me.

'He say he can get you plenty, Gerry. *Il y a* plenty in the forest. He wants to know how many you want.'

'Well, I want at least six ... But what price does he want?'

For ten minutes Rafael and the Indian bargained, and then Rafael turned to me.

'It is good for five *guarani*?' he asked.

'Yes, that's a reasonable price. I'll pay him that. Look, Rafael, ask him if he can show me the place where these things live, will you?'

Again Rafael and the Indian conferred.

'Yes, he say he can show you ... but it is in the forest, Gerry ... We must go on horse, you know.'

'Fine,' I said, delighted. 'Tell him to come back this afternoon and we'll go out and look for some.'

Rafael relayed my suggestion, and the Indian nodded his head and gave me a wide, friendly smile.

'*Bueno ... muy bueno,*' I said, smiling at him; 'now I'll go and get his money.'

As I sped away into the house, the armadillo still lovingly clasped in my hands, I heard Paula give a despairing yelp of horror, but I was in no mood to consider her outraged feelings. I found Jacquie still sitting up in bed, moodily contemplating the mosquito bites on her arms.

'Look what I've got,' I said gleefully, and rolled the creature on to her bed.

In my delight at receiving such an unusual specimen I had forgotten that my wife was, as yet, not quite used to the delights of collecting. She emerged from her cocoon of bed-clothes and landed on the opposite side of the room with a leap that any ballerina might have envied. From this safe vantage point she glared at my offering.

'What is it?' she inquired.

'Good Lord, darling, what are you leaping about like that for? It's an armadillo ... it's perfectly harmless.'

'And how was I supposed to know?' she inquired; 'you rush in here and hurl the thing at me like that. And do you mind taking it off my bed?'

'But it won't hurt you,' I explained. 'It's quite harmless, honestly.'

'Yes, I'm sure it is, darling, but I don't want to romp about in bed with it at five in the morning. Why can't you put it on your bed?'

I placed the offending animal tenderly on my bed, and then went out to pay the Indian. Rafael and I returned to the house to find Jacquie sitting in her bed, wearing a martyred expression. I glanced at my bed, and, to my horror, saw that the armadillo had disappeared.

'Don't worry,' said Jacquie sweetly; 'the dear little thing's only buried itself.'

I dug down among the bed-clothes and felt the armadillo

scrabbling frantically in a tangle of sheets. I hauled him out, and he immediately rolled into a tight ball again. Sitting down on the bed, I examined him. Rolled up, he was about the size and shape of a small melon; on one side of the ball were the three bands from which he got his name, horny stripes which were separated from each other by a thin line of pinkish-grey skin that acted as a hinge; on the other side of the ball you could see how his head and tail fitted into the general scheme of armour-plating. Both these extremities were guarded on top by a section of armour-plate, very gnarled and carunculated, shaped like an acute isosceles triangle. When the head and tail were folded into the ball, these two pieces of armour lay side by side, base to point, together forming a broad triangle which effectively blocked the vulnerable entrance that led to the armadillo's soft undersides. Seen in the light, this armour-plating was a pale amber colour, and appeared as though it had been constructed from a delicate mosaic work. When I had pointed out to my audience the marvels of the creature's external anatomy, I put him on the floor, and we sat in silence, waiting for him to unroll. For some minutes the ball lay immobile; then it started to twitch and jerk slightly. I saw a crack appear between the triangle of head and tail and, as it widened, a small pig-like snout was pushed out. Then, with speed and vigour, the armadillo proceeded to unroll himself. He just split open like some weird bud unfolding, and we had a quick glimpse of a pink, wrinkled tummy covered with dirty white hair, small pink legs, and a sad little face like a miniature pig's, with circular protuberant black eyes. Then he rolled over and righted himself, and all that was visible beneath the shell were the tips of his feet and a few wisps of hair. From the back of his humped shell his tail protruded like one of those ancient war-clubs, covered with spikes and lumps. At the other end his head stuck out, decorated with its triangular cap of knobbed plating, on either side of which had blossomed two tiny, mule-like ears. Beneath this cap of horn I could see the bare cheeks, pink nose, and the small, suspicious eyes gleaming like drops of tar. His hind-feet were circular, with short blunt nails, and looked rather like the feet of a miniature rhinoceros. His fore-feet were so completely different that they might have belonged to another species

of animal: they were armed with three curved nails, the centre one of which was the largest, and resembled the curving talon of some bird of prey. The weight of his hind-quarters rested on his flat hind-feet, but that of his fore-quarters rested on this large nail, so the sole of the foot was raised off the ground, making it seem as though he were standing on tip-toe.

For a moment or so he stood motionless, his nose and ears twitching nervously; then he decided to move. His little legs leapt into motion, moving so fast that they were only a blur beneath his shell, and his claws hit the cement with a steady clickity-clickity-click sound. The complete absence of body

movement, combined with the rhythmic clicking of his nails, made him appear more like some weird clockwork toy than an animal, a resemblance which was even more marked when he ran straight into the wall, which he apparently had not noticed. Our burst of laughter made him pause for a moment and hunch himself defensively, in readiness to roll up; then, when we were silent again, he sniffed at the wall and spent a fruitless five minutes scrabbling at it with his claws in an effort to dig his way through. Finding this an impossibility, he swung round and clickity-clicked his way busily across the room, disappearing beneath my bed.

'He looks just like a gigantic wood-louse,' whispered Jacquie.

'I like this *bicho*, Gerry,' said Rafael, in a stage whisper, beaming through his spectacles; 'he walks just like a tank, no?'

The armadillo, having clicked about under my bed for some time, suddenly reappeared and scuttled off in the direction of the door. It was unfortunate that Paula chose that precise moment to waft massively into the room, bearing a tray on which was our morning tea. Her entrance, with bare feet, was silent, and so the armadillo (whose sight apparently left much to be desired) was unaware of her presence. Paula, her vision of the floor impeded

70

by a combination of bosom and tray, paused in the doorway to beam at us.

'*Buenos días*,' she said to Jacquie, '*el té, señora.*'

The armadillo bustled up to Paula's feet, stopped, and sniffed at this new obstacle, and then decided, since it appeared to be soft, that he would dig his way through. Before any of us could do anything, he stuck an experimental claw into Paula's big toe.

'*Madre de Dios!*' screamed Paula, surpassing in that short exclamation all her previous vocal efforts of the morning.

She sprang backwards through the door, miraculously keeping hold of the tray, but as she disappeared into the darkened living-room the tray tilted and a jug crashed to the floor, spreading a great pool of milk in front of the animal. He sniffed at it suspiciously, sneezed, sniffed again, and then started to lap it up quickly. Rafael and I, weak with laughter, hurried into the living-room to soothe our palpitating housekeeper and relieve her of the tray. When I carried the tray into the bedroom I found

that the armadillo, uneasy at the noise, had pattered off and sought refuge behind a pile of suitcases. Some idea of his strength may be gathered from the fact that the pile of cases was filled with film, batteries, and other equipment, and were so heavy that it took me all my time to lift one of them. Yet the little creature, having decided that

sanctuary lay behind them, stuck his nose into the crack between the cases and the wall and proceeded to push them to one side as easily as though they had been cardboard boxes. He disappeared from view, scrabbling wildly, and then lay still. I decided to leave him there until we had

finished tea. Rafael reappeared, mopping his spectacles and tit-
tering.

'That woman,' he said, 'she makes much noise.'

'Is she bringing some more milk?'

'Yes, I tell her. You know, Gerry, she not understand why you
want *bichos*. No one tell her we come here for *bichos*.'

'Well, did you explain?'

'Oh, yes, I tell her that we come to the Chaco special for
bichos for *zoológicos*.'

'And what did she say to that?'

'She said that all gringos were mad and hoped God would
protect her,' said Rafael, grinning.

After breakfast, served by a still-trembling Paula, we set to
work and made a cage for the armadillo, optimistically making
it big enough to contain several others, should we be lucky enough
to get them. Then I went and dug the little beast from his sanctuary behind the suitcases; it was quite a job, for he was wedged
between the cases and the wall as snugly as a nail in wood. As
soon as I had extracted him, he half rolled himself, and uttered a
few faint hissing sounds; each time I touched his nose or tail he
would hunch himself and give a tiny irritable snort. I yelled for
Jacquie to bring the recording machine, and when it was placed
in position, and the microphone was hovering only a few inches
from the animal, I touched him gently on the nose. He promptly
and silently rolled himself into a tight ball and lay there immobile; no amount of cajoling, tapping, or scratching would
induce him to repeat the sound. Eventually, in disgust, we pushed
him into his cage and left him to his own devices; it was not until
the next day that we managed to record his Lilliputian snorts of
annoyance.

That afternoon the Indian reappeared, leading three depressed-
looking horses, and, arming ourselves with bags, string, and
other impedimenta of the collector, we set out on the hunt for
more orange armadillos. We rode through the village, and for
some two miles followed a track that ran alongside the railway
line; then our guide's horse plunged down the side of the embank-
ment, and made its way along a narrow, twisting path through
the dense, thorny scrub and sprawling cacti. A humming-bird,

glittering green-gold through a misty blur of wings, hung feeding from a white convolvulus flower some three feet above my head; I reached up my hand as we passed beneath it, there was a sudden purring sound and the bird vanished, leaving the trumpet-shaped flower dipping in the breeze caused by its wings. The heat at this hour of the afternoon was intense: a dry, prickly sort of heat that seemed to suck the moisture out of you; even under the broas brim of my hat I had to screw up my eyes against the ferocioud glare. All around, the cicadas sun-worshipped with such a penetrating shrillness that it seemed as though the noise did not come from outside, but was manufactured in the echoing recesses of your own skull.

Presently the dense, thorny growth ended abruptly, and we rode out into a great grass-field decorated with row after row of enormous palms, shock-headed and still in the sun, the shadows of their trunks tiger-striping the golden grass. A pair of black-faced ibis, with neat black moustaches and cinnamon, grey-and-black bodies, paced through the grass, probing the water-filled earth below with their long, sickle-shaped beaks. When they saw us, they flapped up between the palm trunks, crying 'Cronk ... cronk ... arcronk' in deep, harsh voices. Half-way across the grass-field we found that it was divided in two by a wide, meandering strip of wonderful misty blue flowers which stretched away in either direction like a stream; as we got close to it I discovered that it was really a stream, but a stream so thickly overgrown with these blue water-plants that the water was invisible. There was the haze of blue flowers and, underneath, the glint of glossy green leaves growing interlocked. The blue was so clear and delicate that it looked as though a tattered piece of the sky had floated down and settled between the ranks of brown palm-trunks. We took our horses across the river, and their hooves crushed the plants and flowers and left a narrow lane of glittering water. Black-and-scarlet dragon-flies droned smoothly around us, their transparent wings winking in the sun. When we reached the other side and entered the shade of the palm-forest again, I turned in my saddle and looked back at the magnificent lane of blue flowers, across which was marked our path in a stripe of flickering water, like a lightning flash across a summer sky.

We passed through the hot shadow of the palms and re-
entered the thorny scrub, startling a solitary toucan. With its
monstrous marigold-yellow beak, the blue patch round the eye,
and the neat black plumage and white shirt-front, it looked like a
clown who, having put on a dress-suit, has forgotten to remove
his make-up. It watched our approach, turning its head from side
to side, uttering soft wheezing and churring noises, reminding me
of an ancient, unoiled clock about to strike. One of the horses
gave a loud snort, the toucan took fright and, clicking its great
beak and giving strange yelping cries of alarm, it dived into the
tangle of branches.

Gradually the thorn scrub became less and less thick, and soon
it was broken up into clumps and patches, interspersed with
areas of whitish, sandy soil, dotted with clumps of grass and
cacti. The grass was bleached almost white by the sun, and the
soil had a hard crust baked over it, through which the horses'
hooves broke with a soft scrunch. Only the cacti were green in
that area of sun-white grass and sand, for they, with the curious
alchemy of their family, could capture the dews and infrequent
rain, store it in the flesh of their prickly limbs and live on it, as a
hibernating animal lives in the winter off the autumn's accumu-
lated layer of fat. This region was not flooded and soggy as the
other parts of the country had been, for it was raised a few inches
above the surrounding area; the contour was almost impercept-
ible, but sufficient to make it a dry island in the swampy lands
around. Any piece of land that raised itself six inches above the
surrounding territory could almost be classified as a mountain in
the vast uniform flatness of the Chaco. Rafael and our guide had
a rapid conversation, and then Rafael pushed his horse up alongside mine.

'Here we find the *tatu*, Gerry,' he explained, his eyes gleaming
through his spectacles in anticipation; 'we no ride close together,
eh? We make a line, no? When you see the *tatu*, make your horse
go fast, and the *tatu* she will make a ball.'

'You mean it won't run away?'

'No, the Indian he say she stop and make a ball.'

'That sounds very unlikely to me,' I said sceptically.

'No, it is true, Gerry.'

74

'Well, it must be a damn stupid animal, then.'

'Yes, the Indian he say it is *muy estúpido*.'

We rode in silence, fifty yards apart, manoeuvring our horses in and out of the clumps of thorn-bushes. The only sounds were the brain-probing cries of the cicadas, the soft scrunch of the horses' hooves, and the gentle creak and clink of leather and metal. My eyes ached with searching the heat-shimmering undergrowth ahead. A flock of ten guira cuckoos burst from a thorn-bush and flew off, cackling harshly, looking like small fawn-and-brown magpies, with their long and handsome tails.

Suddenly, fifty yards to my right, I saw the hunched shape of an armadillo, clock-working his way between the clumps of grass. With a yell of triumph, I dug my heels into my mount's sides, and he responded with such vigour that I only saved myself from a fall among the cacti by an undignified clutch at the saddle; the horse broke into a lumbering canter, the white sand spurting spray-like beneath his hooves as we bore down upon the quarry. We were within about fifty feet of him when the creature heard us; he swivelled round, sniffed briefly, and then with astonishing rapidity rolled himself into a ball and lay there. I was rather disappointed that the beast had lived up to his reputation for stupidity, for I felt he should have had the sense to try to make a dash for a clump of thorns. I stopped within twenty-five feet of him, dismounted, tied my horse to a clump of grass and then walked forward to collect my prize. To my surprise, I discovered the grass, which had appeared quite short when I was up on my horse, was really quite high, and I could not see the armadillo at all; however, I knew he was not far and in which direction he lay, so I walked forward. Presently I stopped walking and looked around: my horse was now a good distance away – certainly more than twenty-five feet. I decided that I must have walked in the wrong direction, and, cursing myself for my carelessness, I retraced my steps, zig-zagging through the undergrowth and reaching my horse without seeing the armadillo. I felt rather crestfallen and annoyed, for I decided that the little animal must have made a dash for it when I walked past him. Muttering angrily to myself, I remounted and sat there transfixed with surprise, for in the same position, about twenty-five feet away, lay the armadillo. I dismounted again and walked forward, stopping every now and then to look carefully around me. When I reached the area in which I knew he must lie, I paced slowly backwards and forwards, and even then I passed him twice before I noticed him. As I picked up the creature, heavy and warm from the sun, I mentally apologized to him for having thought that his tactics were stupid. I rode after Rafael and the Indian, and for the next two hours we worked our way carefully over the island of dry soil, and by the same simple means we managed to catch three more of them. Then, as it was getting late, we set off homewards, through the shadowy trees. Crossing the river of blue flowers, the mosquitoes rose in a shrill cloud and settled on us and the horses, gorging themselves so that their transparent abdomens, swollen with our blood, looked like scarlet Japanese lanterns. It was dark when we reached the village and our horses clopped their way tiredly down the muddy road, past bushes alive with the green lights of fireflies, and the bats flicked across our path, uttering their microscopic squeaks of amusement.

In our house we found Jacquie sitting at the table, writing, while our first armadillo trotted importantly round and round the room. It turned out that he had spent an exhilarating afternoon tearing the wire front from his cage and was just disappearing into the hibiscus bushes when Jacquie discovered him. Having recaptured him, she had let him loose in the living-room to await our return. While we had our evening meal, we turned all the armadillos out on to the floor, where they clattered and clicked their way about like a flock of castanets. Rafael and I spent the rest of the evening stripping the wire from the cagefront and replacing it with wooden bars. Then we left the cage in the living-room all night, just to make sure that it could hold the animals. In the morning the bars looked a bit battered, but they still held firm, and the armadillos were all curled up asleep in their bedroom.

Having solved the caging problem, I felt that the three-banded armadillos ought to be plain sailing, for, normally, armadillos are the easiest of creatures to keep in captivity. They will live happily on a diet of meat and fruit, and they are not particular about the freshness of the offerings, for in the wild state they will eat meat that is suppurating and maggot-ridden. According to the textbooks, the three-banded armadillo, in the wild state, lives on a diet of insects and grubs; I thought that if we first offered our specimens their natural diet we could then get them on to some substitute food. So we spent hours collecting a revolting assortment of the local insect life and presenting it to the armadillos. Instead of falling on it with joy, as we had expected, the beasts seemed positively afraid of the worms, caterpillars, and beetles that we had taken such pains to collect. In fact, they backed away from them hurriedly, displaying every symptom of disgust and revulsion. After this failure, I tried them on the usual armadillo's diet in captivity: minced meat mixed with milk, but though they drank some of the milk, they refused the meat. They carried on in this irritating manner for three days, until I was sure that they would become so weak with lack of food that I should have to release them. Our lives were a misery, for on and off throughout the day one or other of us would have an idea and rush with some fresh offering to the cage, to try to tempt the armadillos, only to have them treat it with disgust. At last, more by chance than anything else, I invented a mixture that met with their approval. It consisted of mashed banana, milk, minced meat, and raw egg mixed up with raw brain. The result looked like a particularly revolting street accident, but the armadillos adored it. They would rush for the plate at feeding time and stand round the edge, jostling each other, their noses buried deep in the slush, snorting and snuffling, and occasionally sneezing violently and spraying each other with the mixture.

Having got the little creatures on to a substitute diet, I felt that this had been the final obstacle, and that by all the laws of collecting we should have no more trouble with them. For a time all went well. During the day they would sleep in their bedroom, either curled up into a ball, or else lying on their sides, half unrolled, one armadillo fitting into the other. At three-thirty they would wake up and come out of their bedroom to tip-toe round the cage, like ballerinas, occasionally tick-tacking up to the bars and sticking their heads through to test the breeze with their pink noses to find out if the food was on its way. Very occasionally, the males would have a fight. This consisted of one armadillo barging another into a corner, and then endeavouring to get his head under the edge of his opponent's shell, in order to turn him over; once he was on his side, the victor also turned on his side and scrabbled frantically in an effort to disembowel him. As soon as I noticed these tournaments, I kept a close watch on them. Though they never seemed to do each other any harm, I saw that the big ones were fighting the smaller ones at feeding time, and, by their superior size and weight, keeping the smaller and lighter ones from the food. I decided the best thing would be to keep them in pairs, male and female of approximately the same size. So I built a cage that Jacquie used to call Sing-Sing: it was a series of 'flats', one on top of the other, each with its own bed-room. By this time we had acquired ten of these little armadillos, consisting of four pairs and two odd males. It was a curious thing that the females seemed to be in the minority, for any number of males were brought to us, but only very occasionally did a female get caught. The married couples settled down very well in the Sing-Sing apartments, and there were no more tournaments at feeding time.

One day Jacquie had just finished giving them their food, and she appeared holding one of the large males in her hand. By this time they had become so used to handling that they no longer curled into a tight ball when touched. Jacquie looked worried, but the armadillo lay blissfully on his back in her cupped hands, while she stroked his pink, furry tummy.

'Just look at this one's feet,' she said, holding out the beast for my inspection.

'What's the matter with them?' I inquired, taking the semi-hypnotized beast and looking at it.

'Look ... the soles of his hind-feet are all raw.'

'Good Lord! So they are. I wonder what he's been doing?'

'It strikes me,' said Jacquie, 'that these animals are going to be more trouble than they're worth ... they've already caused us more worry than the rest of the collection put together.'

'Are the others all right?'

'I didn't look. I wouldn't have noticed this one, only he came rushing to the door and fell out when I put the plate in; when I picked him up I noticed his feet.'

The Orange Armadillos

We went and examined the others, and discovered to our consternation that all of them had these circular, sixpenny size raw patches on their hind-feet. The only reason for this that I could think of was that the wooden floors of their cages were too hard for them, and, trotting about as much as they did, they had worn the delicate skin off the soles of their hind-feet. So every day all the armadillos had to be taken out of Sing-Sing and laid on the ground, like a row of pumpkins, while we anointed their hind-feet with penicillin ointment. Then something had to be done about the floor of their cages, and I tried covering them with a thick layer of soft earth. This was quite useless, for at feeding time the armadillos splashed their food about with wild abandon, and then trod the sticky mixture of mud and brain into a paste that set as hard as cement, not only on the floor of the cage, but on the soles of their hind-feet as well. After some experiment, I discovered that the best flooring consisted of a deep layer of sawdust, covered by another layer of dry leaves and grass. This acted very well, and within a few weeks their feet had healed up nicely, and we had no recurrence of the trouble.

To the average person it would no doubt seem as though we had taken a lot of unnecessary trouble over a small and unimportant beast, but to us it represented a major triumph. To find and capture a difficult and delicate creature, to house it properly, teach it to eat a substitute food, cope successfully with its illnesses and other problems – these are some of the most irritating, heart-breaking, and worrying of a collector's jobs, but the accomplishment of them is by far the most exciting and satisfying. A creature which settles down well in captivity, never becomes ill, and eats whatever it is given, is regarded with affection by the collector; but the tricky, stubborn, and delicate animal is regarded as a challenge which, though it may be exhausting, is much more satisfying when one achieves success in the end.

CHAPTER FIVE

BEVY OF *BICHOS*

Our own efforts, combined with the help of the local male population (under orders from Paula), soon produced a flood of local fauna; and Jacquie, Rafael, and I were kept hard at work all day, cage-building, cage-cleaning, feeding and watering, recording and photographing. Even with the three of us working, we were still hard put to it to cope with all the work. Reluctantly, I decided that we would have to employ a carpenter to deal with the caging. I say reluctantly, because I have had a good deal of experience of these craftsmen in various parts of the world. Carpenters, as a breed, I have discovered, have one-track minds: employ them to make a door or a table, and, however unskilfully, they will produce the article required. But engage a carpenter and tell him that he must make a variety of cages for animals, and he immediately goes all to pieces. By the time you have taught him the rudiments of cage-making, it is generally time for you to leave. So it was with certain misgivings that I asked Rafael to get Paula to obtain a carpenter for us. The following day he turned up, a short, plump little man with a face so devoid of expression that he might have been a goldfish. In a hoarse voice he confided to us that his name was Anastacius. We spent an exhausting half-hour explaining to him what we wanted, and then gave him a box and told him to convert it into a bird-cage. We very soon discovered that Anastacius had two most irritating habits; first, he whistled loudly and tunelessly while he worked, and, secondly, he seemed to be under the impression that nails had a life of their own, or were possessed of malignant spirits. He would hammer a nail into the wood with a series of tremendous blows that continued to rain down long after the head was flush with the board. Then he would pause and survey the nail narrowly out of the corner of his eye, presumably waiting for it to start creeping out of the wood. Usually the nail remained immobile, but occasionally Anastacius would notice some slight movement, and he would leap forward and bring the hammer down with devastating violence until he was sure that the nail had succumbed. As soon as he had successfully killed a nail, he would break into a loud, tuneless whistle of triumph. So he toiled for two hours over his first cage, and then, when we all had splitting headaches, he produced the result for my inspection.

Now, a bird's cage is one of the simplest things to construct: all it needs is a wire front, with a half-inch gap at the bottom for cleaning purposes; two perches; and a door just big enough to admit one's hand. Anastacius' effort was a masterpiece: the woodwork was a mortuary of dead nails, mostly twisted and crushed, and the wire front had several large dents in it where the creator had swung too wildly in his pursuit of a nail. The door was so contrived that, once shut, it was almost impossible to open, and, once open, it was impossible for me to get my hand inside. The gap he had left for cleaning out was so ample that anything, except a very fat vulture, could have flown through it with ease. We contemplated it in gloomy silence.

'I think it better we do ourselves, Gerry, no?' said Rafael at last.

'No, Rafael, we've got too much to do – we'll just have to put up with this butcher and hope he'll improve.'

'It couldn't be difficult to improve on *that*,' said Jacquie.

'What on earth are we going to put in it? It'll have to be something tame, so that if it escapes we can catch it again easily.'

For a week the Butcher, as we called him, produced a series of cages each worse than the last. The climax came when I asked him to make me a cage for a creature which needed its housing lined with tin. He had attached the tin to the inside of the cage by the novel method of drawing huge nails through from the outside. The result was that the inside of the cage was full of jagged bits of tin and a forest of nail-points. The whole construction looked rather like some strange medieval device for torture.

'It's no good, Rafael, he'll have to go – I can't stand any more of this – the man's obviously mental. Just look at this effort; one would think we wanted to kill the animals, instead of keeping them alive,' I said. 'Tell him he's sacked, and tell Paula we want someone else – someone who at least has some rudiments of intelligence.'

So the Butcher returned to whatever work of demolition he'd been engaged on in the village, and the next morning Paula appeared leading a thin, shy young man wearing a peaked cap. Paula introduced him as the new carpenter, and held forth at great length on his prowess, personality, and intelligence. Rafael showed him the cages that we had made, and the man examined them carefully, and then said he thought he would be able to construct similar ones.

'Good,' I said, when all this had been translated to me. 'What's his name, Rafael?'

'*Como se llama?*' asked Rafael.

'Julius Caesar Centurian,' said the man, giving a nervous giggle.

So Julius Caesar Centurian came into our midst, and a charming, resourceful, and likeable character he turned out to be. What was more important, he was an excellent carpenter as well. As soon as he took over the caging, we found we had far more time to concentrate on the animal work.

In any collection of animals there are bound to be two or three which endear themselves to you particularly; they need not necessarily be very rare or exotic, nor overburdened with intelligence. But the moment you see them you realize they are possessed of those rare and indefinable qualities, charm and personality, and that they are destined to become characters in camp. To begin with, we had three such beasts in the Chaco; later this trio was joined by a fourth who outshone them all – but more of her anon. The three beasts were as unlike one another as possible, yet they all possessed the basic qualification to turn them into characters rather than just specimens.

The first of these was Cai, the douracouli monkey. She was brought in one day by a rather repulsive-looking Indian who wore a very battered straw hat with a blue ribbon dangling from it. I was very pleased to get her; apart from liking monkeys, I was particularly interested in douracoulis, since they are the only nocturnal monkey in the world. Cai was about the size of a small cat and clad in lichen-grey fur. On her chest the fur was a pale orange shade fading to cream on her tummy. Her small ears were so deeply embedded in the hair of her head that they were almost invisible. She had enormous owl-like eyes of pale amber and they were surrounded by an area of white fur edged with black. This marking, together with her big eyes and her apparent lack of ears, gave her a most remarkable resemblance to an owl. She was very shabby and unkempt and terribly thin. For the first three days she was intensely nervous, and we could do nothing with her. We kept her tied to a stake with a big box to retreat into, and at first she spent her whole time cowering out of sight. If we made any overtures of friendship she would cringe back, gazing at us with wide-eyed horror, her little hands trembling with fright. She was, of course, half-starved, and ate greedily of the food we gave her. But, however hungry she was, she would never come out of her box to feed until we had retreated some distance. Then, one day, I succeeded in catching a lizard for her. I killed it and, approaching Cai's box, I squatted down and held out the still-writhing reptile on the palm of my hand. Cai took one look at the delicacy, and delight overcame her caution. She leapt out of her box, gave a faint ghost-like scream, and, grabbing the lizard firmly, she squatted down in front of me. Suddenly she realized that I was much closer than she normally allowed me, and she was just proposing to retreat into her box when the lizard's tail gave a convulsive wriggle. Immediately she forgot me, and with a look of intense concentration she bit the tail off and sat there holding it in one hand, munching happily, as though it was a stick of celery. I sat perfectly still until she had finished her meal, and she gazed at me while she ate, with a watchful expression in her enormous liquid eyes. When the last bit of lizard had been chewed, taken out and gazed at, chewed again and finally swallowed, she examined her hands carefully, and the ground around her, to make sure no bits were left. Then she stretched out her hind-leg, scratched her thigh vigorously, got up, and sauntered off to her box. From that day onwards her confidence increased.

We soon discovered that Cai did not care for being tied up in the open. I think it gave her a naked, unprotected feeling. So I set to work and built her a cage. This was a tall, narrow structure, with a little bedroom at the top, into which she could retire when she felt like it. She adored this bedroom and would spend her whole day sitting in there, just her head and front paws poking out of the door. In this position she would go off to sleep. Her eyes would droop half shut, and then suddenly open again; a few seconds later they would droop once more, her head would start to nod, until eventually, after many fits and starts and sudden awakenings, her head would sink down and rest peacefully on her paws. But let anything interesting or unusual happen, and her great eyes would fly open and she would crane out of her bedroom to see what was going on, sometimes, in her excitement, twisting her head round so that it was completely upside down and you feared that another half an inch and it would drop off. She could also turn her head round and look over her back, with an almost owl-like ability. She was intensely curious and could not bear to stop watching something, even if it frightened her. Sometimes she would witness the arrival of a new snake and, uttering a series of her faint, squeaky sighs, would come down and peer at it through the wire, wide-eyed with horror, glancing continually over her shoulder to make sure her line of retreat was secure. If she thought the snake was too close, she would leap on to the branch near her bedroom and sit facing the door, and then screw her head round and continue to watch the snake over her shoulder. Thus her body was facing the exact way for a rapid retreat to safety, and she could still keep one eye on the reptile.

For a nocturnal creature she spent an awful lot of the day awake, and scarcely anything happened in camp that her big eyes did not notice or her faint voice remark on.

One day when I was hacking up a rotten log for the woodpecker, I discovered some large and juicy cockroaches hiding under the bark. Thinking I would give Cai a treat, I captured them and carried them to her. She was spread-eagled on the floor of the cage, having a sun-bath, eyes closed, mouth half open in ecstasy. She woke up when I called her, and sat blinking in a bemused fashion. I opened the door of her cage and dropped in the largest and most agile cockroach, thinking that it would amuse her to catch it for herself. But Cai, half-awake, only saw that I had put something in her cage which was alive, and she was not going to hang about and see what it was. She disappeared into her bedroom in a flash, while the cockroach stalked about the floor of the cage, waving its antenna in a vague sort of way. Presently Cai poked her head cautiously out of her bedroom door to see what my offering was. She gazed down at the cockroach with suspicion, her face, as always when she was nervous or excited, seeming to be all eyes. After due consideration, she decided that the insect was harmless, and possibly edible, and so she climbed down and sat contemplating it closely for a while. The cockroach ambled about for a bit and then stopped for a quick wash and brush-up. Cai sat, hands folded over her stomach, watching it with absorbed interest. Then she stretched out a cautious hand and very delicately, with one finger, tapped the cockroach on the back. The insect immediately scuttled frantically across the floor, and Cai leapt backwards in fright and wiped her hand hurriedly on her chest. The cockroach, legs and feelers working overtime, reached the front of the cage and started to squeeze through the wire. With a shrill twitter, Cai leapt forward and grabbed it, but she was too late. I caught the insect and reintroduced it into the cage, and this time Cai followed it about, tapping it on the back and then smelling her fingers. Finally she decided that, however revolting its appearance, it must be edible, and so, closing her eyes tightly and screwing up her face into an expression of determination tinged with disgust, she grabbed at it with both hands and stuffed it into her mouth, so that the wriggling legs stuck out like a walrus moustache. Ever after that I used to kill her cockroaches before giving them to her, otherwise she would take so long plucking up the courage to catch them that they always escaped through the wire.

As soon as she knew she had her bedroom to retire to in moments of stress, Cai became very tame and trusting, even allowing us to stroke her. Jacquie would hold a piece of banana or a grape in her clenched hand, and offer it to Cai. She would come down from her bedroom and sit there solemnly opening Jacquie's hand, finger by finger, until she could get at the delicacy. With plenty of fruit and insect life, and two bowls of milk with raw egg and vitamins beaten in it a day, she soon put on weight, and her fur became glossy and thick as a powder-puff. You would not have recognized her as the frightened, faded scrap of fur she had been when we first got her. The credit for her well-being was Jacquie's, for Cai liked her better than she liked me, and so Jacquie had the task of cleaning and feeding her, tempting her appetite with delicacies, and playing with her so that she did not become bored. I can honestly say (without vanity, since it was not my handiwork) that when we landed Cai in England I have never seen a douracouli like her in any zoo.

For some time Cai reigned supreme as Queen of the Camp, and then one day there arrived another creature to share her throne. On being tipped out of the basket, this new addition resembled a very small, very fluffy chow puppy, with a black-and-white ringed tail, and wearing, for reasons best known to himself, a mask of black fur across his face, from which two wistful, rather sad brown eyes contemplated us. He stood there on immensely large and very flat feet, looking like a dismal highwayman who has lost his pistol. The soles of his paws, we noticed, were pink, and his fingers and toes long and slender, of the type that is generally known as artistic. He was a baby crab-eating raccoon, and we soon decided to call him Pooh, for he closely resembled the famous bear of that name, and it was generally the first thing we said when we went to clean out his cage in the morning.

I put Pooh into a nice roomy cage with wooden bars and a neat door with a latch, gave him a couple of buckets of sawdust to sit in and left him to settle down. He behaved, to begin with, with the utmost decorum, squatting on his ample behind and gazing through the bars, looking like Dick Turpin awaiting trial. When we came back after lunch, however, we found Pooh had been busy. He was sitting with an air of depressed innocence, surrounded by our day's egg supply, or, to be more accurate, he was surrounded by the shells, while his paws, face, and coat were sticky with yolk or white. He gazed at us, when we scolded him, with the expression of one who has always found life harsh and is beyond expecting sympathy or understanding. I decided that his burglar-like method of getting out of his cage deserved further study, for I could not see how he had managed it. I put him back inside the cage, securely latched the door and then kept a wary eye on him from a distance. After a long pause, a black nose appeared through the bars and whiffled to and fro; having decided the coast was clear, this was withdrawn and its place taken by a long, slender set of fingers and a pink paw which groped in the most human fashion round the bars in the direction of the latch. Having located it, one of the artistic fingers was inserted under the hook, and with an expert flick it knocked the latch up. The door was pushed open guiltily and Pooh's face appeared slowly and thoughtfully round the edge. The next quarter of an hour I spent fixing a bolt to the door, as well as the latch, and it took him three days to learn the intricacies of this and escape again. By the end of the week the door of his cage bristled with an assortment of bolts, latches, and hooks that would have made Houdini think a bit, but the only result was that we took longer to open the door than Pooh did. In the end, I had to fix a padlock on the door, and that did the trick. But Pooh would sit for hours with his paws stuck through the bars, fondling the padlock with his sensitive, pink paws, occasionally sticking a finger into the keyhole in a hopeful sort of way.

Now a sentimentalist might argue that Pooh was trying desperately to escape from his wooden prison to the gay, abandoned freedom of the forest. This, however, would be exaggerating. Whenever Pooh escaped, he had only two objectives: firstly, the food-table, and, if this was empty, the bird-cages. If food was available, Pooh would be found in the midst of it. If there was no food, he would send the birds into an hysterical twitter by peering through the wire at them and licking his lips. It might be argued that, if Pooh was not interested in regaining his lost freedom, he was merely escaping in order to secure a square meal which we denied him. To counter this, I should like it to go on record that Pooh, for his size, ate more than any other animal I have ever come across. This walking stomach had a daily ration consisting of two raw eggs, vitamins, and cod-liver oil, beaten up in half a pint of milk, a quarter of a pound of minced steak or heart, and fruit in the shape of bananas, guavas, or pawpaws. Having consumed all this in the space of an hour, he would, after a slight doze, be ready for more.

When Pooh discovered that the padlock would not yield its secrets to him, he did not give up hope, but devoted half an hour a day to it, and the rest of the time he devoted to other good works. Among these were his spring-cleaning activities. Every day, having indulged in the herculean task of cleaning his cage, we would spread a layer of clean sawdust in the bottom of it. Pooh would then be seized with what appeared to be a housewifely desire for tidiness. The fact that the sawdust was spread all over the cage would get on his nerves. Starting in one corner, he would begin to work backwards, sweeping the sawdust with his front paws and shooting it out between his hind legs to be bulldozed along by his ample bottom. He would solemnly work his way over the cage like this until the floor was not marred by one speck of sawdust, while in one corner his bottom had amassed a huge conical pile of the stuff; needless to say, the corner with the sawdust in it was the one he did not use for those functions of nature for which this commodity had been provided. Instead, he used it as a couch, a sort of sawdust chaise-longue, against which, during the heat of the afternoon, he would recline, on his back, plucking meditatively with his long fingers at the hair on the enormous mound of his stomach. He liked nothing better, while wrapped in these Buddhist meditations, than to have a piece of fat to play with. Holding one end in his mouth and the other end between his hind-paws, he would

pull alternately with his teeth or toes, thus producing a gentle rocking-chair-like motion which was apparently very conducive to slumber.

In order to give Pooh more exercise, I thought it would be a good idea to put him out on a lead for a few hours every day, so I drove a stake into the ground, fashioned a collar out of plaited string, and a lead out of rope. Within half an hour Pooh had gnawed his way through the rope, visited the food-table, and had eaten twenty-four bananas. I tried a variety of different materials as leads, and the one that took him longest to get through was a thong of rawhide, but even this gave up the unequal struggle eventually. In the end I procured a length of chain which had, originally, been intended for other purposes, and this, though short, at least resisted all Pooh's efforts to bite through it. In spite of Pooh's flat-footed, slow, shuffling walk and his air of benign obesity, he was really a most active creature, rarely still and always on the look-out for something to stick his paws into. Being so active, he was easily bored, and sometimes we had to exercise the utmost ingenuity in finding things to occupy him. A length of old ciné-film kept him amused for days: he would stroll back and forth with yards of celluloid trailing from his mouth, or else lie on his back, holding the film in his paws and peering at it short-sightedly, looking like a plump and rather melancholy film mogul contemplating his latest epic.

The day I found the husk of an old coconut was a red-letter one for Pooh. At first he was a bit suspicious of it and approached it with a curious sideways shuffle, ready to run for

it should the coconut attack him. Then he touched it delicately with one paw and discovered to his pleasure that the coconut would roll about. He spent a happy half-hour chasing it to and fro; and several times he grew over-excited and knocked it outside the limit of his chain, so he had to give his loud yarring screams until Jacquie or I retrieved it for him. Then Jacquie had an idea and suggested I should bore a hole in the husk. This simple action transformed the coconut from being a passing fancy to being Pooh's favourite toy. Now he would sit for hours with it clasped between his hind legs, one arm and paw delving deep inside it and occasionally surfacing with some microscopic fragment of shell. The first time, he delved so enthusiastically that he got stuck, and, having extricated him, I had to enlarge the hole. So Pooh would spend the day with his coconut, playing football with it, plunging his hand into it like a child with a bran-tub, and eventually, when he was tired, falling asleep draped over it.

Our third animal character was known by the rather unimaginative name of Foxey. He was a small, delicately made, grey pampas fox, with slender legs and enormous brush and eager brown eyes. Foxey had been procured by a Paraguayan at a very tender age, and when he came to us he must have been some three or four months old. He was about the size of a wire-haired terrier, and he had obviously given up all ideas of behaving like a fox. In fact, I think that privately he was convinced he wasn't a fox, but a dog, and he had certainly developed some most unfox-like habits. We kept Foxey on a collar and chain, which was, in turn, attached to a ring. Through the ring was threaded a wire stretched between two posts. In this way he would have a greater area to run about in and yet his leash was short enough to ensure he did not get tangled up in it. At night he slept in a large, grass-filled cage. Every morning when he caught sight of us he would greet us with loud and prolonged yowls of joy, and as soon as his cage was opened he would wag his great tail frantically from side to side, lift his upper lip and display his baby teeth in the most endearing grin of delight. His final moment of ecstasy came as he was lifted out of his cage, and then you had to be careful how you held him, for he would be so overcome with joy at seeing you again that he could no longer contain himself, and the resulting stream could drench you if you were not careful.

Shortly after he arrived we discovered he had two passions in life: one was chickens, and the second was cigarette butts. Chickens, or for that matter any birds, fascinated him. Occasionally one or two members of Paula's fowl-run would invade the collection and wander near to where Foxey was tethered. He would crouch down, head on his paws, ears pricked, and his tail moving gently from side to side. The hens would approach, pecking and uttering hiccupping, slightly inebriated, chucks, and the closer they got, the brighter grew Foxey's eyes. The hens' vacant meanderings always took some time, and Foxey could not contain himself. Long before they were within range, he would gather himself together and charge to the limit of his leash, yapping excitely. The hens would scuttle off, squawking hysterically, and Foxey would squat down and beam over his shoulder at us, creating a miniature dust-storm with the frantic wagging of his tail.

His interest in cigarette butts amounted to almost an obsession. Whenever he found one he would pounce on it and devour it, with the expression of utmost loathing on his face. Then he would spend an uncomfortable half an hour coughing violently, have a long drink of water and be ready for the next butt-end.

One awful day, however, Foxey learnt his lesson. Carelessly I had left a nearly full packet of cigarettes within his reach, and before I had discovered it Foxey had eaten the lot. To say that he was sick would be a vast understatement. His stomach performed the emesis of all time, and every last shred of paper and tobacco was returned to the light of day, tastefully mixed with Foxey's breakfast. He was so exhausted by this effort that he just lay and let a chicken walk right past him, and never even twitched an ear. By evening he had recovered enough to eat a couple of pounds of meat and two raw eggs, but the offer of a cigarette caused him to back away, sneezing indignantly. Never again did he sample tobacco in any shape or form.

CHAPTER SIX

FAUNS, FROGS, AND FER-DE-LANCE

ONE day we learnt that on the following morning an *autovia* was travelling some twenty-five kilometres up the line to a place that delighted in the name of Waho. Apart from the name, which attracted me, Waho seemed worth a visit, for I had been told that it was the best area for jaguar, and I wanted to see the overseer about setting some traps. Also, being a cattle-station, Waho had quite a substantial population – at least fifty people, which is substantial by Chaco standards – and I thought that they might have some pets which they would be willing to part with.

We had been told that the *autovia* would start at four in the morning and could not, on any account, wait for us if we were late. With a considerable effort we managed to get Rafael out of bed and semi-conscious by this hour, and we stumbled down the road to the railway line, past the canals where the frogs and toads were still holding their nightly jazz club, and through the dark and lifeless village, shrouded in mist from the river. We found the *autovia* squatting on the line, and climbed in and sat dozing on the hard seats for half an hour, waiting for the driver. He appeared at last, yawning prodigiously, and informed us that we could not start until five, as they had forgotten to give him the mails for Waho, and he had had to send someone to collect them. We sat in an irritated silence, listening to the village cockerels starting up, and presently a small boy appeared out of the mist, bearing the sack of mails. The driver flung the sack into the back of the *autovia*, engaged his gears with a retching sound that any of the cockerels would have envied, and we clattered off down the buckled lines into the mist.

Gradually, as the line curved inland and away from the river, the mist grew thinner, and eventually disappeared altogether, except for small eiderdown patches of it that hung over the pools and streams we passed. The sky ahead turned steel grey, and against it the tangled crest of the forest was etched with microscopic exactness. Gradually the grey faded, to be replaced by a purplish-red which spread across the horizon like a bruise. This, in its turn, rapidly faded to pale pink, and then to blue, as the sun rose over the rim of the forest. In the first slanting rays the whole landscape gained perspective and became alive. The forest was no longer a flat black silhouette, but a solid, interlaced crochet work of branches, vines, and thorns, its leaves glossy with mist. Flocks of guira cuckoos sat preening the moisture from their feathers, or crouched with drooped wings in the first heat of the day. We passed a small lake, the edge of which was trembling with the movement of birds: ibis strolling in groups, probing the mud eagerly with their curved beaks; an openbill stork, lank and dark, standing in rapt contemplation of his own reflection; two jacanas bathing, their underwings flashing buttercup yellow as they threw up a glittering spray of water over their heads and bodies. A small grey fox, returning from his night's hunting, scuttled on to the line and then galloped ahead of us for about fifty yards before swerving off into the undergrowth. We chugged on, and very soon we passed a small grass-field that was an incredible sight.

It was some two acres in extent, neatly fenced in with tall palms, and in it the great chaco spiders had been at work. These spiders have a body the size of a hazel nut, spotted with pink and white, and mounted on long, slender legs covering the area of a saucer. The silk they spin is thick, elastic, and the colour of gold. In this small grass-field they had covered every available bush and grass tussock with their great golden webs, each one the size of a cartwheel. In the centre of each web a spider was spread-eagled, and around it each delicate thread and spoke of their kingdom was decorated with dew, like diamonds on cloth of gold. The decorative effect was breathtakingly beautiful as they shimmered and glittered in the early sunlight.

We reached Waho at about seven-thirty. The line swept out of the forest into an immense field, glinting here and there with water. In the grass at the edge of the line flocks of black-headed conures were feeding. These small parrots had the most vivid grass-green plumage with coal-black heads and necks. They flew up and wheeled, glittering, through the sky as we passed, screaming shrilly. The line ended here, in an area of churned mud; it was the usual sort of Chaco out-station, with a long, low, whitewashed house for the overseer, and a collection of dilapidated palm-log huts that housed the workers. The *autovía* drew up with an important chuffing and rattle, and Fernandez, the overseer, appeared, striding over the sea of mud to greet us. He was a tall, powerful man with a handsome, rather Mongolian face and very fine teeth. He had the most charming manners, and greeted us as though we were royalty, ushering us into the living-room of his house and sending his small, dark wife bustling round to prepare us some *mate* with milk. While we drank this thick, sweet, and rather sickly drink, I spread out my books and drawings on the table, and with Rafael acting as interpreter, I went into the subject of the local fauna with Fernandez. He recognized all the creatures that I particularly wanted, and promised to do his best to try to obtain some for me. Jaguar and ocelot were very common, he told us, some cows having been killed by a jaguar only a week before; however, they were wary and not easily caught. He promised to set traps in all the likely places, and should he be successful in catching anything he would send me a message at once. When I questioned him about the smaller creatures – the frogs, toads, snakes, and lizards – he gave a disarming grin and said that we had better go over to an area of the out-station where they were clearing a section of the forest; here, he told us, they were finding any number of small *bichos*. While we hastily gulped down our drinks, Fernandez called two Indians, and we set off to look for small *bichos*.

We followed a narrow, muddy path that zig-zagged through the long grass from which the mosquitoes rose in clouds. We passed by the cattle-slaughtering pen, a large corral some seventy feet square, with walls made of palm logs. The top of the walls was decorated with a frieze of black vultures, sitting in their usual hunch-backed, rather menacing way, waiting for the next killing. They were so bold that we walked within six feet of them and they did not take wing, but merely surveyed us appraisingly, looking like a convention of elderly undertakers. Fernandez led us down the path for about half a mile, until it left the grass-field and entered the forest. Here we found a group of Indians hacking away at the thorny undergrowth with machetes, chattering and laughing, their huge straw hats bobbing about like animated mushrooms in the tangle of scrub. Fernandez called them together and explained what we wanted, and the Indians glanced shyly at us and grinned at each other; then one of them addressed Fernandez and pointed to a large log lying half-hidden in the undergrowth. Fernandez relayed the information to Rafael, who, in turn, translated for me.

'The Indian say they find a snake, Gerry, but she run very fast and she is sitting under that tree.'

'Well, ask Señor Fernandez if the Indians can help us shift it, and then I can have a shot at catching it.'

Once again there was a pause while my request was translated, and then Fernandez gave an order, and the group of Indians sped towards the log, giggling and pushing each other like school-children, and started to hack the undergrowth away from its length. When a sufficient space around the log had been cleared, I cut myself a suitable stick and prepared for action. To Rafael's extreme irritation, I would not let him help, for, as I explained, I had promised his mother that, whatever else I let him do, I would not let him mess about with snakes. After some argument, during which Rafael almost came to the point of rebellion, I persuaded him to retreat to a safe distance. Then I nodded to the Indians, they stuck their machetes under the curve of the log and with a quick heave turned it over and took to their heels.

As the log rolled over, a thick, brown snake about four feet long wriggled elegantly out of the depression, travelled for about six feet, when it suddenly saw me approaching, and stopped. As I leant forward to pin it down with my stick, it did something which shook me considerably: it raised its blunt, rather heavy-looking head, and some six inches of its body, from the ground, and proceeded to inflate the skin of its neck. Slowly the skin expanded until I was looking at what appeared to be a cobra with its hood up. Now, there is more than one species of snake in the world that can inflate the skin of its neck like a cobra, but this generally results in a slight balloon-like expansion which could not compare with the beautifully flattened hood of that reptile. Yet here, in the middle of the Chaco, in a Continent which does not contain cobras, I was confronted by a snake that looked so like one that even an Asiatic snake-charmer might have been forgiven for getting out his flute. I lowered my stick gently to try to pin it to the ground, but the snake was well aware of my motives. It lowered its hood and proceeded to glide towards the nearest bit of forest with considerable agility. I made one or two ineffectual attempts to pin it down, and then, in desperation when it neared the undergrowth, I slid the stick under the gliding body, lifted it up, and flipped it back into the clearing again. This obviously irritated my quarry, for it paused for a moment and glared at me with open mouth before once more setting off determinedly in the direction of the nearest bush. Once more I pursued it, slid my stick under it, and lifted it into the air, preparatory to giving it the backward flick that would keep it away from the undergrowth, but this time the snake had its own ideas on the subject. It gave a violent wiggle as it felt itself lifted, and, while still in mid air, expanded its hood to the fullest extent and flung itself sideways at me with open mouth. Luckily, I realized what was happening and scuttled backwards, and the snake missed my trouser leg by a fraction. It fell to the ground and lay there quite quietly; presumably, having tried out all its tricks and failed, it decided to give up the unequal struggle. I picked it up by the back of the neck and put it into a bag without any further trouble. Jacquie came forward and gave me a bitter look.

'If you insist on doing things like that,' she said, 'I'd be glad if you did them when I wasn't around.'

'Nearly she bite you,' said Rafael, his eyes large behind his spectacles.

'What sort of snake was it, anyway?' asked Jacquie.

'I don't know. I can't place that hood, although I have a feeling that I've read about the thing somewhere. I'll look it up when we get back.'

'She have poison?' asked Rafael, seating himself on the log.

'No, I don't think it's poisonous ... only mildly so, anyway.'

'I seem to remember that a snake you identified as being non-poisonous in Africa turned out to be exactly the opposite, after it had bitten you,' said Jacquie.

'Oh, that was different,' I explained – 'that one looked just like a non-poisonous kind, and I picked it up.'

'Yes, and this one looks just like a cobra, and you picked it up,' retorted my wife, crushingly.

'Don't sit on that log, Rafael,' I said, changing the subject; 'it might have scorpions under the bark.'

Rafael shifted rapidly, and, borrowing a machete from one of the Indians, I approached the log and began to hack away at the rotten bark. The first blow of the blade brought forth a shower of beetle larvae and a large centipede; the second, more beetle larvae, two beetles and a depressed-looking tree-frog. I worked slowly down the length of the trunk, sticking the point of the machete in and then levering the bark up and ripping it off with a soft scrunch. There seemed to be nothing except this wonderful array of insect life. Then I stripped the piece of bark away near the place where Rafael had been sitting, and a snake some six inches long and as thick as a cigarette fell out. It was gaily banded with black, cream, grey, and fire-engine red, and was very handsome.

'Oh, migosh!' said Rafael, as I picked it up, 'I sit there, no?'

'Yes,' I said severely. 'You should be careful where you're sitting. You might have killed it.'

'What is it?' asked Jacquie.

'A baby coral snake ... we seem to be having a rather snaky day today.'

'But they're deadly, aren't they?'

'Yes, but not so deadly that they could kill Rafael through half an inch of bark,' I said.

Putting the snake into a bag, I investigated the rest of the log, but found nothing more of interest. Fernandez, who had been watching fascinated from a safe distance, now suggested that we should make our way back to the out-station and make a tour of the huts to see if they contained any pets. As we wandered back along the path, I caught the glint of water through the trees, and insisted we should all go and investigate. We found a large pond, its waters stained by decaying leaves to the colour of rum, from which rose the intoxicating smell of rotting leaves. I started to potter happily round the edge in search of frogs, and was still doing this some ten minutes later when I was brought to earth by an uproar that broke out at the far end of the pond. Looking up, I saw Fernandez, Rafael, and the two Indians dancing round Jacquie, shouting, while she was calling me loudly. Above the uproar a strange sound was wafted to me: it sounded like some-one blowing prolonged blasts on a toy trumpet. I hurried round the pool to see what was happening. I found Jacquie clutching something in her hands which was producing the trumpet-like sound, while Fernandez and the Indians kept shouting ' *Venenosa, muy venenosa, señora*,' in a sort of despairing chorus.

Rafael approached me, looking very startled.

'Gerry, some bad *bicho* Jacquie catch. They say she is very bad,' he explained.

'It's only a frog,' said Jacquie, raising her voice above the jabbering of the Indians and the irritated blasts from her capture. 'Let's have a look at it.'

She opened her hands and displayed the most extraordinary amphibian imaginable. It was black with a pale yellowish-white belly, and was almost completely circular in shape. Its golden

eyes were perched up on the top of its broad, flat head, like those of a miniature hippo. But it was the mouth of the beast that startled me: it had thick, yellow lips which stretched from side to side of the frog's head in a great, grinning curve, exactly like the Tenniel illustration of Humpty Dumpty. As I watched it, it suddenly blew up its body like a balloon, stood up on its short, stubby legs, opened its mouth wide (showing that the inside was a bright primrose yellow) and proceeded to give another series of yarring trumpet-blasts. When I took it in my hand, it struggled wildly, so I put it on the ground. It stood up on its small legs, opened wide its mouth, and took little jumps towards me, snapping its mouth fiercely and giving trumpet-blasts of rage. It was an enchanting beast.

'Where did you catch it?' I asked Jacquie.

'Just there. It was sitting in the water with just its eye showing, rather like a hippo, so I grabbed it. What is it?'

'I haven't the faintest idea. It looks like a horned toad in some ways, but it's not the ordinary sort. Whatever it is, it's jolly interesting ... might even turn out to be something quite new.'

Filled with enthusiasm, we searched the little pond and managed to capture three more of these peculiar frogs, which elated me considerably. At the time I thought they might well turn out to be a new species, related to the horned toads which, in some respects, they resembled closely. However, on return to England, they were identified as being a Budgett's frog, a name which I think is singularly appropriate to their portly form and demeanour. But, although they had already been scientifically described, they were considered very rare, and the Natural History Museum had only one specimen.

101

As we approached the cluster of dilapidated huts we could see that the cattle-men had returned for their midday meal and siesta. The horses were tethered near the houses, and close by was a cluster of the heavy, sheepskin-covered saddles. The men, their straw hats tilted on to the backs of their heads, leaned against the walls of the houses, sipping their *mate* out of the little pots. They were dressed in tattered shirts, grey with sweat, and the thick leather chaps over their *bombachas* were ripped and scarred by the thorns they had ridden through. In the lean-to kitchens their wives crouched over smoky fires, cooking the meal, while around them sprawled broods of dirty-faced, dark-eyed children and mangy dogs. As we approached the first of the houses, Jacquie imparted some advice.

'Now, if they have got any pets, for goodness sake don't leap at them with cries of delight. They double the price straight away,' she said.

'No, no, I won't,' I promised.

'Well, you did it the other day with that bird. If you hadn't looked so delighted with it, we'd have got it for half the price. Just pretend you're not really interested in whatever it is they've got.'

'I shouldn't think they'll have much here, anyway,' I said, surveying the decaying group of shanties.

We moved slowly from house to house, and Fernandez explained to the men what we wanted. They laughed and chattered among themselves, promising to try to catch specimens for us, but no pets were forthcoming. Outside one hut we were talking to

the owner, a villainous, unshaven man, who was holding forth at great length about jaguar, when something appeared in the doorway of the house and trotted out into the open. At first, seeing it out of the corner of my eye, I thought it was a dog. The next thing I knew, Jacquie had uttered a shrill cry, and, turning, I found her embracing a small spotted faun, who was regarding her suspiciously from large dark eyes.

'Just look at this ... isn't it sweet?' she cried, regardless of the fact that the faun's owner was standing within two feet of her. 'Isn't it adorable? Just look at its eyes ... We must have it. D'you think they'll sell it?'

I looked at the creature's owner, noted the gleam in his eye, and sighed.

'After watching your display of indifference to the beast's charms, I should think he's only too willing to sell,' I said bitterly. 'Rafael, ask him how much he wants for it, will you?'

The man, after devoting ten minutes to telling us how attached he was to the little deer, and how heartbroken he would be to part with it, named a price that made us all wilt. Half an hour later the price had dropped considerably, but was still much more than the animal was really worth. Jacquie gazed at me mutely.

'Look,' I said desperately, 'he wants twice what the little wretch is worth. We'd have got it for a quarter the price if you hadn't started to drool over it the minute it appeared.'

'I didn't drool,' said Jacquie indignantly; 'I was just drawing your attention to it.'

This monstrous understatement struck me speechless; silently I paid the man, and we made our way back towards the railway line, Jacquie clutching the faun in her arms and whispering endearments into its silky ears. As we got into the *autovía*, the driver leant forward and stroked the little deer's head, beaming at it.

'*Lindo*,' he said, '*muy lindo bicho*.'

'*Lindo* means beautiful, doesn't it?' asked Jacquie.

'Yes, that is right,' said Rafael. 'Why, Jacquie?'

'I think it would be a good name for her, don't you?'

So, Lindo, the beautiful, she became forthwith. She behaved with the utmost decorum, sniffing interestedly round inside the *autovía*, and then going to Jacquie and nuzzling her with a moist,

103

black nose. But with the first jerk of the *autovia* starting she decided that she did not approve of this form of travel, and made a wild leap for the tailboard of the vehicle. She sprawled over it and was just about to crash on to the line when I managed to grab her hind legs and haul her back. She fought like a demon, lashing out with her sharp little hooves and uttering prolonged and piercing 'barrrs'. Fauns are extremely difficult things to handle when they become frightened; their hind legs must be held, or they kick violently and are liable to rip you to bits with their sharp hooves. On the other hand their legs are so fragile that there is always the danger that you might break one if you hold them too tightly. After a hectic five minutes we managed to subdue Lindo, and then I took off my shirt and wrapped her in it, so that even if she did struggle she could not damage herself or us. The driver was so tickled with the sight of a faun wearing a shirt that he narrowly missed overturning the *autovía* at a sharp corner.

As we walked down the road towards our little house we were surprised to see a group of some thirty people standing outside the gate, forming a circle round a man with a large wooden box. This man, and the crowd around him, were all waving their arms and chattering. On the veranda of our house stood the mountainous form of Paula, clutching in her hands a rusty shot-gun with which she was menacing the crowd. We pushed through the people and made our way on to the veranda, to find out what was going on. Paula greeted us with evident relief, and proceeded to spout Spanish at us, rolling her eyes, clutching her brow, and pointing the shot-gun at each of us in turn with complete impartiality. I removed the weapon from her reluctant hands, while Rafael listened to her story. That morning the señor had asked her to procure a shot-gun, in order to shoot some small birds for the *lechuchita*, the little owl, no? Well, she had gone to the village and procured this fine gun for the señor. On her return she had found that creature (here she pointed a trembling finger at the man with the box), sitting on the veranda. He said that he had brought a *bicho* for the señor. She, being curious, had asked him what sort of *bicho*, and he had removed the lid of the box and displayed to her horrified gaze a large and obviously angry *yarará*. Now, of all the dangerous creatures found in the Chaco, the *yarará* is the most feared, for a *yarará* is a fer-de-lance, one of the most poisonous and bad-tempered of South American snakes. Paula had not hesitated for a minute. She had ordered the man to remove his offering to a safe distance from the house. As it was very hot outside, and the veranda was shady, the man refused to do this, whereupon Paula had loaded the shot-gun and driven him off by force. The man, who turned out to be a trifle weak-minded, was not unnaturally rather upset at this reception. After having been brave enough to capture a *yarará*, he felt that he ought to be received with due solemnity and congratulation, not driven away by an irate outsize female with a shot-gun. Standing outside the gate, he had howled abuse at Paula, while she mounted guard over the front door with her gun. Our arrival, luckily, put an end to the whole business; we despatched Paula to the kitchen to make us some tea, and called the man inside.

The fer-de-lance, having been bumped about in the hot sun all afternoon, was not in the best of tempers, and as soon as I lifted the lid of the box to take a look at him he leapt at the opening and struck at me viciously. He was quite a small specimen, being only about two and a half feet long, but what he lacked in length he made up for in pugnacity, and it was a long time before I could get a noose round him and grab him behind the head. He was a very handsome reptile, the whole of his body being ashy grey, patterned with a series of diamond-shaped charcoal-black patches, bordered with creamy-white, that extended from head to tail. His head was flattened and arrow-shaped, with fierce, golden-flecked eyes. I managed to get him into a shallow snake-box with a gauze top, and he lay among the twigs and dead leaves, hissing loudly and vibrating his tail so rapidly that it struck among the leaves and rattled like a rattlesnake. If the slightest shadow fell across the box, he would strike up at the wire gauze, his fangs coming right through the mesh. I would never have believed this unless I had seen it, for normally a snake cannot make any impression on a completely flat surface. His gape was tremendous, and he would throw his head right back as he struck, to get the maximum force behind his long, curved fangs. Within half an hour there were several spots of golden venom on the wire gauze, and he was still striking wildly. I was forced, in the end, to put another layer of gauze half an inch above the first, to prevent accidents.

That evening, as Paula surged round the table, serving the meal, she treated us to a long discourse on *yarará* and their habits. It appeared that nearly every member of her family had, at one time or other during their lives, been within inches of death from a *yarará*. One received the impression that the entire fer-de-lance population of the Chaco spent its time stalking Paula's relatives. As they all escaped with monotonous regularity, the snakes must have led the most frustrating lives. Our meal over, Paula came in to say good night. She cast a black look at the fer-de-lance box in the corner of the room and observed that she would not spend the night in a house with a *yarará*, even if she were paid to do so, added a prayer that she would find us all still alive in the morning, and swept off in the direction of her home in the village. As it turned out, it was not snakes that disturbed us that evening.

Rafael was strumming on the guitar, singing a Gaucho ditty, in which alliteration appeared to be nicely blended with vulgarity; Jacquie had retired to bed with a month-old copy of the *Buenos Aires Herald*, which she had unearthed from somewhere; and I was examining the gun which Paula had procured for me. It was a Spanish make which I had not come across before, but it seemed in reasonable condition. As far as I could see, there appeared to be only one thing wrong with it.

'Rafael,' I said, 'this gun's got no safety-catch.'

He came across the room and peered at it.

'Yes, Gerry . . . see, that is the safety.'

'What, this little lever?'

'Yes, that is safety,' he said.

'It isn't, you know. I've tried it in both positions and the hammer still falls.'

'No, no, Gerry . . . she go click, yes. But she no go bang.'

I looked at him sceptically.

'Well, it seems very queer to me. A safety-catch is a safety-catch, and when it's on you should be able to pull the trigger without anything at all happening,' I pointed out.

'No, Gerry, you no understand . . . she is Spanish gun . . . I show you how she work,' he said.

He loaded the gun, pressed the small lever down, pointed it out of the window, and pulled the trigger. There was a shattering roar, all the dogs in the village started barking, and Jacquie appeared suddenly out of the bedroom, under the impression that the *yarará* had escaped from its box. Rafael straightened his spectacles and stared at the gun.

'Well,' he said philosophically, 'this way must be safety.'

He pressed the lever up, reloaded, aimed out of the window and pulled the trigger again. For the second time the gun went off with a roar, and the village dogs became almost hysterical.

'You can tell it's a Spanish gun,' I pointed out to Jacquie, 'because you can shoot yourself just as easily with the safety-catch on or off.'

'No, Gerry, she is good gun,' said Rafael indignantly, 'but I think she is broke inside.'

'I'm sure she is broke inside,' I agreed.

We were still arguing about this some ten minutes later when there came a thunderous knocking on the front door. Mystified, for it was quite late, Rafael and I went to see who our visitors were. On the veranda we found two rather scared Paraguayans, dressed in tattered green uniforms, peaked caps, and clutching in their hands a brace of antiquated and rusty rifles. As they saluted in unison, we recognized them as two members of the local constabulary. Having said good evening, they asked us if we had fired a gun, and if so, who was dead. Rafael, rather taken aback, said the gun had gone off by accident and that no one was dead. The policemen shuffled their bare feet in the dust and looked at each other for inspiration. Then they explained, rather hesitatingly, that they had been sent out by the chief of police to arrest us and bring in the corpse of our victim. As there was no corpse, they were not quite sure what to do next. They would, they explained earnestly, earn the wrath of their chief if they returned without us, even though we had killed no one. They looked so woebegone and puzzled by the whole matter that Rafael and I took pity on them, and offered to accompany them to the police-station and explain to the chief of police ourselves. They were pathetically grateful for this, and saluted a great number of times, smiling and saying, '*Gracias, señor, gracias.*'

We made our way down the moonlit village street, our captors trotting ahead, occasionally stopping to steer us carefully round a puddle or a patch of mud. At the other end of the village we came to the police-station, a two-room, whitewashed shack, shaded by a large, golliwog-headed palm tree. Our escort led us into a bare little room where, behind an ancient table piled high with an impressive array of documents, sat the chief of police. He was a lank and scowling man, whose polished boots and belt proclaimed his importance; he had only recently taken over this post, and it was obvious that he intended to prove to the inhabitants that crime did not pay. Our escort saluted, stood more or less to attention, and proceeded, in a chorus, to give an account of the incident. Their chief heard them out, scowling impressively, and when they reached the end of the story he gave us a searching look through narrowed eyes; then, with a magnificent gesture, he pulled a cigarette butt from behind his ear and lit it.

'So,' he hissed melodramatically, blowing smoke through his nose, 'you are responsible for the outrage, eh?'

'*Si, señor,*' said Rafael meekly, his lips twitching, 'we are responsible.'

'Ah! So you admit it?' said the chief of police, pleased at having trapped us into a confession.

'*Si, señor,*' said Rafael.

'So,' said the chief of police, sticking his thumbs in his belt and leaning precariously back in his chair, 'so, you confess, eh? You come here to the Chaco and you think you can commit these outrages with impunity, eh? You think that here it is *incivilizado,* and that you can get away with this sort of thing, eh?'

'*Si, señor,*' said Rafael.

There is nothing so irritating as having a purely rhetorical question answered, and the chief of police glared at him.

'But you didn't realize that there were laws here, the same as anywhere else, did you? You did not realize that you had a police force to contend with, did you, eh?'

The police force had, meanwhile, relaxed, content to let their chief handle the matter. One of them was picking his teeth very thoroughly, while the other was sticking his finger down the barrel of his rifle, and then pulling it out and examining it with a worried expression: presumably the gun was due for its annual clean.

'Look, señor,' said Rafael patiently, 'we haven't committed any crime. All we did was let off a gun by accident.'

'That's not the point,' said the chief of police cleverly; 'you *might* have been committing a crime.'

In the face of such astute reasoning, Rafael was struck dumb.

'As it is,' the chief went on magnanimously, 'I will not arrest

109

you at once. I will consider the matter. But you must report here first thing tomorrow morning with your police permits. D'you understand?'

It was useless to argue, so we just nodded. The chief of police rose to his feet, bowed to us, and then clicked his heels together with such vigour that one of the constables dropped his rifle, and had to salute hurriedly to cover up his clumsiness. Rafael and I managed to get out of earshot of the police-station before dissolving into helpless mirth over our interview. When we got back to the house, Rafael gave a wonderful imitation of the chief of police for Jacquie's benefit, and was so amused by his own act that the tears of laughter ran out from under his spectacles.

The next morning, while we had breakfast, we related the whole incident to Paula. Instead of being amused, as we thought she would be, she was shocked and revolted by the whole thing. She described the chief of police in terms no lady should use, and told us that he was far too full of his own importance; once before she had been forced to have words with him, when he had tried to stop her girls going on board the river steamer. But this treatment we had received was the last straw. This time he had gone too far, and she herself was going to come down to the police-station and tell him where he got off. So after breakfast she draped her massive shoulders in a purple-and-green shawl, pinned a large straw hat covered with scarlet poppies to her head, and accompanied us, breathlessly indignant, down the road to the village.

When we reached the police-station we saw outside it an enormous double bed placed in the shade of a palm tree, and in it, snoring blissfully, lay the chief of police himself. His unshaven face wore a seraphic expression, and a couple of empty bottles by the bed argued that he had celebrated our arrest in a lavish fashion. Paula, at the sight of him, uttered a grunt of derision, and then, waddling rapidly forward, she drew back her hand and slapped vigorously at the heap of bed-clothes that presumably covered the chief of police's rear end. It was a fine, powerful blow, delivered with the full weight of Paula's massive body behind it, and the chief sat bolt upright in bed and stared wildly around; then he recognized Paula, and modestly drew the bedclothes up to his chin while giving her good morning. But Paula was in no mood for niceties, and she swept aside his greeting and launched her attack. Bosom heaving, eyes flashing, she hung over the bed and proceeded to tell him what she thought of him in a voice so shrill and so clear that half the village could hear. I began to feel rather sorry for the poor man; pinned down as he was, in his own bed and in full view of the village, he was forced to lie there while Paula loomed over him like a great avalanche of brown flesh, pouring scorn, ridicule, slander, and threats over him in a remorseless stream that flowed so steadily he had no chance to get a word in. His sallow face turned from indignant pink to white, and then, when Paula got on to the more intimate details of his love life, it turned a delicate shade of green. All the inhabitants of the nearby houses had gathered in their doorways to watch the fun and shout encouragement to Paula, and it became apparent that the chief of police was not a popular member of the community. At length the poor man could stand it no longer; he flung back the blankets, leapt out of bed, and scuttled into the police-station, clad only in his vest and a pair of natty, striped underpants, to the raucous delight of the assembled villagers. Paula, panting but triumphant, sat down for a short rest on the vacated bed, and was then able to accompany us homewards, stopping at various houses *en route* to receive the congratulations of her admirers.

The sequel to this episode came that evening, when one of the constables turned up at the house, looking distinctly embarrassed, clutching in one hand his trusty rifle and in the other a large and disorderly bunch of canna lilies. He explained that the chief of police had sent this floral offering for the señora, and Jacquie accepted them with suitable expressions of gratitude. After that, whenever we met the chief striding importantly about the village, he would come to attention and salute smartly, and then sweep off his peaked cap and beam at us. But he never did get around to seeing our police permits.

CHAPTER SEVEN

TERRIBLE TOADS AND A BUSHEL OF BIRDS

By the time we had been in the Chaco two months our collection
had reached such proportions that it took us all our time to cope
with it. Our day would begin just before dawn, when Paula would
surge into the bedroom with the tea. The reason we arose at such
an ungodly hour was not, I regret to state, because we liked early
rising, but simply that we found it paid to get the heavier work
done before the sun got too high and the temperature shot up.

Our first job was the cleaning out – a long, tedious, and messy
business that generally took us a couple of hours. The length of
time taken over a cage depended entirely on the occupant: if it
was bad-tempered, a longer time was needed in order to avoid
being bitten or pecked; and if it was playful, a lot of time was
wasted trying to persuade it that the cleaning out was not a game
designed for its benefit. Most of the specimens very soon learnt
the routine and would stand patiently to one side while half the
cage was cleaned out, and then they would skip over into the
clean section while the other half was dealt with. After the cleaning out was done and all cages had received a fresh bed of dry

leaves or sawdust, we could start preparing the food. First of all came the fruit, which had to be peeled or cut up. Now, this sounds a fairly straightforward job, and it would have been so if we could have prepared the fruit in exactly the same way for every member of the collection, but, unfortunately, it was not quite as easy as that. Some birds, for example, liked their banana split lengthwise, put on a hook and hung on the wire front of their cage; others liked their bananas cut up into small pieces, just the right size to swallow. Some would not touch their mango unless it was mixed into a slush with bread and milk, while others demanded (before they would touch anything else) that they should have a slice of over-ripe pawpaw with the seeds left in. Remove the seeds and they would not touch it, although they did not eat the seeds but merely plucked them out of the soft orange flesh and scattered them about the cage. So preparing the fruit was a long job that required a good memory for the animals' likes and dislikes.

After the fruit, the next big task was the meat. We used fourteen pounds a day: a sort of gigantic mixed grill that was composed of heart, liver, brain, and steak, all of which had to be chopped or minced into an acceptable form. Preparing fourteen pounds of meat when the temperature is over a hundred in the shade is no joke, and, in order to try to facilitate this operation, I had purchased in Asunción a gigantic mincing machine. On its base was proudly embossed 'Primero classe', but in spite of its rash boast this ponderous piece of mechanism was the bane of our lives. Bits dropped off off it at the slighest provocation, and no matter how small the pieces of meat we inserted into its maw, they always managed to stick, which meant that the whole thing had to be dismantled. Even when working properly, it shuddered and groaned, emitting at intervals a piercing shriek calculated to try the sternest nerves.

The meat prepared, the next job was to wash all the food- and water-pots. Anyone who thinks that by taking up collecting they will be rid of such domestic chores as washing up are sadly mistaken. Towards the end of our trip we had some fifty cages, and all of these had at least two pots in them, while some had three and even four. Every one of these had to be scrupulously scrubbed and rinsed before feeding could begin. In that heat any small bits of food left in the pots would soon start to decay, infect the fresh food, and probably kill the specimens.

To someone who has never been collecting, it may seem as though we gave ourselves a lot of unnecessary trouble by pampering our animals. The answer is, of course, that unless you pamper them you will get precious few back alive. In every collection there is a nucleus of creatures of such phlegmatic disposition that they will put up with almost any sort of treatment, but for every one animal like this there will be twenty which are just the opposite.

Having got through the routine work, we could then devote ourselves to the more unusual and sometimes complicated jobs, such as bottle-feeding baby animals, doctoring any sick specimens and dealing with any new arrivals. These would turn up at any time of the day or night, and most of them caused trouble before we had them settled. Most specimens are fairly straightforward and are not much trouble once they are used to the routine, but occasionally we would get a creature which appeared to go out of its way to cause extra work. In a lot of instances this would be an animal which, by normal collecting standards, should be the easiest thing on earth to keep in captivity.

There is found in certain parts of South America a toad which must be one of the most bizarre looking of the batrachians. It is called the horned toad, and, as toads as a general rule are easy enough to keep, I thought the horned toad would be simple. For some reason, I had an overwhelming desire to obtain some of these toads while we were in the Chaco. I knew that they were found there, that the local name for them was *escuerzo*, but there, so to speak, the matter ended. It is one of the strange things about collecting that a creature you are most anxious to capture, no matter how common it was before, immediately becomes non-existent as soon as you ask about it. So it was with the horned toad; I showed everyone pictures of it, I offered fabulous rewards for its capture, and I nearly drove Jacquie and Rafael mad by forcing them out of bed at two o'clock in the morning to investigate marshes with me in the hope of catching some, but with no success. If I had known the trouble that the horned toads were to cause me, I would not have made such efforts to try to obtain them.

One lunch-time I found a battered tin can, the mouth plugged with leaves, waiting for me on the veranda. Paula could give me no more information than that it was a *bicho*, which was fairly obvious, and that it had been brought by an elderly Indian. I removed the plug of leaves circumspectly with a stick. Peering into the rusty inside, I saw, to my surprise, a gigantic horned toad squatting placidly on the backs of two smaller ones.

'What is it?' inquired Jacquie, who had kept a discreet distance with Paula.

'Horned toads ... three beauties,' I answered delightedly.

I tipped the tin over, and out spilled the toads on to the veranda in a tangled heap. Paula let out a whoop and disappeared into the house; from behind the safety of a window she looked out, palpitating.

'Señor, señor, look out,' she wailed; '*es un bicho muy malo, señor, muy venenoso.*'

'Rubbish,' I said. '*No es venenoso ... no es yarará ... es escuerzo, bicho muy lindo.*'

'*Madre de Dios,*' said Paula, rolling her eyes to Heaven at the idea of a horned toad being called beautiful.

'Are they poisonous?' inquired Jacquie.

'No, of course not ... they just look as though they ought to be, that's all.'

By now the toads had sorted themselves out, and the largest was squatting there, regarding us with an angry eye. He was about the circumference of a saucer, and three-quarters of his bulk seemed to consist of head. He had short, thick legs, a paunchy body, and this enormous head in which were set two large eyes filigreed with a pattern of gold and silver. Above each of these the skin was raised into an isosceles triangle, like the horns of a baby goat. His mouth was incredible, for it was so large it almost appeared to split him in two. The toad, with his rubber lips, horned head, and sulkily drooping mouth, managed to achieve an expression that was a combination of extreme malevolence with the arrogant bearing of an obese monarch. His whole air of evil was enhanced by the fact that he was a pale mustard-yellow in colour, covered with rust-red and sage-green patches that looked as though someone, lacking in artistic and geographical knowledge, had tried to draw a map of the world all over him.

While Paula was evoking the aid of the saints and assuring Jacquie that she would be a widow within half an hour, I bent down to get a closer look at our protégé. Immediately he gulped convulsively, blew himself up to twice his previous size, and then exhaled the air in a series of indignant wheezing screams, at the same time taking little jumps towards me and snapping his great mouth. This was a most effective and startling display, for the inside of his lips was a bright primrose-yellow.

At the sound of the toad's war-cry, Paula clasped her hands and rocked to and fro in the window. I thought this would be a most suitable opportunity to teach her some elementary natural history and, at the same time, enhance my prestige. I picked up the toad, who kicked violently and wheezed asthmatically, and approached the window where Paula was posturing like an outsize puppet. '*Bueno*, Paula, *mira . . . no es venenoso . . . nada, nada*,' I said.

As the toad opened his colossal mouth for another bagpipe-like cry, I stuffed my thumb into it. The creature was so surprised that his mouth remained open for a second, and I smiled soothingly at Paula, who appeared to be on the verge of a swoon.

'*No es venenoso*,' I repeated. '*No es . . .*'

At that precise moment the toad recovered from his surprise and snapped his mouth shut. My first impression was that someone had amputated the entire first joint of my thumb with an extremely blunt hatchet. With an effort, I stifled the cry of agony that rose to my lips. Paula was regarding me pop-eyed, and, for the first time, without a sound. I gave a lop-sided sneer, which I hoped she would mistake for a debonair grin, while the toad amused himself by clenching his jaws as hard as he could at half-second intervals, so that the effect was as if my thumb was lying in the path of an extremely long goods train with more than the normal complement of wheels.

'*Santa Maria,*' said Paula, '*qué extraordinario ... no tiene veneno, señor?*'

'*No, nada de veneno,*' I said hoarsely, still wearing my fixed smile.

'What's the matter?' asked Jacquie curiously.

'For Heaven's sake, get the woman away. This damn thing's nearly taken my thumb off.'

Jacquie hastily distracted Paula's attention with a discreet inquiry about the lunch, and she floated off to the kitchen, still ejaculating '*extraordinario*' at intervals. When she had vanished, we turned our attention to saving the remnants of my thumb. This was not so easy, for the toad had an immensely powerful grip but very fragile jaw-bones, and all our attempts at prising open his mouth with a stick caused them to bend alarmingly. Then every time we removed the stick, he would give my thumb a triumphant squeeze. At last, in desperation, I laid my hand and the toad down on the concrete, hoping that this would persuade him to let go, but he just squatted there like a nightmare bulldog, and glared up at me with defiance.

'Perhaps it's the wrong sort of place,' suggested Jacquie helpfully.

'Well, what do you expect me to do?' I inquired irritably. 'Go and sit in a swamp with him?'

'No, but if you stuck your hand into that hibiscus bush, he might feel he could escape if he let go.'

'If he won't let go here, I don't see that crawling about in an hibiscus bush is going to help.'

'Have it your own way. What are you going to do, spend the rest of your life wearing a horned toad on your thumb?'

Eventually I saw that the only alternative to the hibiscus-bush experiment was to risk damaging the toad's mouth in prising it open, so I crawled into the shade of the bush and plunged my hand into the thickest tangle of the undergrowth. Immediately the toad sprang backwards, at the same time spitting out my thumb with every indication of disgust. I re-captured and put him back in the tin, without much opposition beyond a few half-hearted wheezes. My thumb had a scarlet line round it where his jaws had clamped together, and within an hour an ugly bruise had spread across the nail. It was three days before I could use my thumb without pain, and a month before the bruise faded.

It was the last time I attempted to demonstrate to the inhabitants of the Chaco the harmlessness of the horned toad.

The Chaco being such a paradise for bird-life, naturally the specimens in the avian section of our collection outnumbered the others by about two to one. The largest of our birds were the Brazilian seriemas. Their bodies were about the size of a chicken and were mounted on long, powerful legs; their necks were also long and their heads large. Their beaks were slightly curved at the end, and this, with the big, pale silver eyes, made them somewhat like hawks. Their plumage was a soft greyish-brown on the neck and back, with cream underparts. On their heads, just over the nostrils, they had curious tufts of feathers that stuck up in the air. When they walked with their necks curved and the head thrown back, wearing their usual haughty expressions, they reminded me of immensely superior feathered camels. The two we had were perfectly tame, and so we used to let them out each day to wander round the camp.

When they were released from their cage in the morning, they would first walk all round the camp on a tour of inspection. They would stalk along for a few yards, pacing slowly and solemnly on long legs, and then all of a sudden they would stop with one leg in mid-air and freeze in that position, their tattered tiara of feathers quivering, expressions of outraged, aristocratic indignation on their faces. After a moment or so they would unfreeze, the suspended leg would come down and they would continue their constitutional with measured steps before once again becoming immobile a few yards farther on. From their demeanour you would imagine them to be a couple of dowager duchesses who, whilst strolling in the park, had been whistled at by a tipsy soldier.

Occasionally the duchesses would drop their aloof pose and indulge in wild and fantastic dances. One of them would discover a twig, or tuft of grass, and, picking it up in her beak, she would rush towards her companion with great bouncing strides and then toss the offering on to the ground. They would

both stare at it for a minute and then start to pirouette around
it on their long, ungainly legs, bowing courteously to each
other and fluttering their wings, now and again picking up the
twig or grass and tossing it into the air with gay abandon.
Then, as suddenly as it had begun, the dance would stop; they
would freeze, glare at each other with what seemed like glacial
rage, and then stalk off in opposite directions.

The seriemas developed a passion 'for nails, which they
were convinced (rather as Anastacius, the butcher, had been)
were live creatures. They would carefully pick a nail out of
the packet and proceed to bang it on the ground until it was
'dead'. Then they would drop it and pick up another. In a
short time the packet would be empty and the seriemas would
be standing proudly in a sea of 'dead' nails. Fortunately, they
never attempted to swallow them, but the habit grew irritating,
for every time I wanted to construct something I had to spend
a considerable time grovelling about in the dust, collecting the

slaughtered nails which the seriemas had spent a happy morning scattering about the camp.

Apart from the seriemas, the bird that probably amused us most was a rail: a small marsh bird with piercing eyes of rich wine-red, a long, sharply pointed beak, and enormously large feet. This bird had the honour to be the one and only specimen that Paula obtained for us during our sojourn in the Chaco, and, needless to say, no one was more surprised than Paula herself. It happened like this.

One day Jacquie woke up with a slight temperature and shivering fits which indicated a mild dose of sandfly fever, and so I made her stay in bed. After a hurried breakfast, I told Paula that the señora was ill and would be staying in bed, and then left to get on with the animal work. When I returned at lunch-time I was amazed to see Jacquie's bed, with her still in it, out on the veranda, while from inside the house rose a confused cacophony of sounds, among which Paula's steamship-like hoot was predominant.

'What's going on?' I inquired of my wife.

'Thank goodness you've come back,' she said wearily. 'I've had the most exhilarating morning. For the first two hours Paula kept tiptoeing in and out of the room with the most ghastly selection of herb-teas and jellies, but when she found I only wanted to sleep she gave that up and started to clean the house. Apparently she gives the whole place a thorough going over once a week, and this happens to be the day.'

It sounded as if a troop of Cossacks was galloping round and round the house, pursued by several soprano Red Indians. There was a crash and a tinkle of glass, and a broom-handle appeared through a window-pane.

'But what the hell's going on in there?' I demanded.

'Wait a minute and I'll tell you,' said Jacquie. 'Well, just as I was dropping off to sleep, Paula came in and said she wanted to clean out the bedroom. I said that I didn't want to get out of bed and she'd have to leave it until next week. She seemed very shocked at the idea, rushed out here, and screamed for her girls. About ten of them came over, and before I knew what was happening they'd lifted the whole bed up and carried

it out here. Then they set to work to clean out the bedroom ...
the whole crowd.'

There came another crash from inside the house, followed
by shrill squeals and the patter of running feet.

'Is that what they're doing now? It seems a novel way of
cleaning out a bedroom.'

'No, no; they've finished the bedroom. They all trooped
out here to carry me back inside, when Paula gave one of those
screams of hers that nearly took the top of my head off, and said
she could see a *bicho* in the garden. I couldn't see anything,
but all the girls apparently could. Before I could ask them
what sort of *bicho* it was, they'd all dashed down to the end of
the garden and were crashing about in the bushes with Paula
directing operations. Whatever the thing was, it took to its
heels and for some peculiar reason it dashed straight into the
house through the door ... they all followed it inside and
they've been chasing it from room to room ever since. Heaven
alone knows what they've broken in there, but they've been
galloping around for the past half-hour. I've shouted at them
till I'm hoarse, but they won't answer. It's a wonder the beast
hasn't died of heart failure, the row they've been making.'

'Well, there's one thing certain: it must be a harmless kind
of *bicho*, or they wouldn't have chased it in the first place.
Anyway, I'll go and have a look.'

Cautiously I poked my head round the front door. The
living-room was a shambles of overturned chairs and broken
plates. Distant crashes and yelps indicated that the hunt had
ended in the second bedroom. I edged open the bedroom door,
and was almost deafened by the chorus from inside; pushing
the door open further, I peered round it. A broom-handle
appeared from nowhere and swiped viciously downwards, miss-
ing my head by inches. I retreated and closed the door a trifle.

'Hey, Paula, *qué pasa*?' I bellowed through the crack.

There was silence for a moment, and then the door was flung
open and Paula stood on the threshold, quivering like a half-
inflated barrage balloon.

'*Señor!*' she proclaimed, pointing a fat finger at the bed,
'*un bicho, señor, un pájara muy lindo.*'

I entered the room and closed the door. Paula's gang of girls surveyed me with glittering smiles of satisfaction from among the ruins of the room. Their hair was disarranged, they panted with exhaustion, and one of them had lost a large portion of the front of her dress, which left little of her more obvious charms to the imagination. This seemed to cause her more gratification than anything else, and I noticed that she panted more vigorously than the others. The smell of eleven different varieties of scent in such a small space made my senses reel, but I approached the bed and got down on all fours to look under it. The girls and Paula clustered round me in a giggling, asphyxiating scrum as I looked for the *bicho*. Under the bed, covered with bits of fluff and dust, stood a panting, irritated, but still extremely belligerent rail. An exciting five minutes followed: the girls and Paula went round one side of the bed to chivvy the bird out, while I crawled under the bed with a towel and tried to grab him. My first attempt was thwarted because when I came to hurl the towel at him I discovered that Paula was innocently standing on one end. My second attempt was also a failure, for one of the girls in her excitement trod heavily on my hand. The third time, however, I was lucky and scrambled out from underneath the bed with the rail wrapped up in the towel and screaming at the top of his voice. I carried him out to show Jacquie, while Paula marshalled her girls and set them to repairing some of the chaos the rail hunt had produced.

'D'you mean to say that all that row was over *that?*' asked Jacquie in disgust, looking at the dust-covered head of the rail sticking out from the depths of the towel.

'Yes. Ten of them chasing him, and they couldn't get him. Amazing, isn't it?'

'He doesn't look worth getting to me,' said Jacquie; 'in fact he looks a horribly dull brute.'

But there, as it happened, she was quite wrong, for the rail turned out to be a bird which, though exceedingly irascible and short-tempered, had a distinct personality, and he very soon became one of our favourite bird characters.

We soon discovered that he moved about in almost as

unusual and comical a way as the seriemas. Like a lanky school-master, he would stop and lower his head and peer myopically, neck stretched out, as though glaring through a keyhole, in the hope of catching his class misbehaving. Then, apparently satisfied, he would straighten up, give three or four quick flips of his short, pointed tail, and mince off to the next imaginary keyhole. This habit of flipping his tail up and down earned him the apt but regrettable name of Flap-arse. His spear-like beak he never hesitated to employ, lunging wildly at the hand of whoever was cleaning out his cage; this job became one of the bloodier and more painful tasks. I remember, on the day of his capture, putting in a large Player's cigarette tin filled with water. As soon as it appeared through the door, Flap-arse leapt forward and stabbed at it; to our surprise, his beak went straight through the tin, like a needle through cloth. He danced about the cage, wearing the tin on his beak, and it was some time before I was able to catch him and remove it. Flap-arse was kept in a cage with wooden bars, through which he was forever peering hopefully, occasionally uttering a rasping 'Arrrk', in an admonishing tone of voice.

In the cage on top of Flap-arse's lived a bird, one of Jacquie's favourites, whom, to her annoyance, I christened Dracula almost as soon as he arrived. He was a bare-faced ibis, a bird the size of a pigeon, and had stubby, flesh-coloured legs and a long, curved beak of the same shade. His whole body was covered in funereal-black plumage, with the exception of an area round the eyes and base of his beak, which was bare and a pale tallow yellow. From this bald area a pair of small, circular, and sad little eyes peered forth mistily. Dracula was a very dainty feeder, and seemed quite incapable of eating his meat unless it was shredded to a microscopic minuteness and saturated with water. If a little raw brain was mixed into this slush, his happiness was complete and he would dip and patter his beak in the food, giving tiny, wheezing titters of pleasure. Although he was a sweet-tempered and very likeable little bird, there was something rather eerie about the way he would chuckle to himself as he probed the bloody slush of brain and meat, with the enthusiasm of a ghoul that has found a fresh grave.

Another bird that enjoyed brain was a black-faced ibis, known to us simply as B.F.I. He throve on a pure meat diet for some time, until one day, thinking he would like a treat, I mixed some brain with it. B.F.I. could have had no opportunity of sampling this delicacy in the wild state, but he fell on it as though it was his favourite food. Unfortunately, he then decided that meat was too coarse and lowly a fare for him, and vociferously demanded brain at every meal. Whereas Dracula was a dainty feeder, B.F.I. had no pretensions to manners. His idea of feeding was to stand as close to his food-pan as possible (preferably *in* it) and then toss bits of brain all over himself and the cage with the gay abandon of someone throwing confetti, and crying 'Arrr-onk!' loudly and triumphantly with his beak full.

Once a week Flap-arse, Dracula, and B.F.I. had a fish-feed to keep them in condition. This had been difficult to organize, for no one ever dreams of eating fish in the Chaco, so it could not be bought in the local market. Armed with lengths of thick string and fearsome barbed fish-hooks that appeared to have been designed for catching sharks, we would make our way down to the river-bank in the morning. Half a mile below the village was an old landing-stage, now disused, its worm-eaten timbers infested with spiders and other creatures, and almost hidden under a great eiderdown of glossy convolvulus leaves brocaded with pink, trumpet-shaped flowers. By picking our way from beam to beam, moving cautiously, so as not to disturb the great electric-blue wasps that had their nests in the wood, we would eventually arrive at the remains of the small jetty that jutted out into the dark waters, its fragile piles decorated with ruffs of lily leaves. Perched on the end, we would bait our hooks and cast them into the brown waters. It could scarcely be called fishing, for the river was infested with piranhas, and a bloody scrap of meat as bait would soon create a churning, snapping merry-go-round of fish below us, all fighting to be caught. It could not, therefore, be classified as sport, for there was no element of doubt about the outcome, but these fishing expeditions gave us an excuse to sit on the jetty's edge which commanded a wonderful view of the river as it wound away westwards. The sunsets were so magnificent that not even the haze of mosquitoes around us lessened our pleasure. After two months, Rafael had to leave us in the Chaco and return to Buenos Aires. The night before he left, we went fishing, and were rewarded with one of the most spectacular and impressive sunsets I have ever seen.

Somewhere to the north, in the great Brazilian forests, there had been rain, and so the river was swollen and swift with the extra water. The sky was a pale blue, smooth and unclouded as a polished turquoise. As the sun sank lower and lower, it changed from yellow to a deep red that was almost wine colour, and the black river-waters took on the appearance of a bale of shot silk being unwound between the banks. As the sun reached the horizon, it seemed to pause in its descent, and from somewhere out of the vast empty sky appeared three small clouds which looked as though they were composed of a small crowd of black soap-bubbles edged with blood red. The clouds arranged themselves with artistic precision, curtain-like, and the sun sank discreetly behind them. Then, round the bend of the river, appeared the vanguard of the camelotes. The flood-water had brought them down from higher levels, these islands

of lilies, convolvulus, and grass entwined round water-softened logs from the great forests. The sun had sunk and the river was moon-white in the brief twilight; and the camelotes in their hundreds swept past us silently and swiftly on their eager journey to the sea, some only as big as a hat, others a solid tangled mat as big as a room, each carrying their cargo of seeds, shoots, bulbs, leeches, frogs, snakes, and snails. We watched this strange armada sliding past us, until it was too dark to distinguish anything, only now and then becoming aware of the passing of the great fleet of camelotes, for one would brush against the piles of the jetty with a quiet, soothing whisper of soft leaves and grass. Soon, mosquito-bitten and stiff, we made our way silently back to the village, and all night long the endless string of camelotes hurried on, but in the morning the river was as smooth and empty as a mirror.

CHAPTER EIGHT

THE FOUR-EYED BIRD AND THE ANACONDA

ONE morning we received an addition to the collection, which we could hear arriving when it was still a good half-mile down the road. I saw an Indian trotting rapidly towards the camp clearing, endeavouring with moderate success to keep his large straw hat on with one hand while with the other he tried to prevent something from climbing out of a rather frayed wicker basket. The thing, whatever it was, kept complaining about its confinement in a series of rich, base honks which sounded like someone trying to play a complicated Bach fugue on an old bulb motor-horn. The Indian dashed up to me, laid the basket at my feet, then stood back, doffing his big hat and grinning broadly.

'*Buenos días, señor*,' he said, '*es un bicho, señor, un pájaro muy lindo.*'

I wondered what species of bird could possibly produce that

complicated series of organ-like brays. The basket lay on the
ground, shuddering, and more of the wild cries broke out.
Looking down, I found myself staring into a cold, fish-like
eye of pale bronze colour that glared through the wicker-work
at me. I bent down, undid the lid of the basket, and lifted it a
trifle, so that I could see the occupant; I caught a brief glimpse
of a tumble of tawny feathers, and then a long, green, dagger-
shaped beak shot out through the crack, buried itself half an
inch in the fleshy part of my thumb, and was immediately
whipped back into the basket again. Drawn by my yelp of
pain and resulting flood of bad language, Jacquie appeared on
the scene and asked resignedly what had bitten me this time.

'A bittern,' I said, indistinctly, sucking my wound.

'I know, darling, but *what* bit you?'

'I was bitten by a bittern,' I explained.

Jacquie stared at me blankly for a moment.

'Are you being funny?' she inquired at length.

'No, I tell you I was bitten by this blasted bird ... or rather I
was pecked by it ... It's a tiger bittern.'

'Not a jaguar bittern?' she asked sweetly.

'This is no time for silly jokes,' I said severely; 'help me
get it out of the basket ... I want to have a look at it.'

Jacquie squatted down and eased the lid off the basket, and
once more the green beak shot out, but this time I was ready
for it and grabbed it adroitly between finger and thumb. The
bird protested deafeningly, and kicked and struggled violently
in the basket, but I managed to get my other hand inside and
to grab him firmly by the wings and lift him out.

I don't know what Jacquie was expecting, but the sight of
him made her gasp, for a tiger bittern is definitely one of the
more spectacular of the wading birds. Imagine a small, rather
hump-backed heron, with sage-green legs and beak, and clad
entirely in plumage of pale-green colour spotted and striped
with a wonderful, flamboyant pattern of black and tiger-orange
so that the whole bird seems to glow like a miniature feathered
bonfire.

'Isn't he lovely?' said Jacquie. 'What gorgeous colouring!'

'Here,' I said, 'just hang on to his feet a second – I want to look at his wing. It seems to be hanging in a rather peculiar fashion.'

While Jacquie held on to his green legs, I ran my hand down the underside of his left wing, and half-way down the main bone I found the ominous swelling of the muscles that generally denotes a break. I probed the swelling with my fingers, and manipulated the wing gently: sure enough, there was a break about three-quarters of the way down, but to my relief it was a clean break, and not a complicated mass of splintered bone.

'Anything wrong with it?' asked Jacquie.

'Yes, it's broken fairly high up. Quite a clean break.'

'What a shame! He's such a lovely bird. Isn't there anything we can do about it?'

'Well, I can have a shot at setting it. But you know how damn stupid these creatures are about bandages and things.'

'Let's try, anyway. I think it's worth it.'

'O.K. You go and get the money, and I'll try to explain to Daniel Boone, here.'

Jacquie disappeared into the house, while I explained slowly and tortuously to the Indian that the bird's wing was broken. He felt it and agreed, shaking his head and looking very sad. I went on to explain that I would pay him half the value of the bird then, and the other half should it still be alive in a week's time. This was a fairly complicated explanation that taxed my primitive Spanish to the extreme. Also, I find it helpful, when attempting to speak a language other than my own, to use my hands lavishly, for a gesture can explain something when a limited vocabulary would let me down. Clutching the infuriated bittern to my bosom, I could not indulge in gestures to help me out, for one hand held the bird round the body, while the other clasped his beak; in consequence I had to repeat everything two or three times before the Indian got the hang of it. At length he grasped my meaning and nodded vigorously, and we both smiled at each other and gave little bows and murmured '*Gracias, gracias.*' Then a thought struck the Indian, and he asked me how much I was going to pay; this simple question was my undoing. Without thinking, I let go of the bittern's beak, and lifted my hand to show him the

requisite number of fingers. It was the opportunity the bird
had been waiting for, and he did what all members of his family
do in a fight. He looked upwards and launched his beak in a
murderous lunge at my eyes. By sheer luck I managed to jerk
back my head in time, so that he missed my eyes, but I did
not jerk it back far enough; his beak shot squarely up my left
nostril, and the point imbedded itself briefly somewhere near my
sinus.

Those who have never been pecked in the nose by a tiger
bittern can have little idea of the exquisite agony it produces,
nor of the force of the blow. I felt rather as though I had been
kicked in the face by a horse, and reeled back, momentarily
blinded by the pain and stunned by the force of the thrust. I
managed to keep my head well back to avoid a second stab
from the beak, while my nose gushed blood like a fountain
that splashed all over me, the bittern, and the Indian, who had
rushed forward to help me. I handed the bird over to him and
went to the house in search of first-aid; Jacquie busied herself
with wet towels, cotton wool, and boracic, scolding and com-
miserating as she did so.

'What would have happened if he'd got you in the eye?' she
asked, scrubbing at the crust of dried blood on my lips and cheeks.

'I dread to think. His beak's at least six inches long, and if
he'd got a straight peck, with that force behind it, he'd have
gone right through into my brain, I should imagine.'

'Well, perhaps that will teach you to be more careful in
future,' she said unsympathetically. 'Here, hold this cotton wool
to your nose; it's still bleeding a bit.'

I went outside again, looking rather like one of those lurid
anti-vivisection posters, and concluded my bargain with the
Indian. Then I put the bittern into a temporary cage and went
to collect the necessary medical appliances for the operation on
his wing. First, I had to carve two splints out of soft white
wood and pad them carefully with a layer of cotton wool held
in place by lint. Then we prepared a large box as an operating
table, and laid out bandages, scissors, razor-blade. I put on a
thick gauntlet glove and went to fetch the patient. As I opened
the door of his cage he lunged at me, and I caught him by the

beak and pulled him out, squawking protestingly. We bound his feet with a bandage, and dealt in the same way with his beak. Then he was laid on the table, and, while Jacquie held his feet and beak, I set to work. I had to clip off all the feathers on the wing; this was not only in order to make it easier to fix the splint, but also to take as much weight off the wing as possible. When the wing was almost as bare as a plucked chicken, I manoeuvred one of the flat splints under the wing, so that the break lay in the centre of it; then came the delicate and tricky job of feeling until I located the two broken ends of bone, and then twisting and pulling them gently until they lay together in a normal position. Holding them in this position on the splint with my thumb, I slid the other splint on top, and held the break firmly, trapped between the two slats of padded wool. Then the whole thing had to be bound round and round with yards of bandages, and the finished product tied firmly against the body with a sort of sling, so that the weight of the bandages and splints did not drag the wing down and pull the broken ends of bone out of place. This done, our patient was put back in his cage, and supplied with a plate of chopped meat and some fresh water.

For the rest of the day he behaved very well, eating all his food, standing in one position, not attempting to interfere with his wing, and generally behaving as though he had been in captivity for years. Most wild creatures have the strongest possible views about bandages, splints, and other medical accoutrements, and no sooner do you put them on, than their one ambition in life is to get them off again as quickly as possible. I had had a number of irritating experiences in the past with both birds and mammals over this vexed question of first-aid, and so I was surprised and pleased when the tiger bittern seemed to take the whole thing calmly and philosophically. I felt that at last I had found a bird who was sensible and who realized that we were strapping him up for the best possible reasons. However, I was a bit premature in my judgement, for next morning, when we were checking round the collection, Jacquie peered into the bittern's cage, and then uttered an anguished groan.

'Just come and look at this stupid bird,' she called.

'What's he done?'

'He's got all his bandage off ... I thought you were being a little too optimistic about him last night.'

The tiger bittern was standing gloomily in the corner of his cage, glaring at us with his sardonic bronze eyes. He had obviously spent an energetic evening stripping the bandages from his wing, and he had made a good job of it. But he had not reckoned with one thing: the inside edge of his beak was minutely serrated, like a fretsaw, the teeth of which were directed backwards, towards the bird's throat. When he caught fish, these little 'teeth' helped him to hold on to the slippery body, and made sure that it only slid one way. This is a very fine thing when you are catching fish, but when you are unwinding bandages you find this type of beak a grave disadvantage, for the bandages get hooked on to the serrated edge. So the tiger bittern stood there with some twelve feet of bandage, firmly hooked to his beak, and dangling down in a magnificent festoon. He looked like an attenuated, morose Father Christmas whose beard had come askew after a hot half-hour distributing presents. He glared at us when we laughed, and gave an indignant and slightly muffled honk through the bandages.

We had to get him out of his cage and spend half an hour with a pair of tweezers stripping the tattered bandage from his beak. To my surprise and pleasure, I found that he had not succeeded in removing the splints, so the wing-bones were still held in the same position. We bound him up once more, and he looked so contrite that I felt he had learnt his lesson. The next morning, though, all the bandages were off and trailing from his beak, and we had to go through the whole laborious re-bandaging again. But it was no use, for every morning we would be treated to the sight of him standing in his cage, heavily disguised under a patriarchal cascade of white beard.

'I'm getting sick of bandaging this bloody bird,' I said, as Jacquie and I cleaned his beak for the eighth morning running.

'I am, too. But what can we do? We're using up an awful lot of bandage; I wish we'd thought of bringing some sticking-plaster.'

'Or even some plaster bandage ... that would have fooled him. What worries me, though, is that all this messing about isn't going to do the wing any good. For all I know, the bones may have shifted under the splint, and his wing will heal with a damn great bend in it, like a croquet hoop.'

'Well,' said Jacquie philosophically, 'all we can do is to wait and see. We can't do any more than we're doing.'

So, every morning for three interminable weeks, we unpicked, unravelled, and re-bandaged the bittern. Then the great day came when the bones should have healed, and the bandage was removed from his beak for the last time. I seized the scissors and started to cut away the splints.

'I wonder what it'll be like,' said Jacquie.

'Probably look like a corkscrew,' I said gloomily.

But as the splints fell away, they revealed the bittern's wing lying there as straight as a die. I could hardly believe my eyes; it was impossible to see where the break had been, and even when I felt the bone with my fingers I could not have located the break if it had not been for a slight ridge of protecting bone which had appeared at the point where the two broken ends had grown together. The wing-muscles had, of course, grown weak through lack of use, and so the wing dropped considerably, but after a week or so of use he soon regained the power in it, and the wing went back to its normal position. For some time it remained bald, but eventually the feathers grew again, and when he attacked his food-pan with beak snapping and wing flapping, you could not have told that there had ever been anything wrong with him at all. We were very proud of him, not only because he was a good advertisement for our surgery, but also because he was a good example of how worth while it is to persevere with even the most hopeless-looking cases. Of course, we never received any gratitude from the bird himself – unless a savage attack every feeding time could be interpreted as gratitude – but we were repaid in another way, for indirectly the tiger bittern was the cause of our meeting the Four-eyed Bird and the anaconda.

The Indian who had brought us the bittern did not turn up to collect the other half of his money on the appointed date – a most unusual occurrence. But he did appear some ten days later, and seemed genuinely pleased at the good job we had done on the bird. He explained that the reason he had delayed in coming was that he had been trying to catch us a snake of monstrous proportions, '*muy, muy grande*', as he put it, and of incredibly evil disposition. This grandfather of all reptiles lived in a swamp behind his house, and twice in the past three months it had paid a visit to him and stolen one of his chickens. Each time he had followed it into the swamp, but had failed to find it. Now, the night before, the snake had made a third raid on his chickens, but this time he was fairly sure he knew the area in which it was lying up to digest its meal. Would the señor, he inquired diffidently, care to accompany him to catch it? The señor said that nothing would give him greater pleasure, and the Indian promised to come back early the next morning to guide us to the serpent's lair.

I felt that this hunt for – and I hoped capture of – the anaconda (for that was obviously what the snake was) would make an ideal subject for our ciné-camera, so I made arrangements for an ox-cart to come the next morning, in which Jacquie and the camera could travel. These ox-carts are fitted with gigantic wheels, some seven feet in diameter, which enable them to get through swamp-land that would bog down any other form of vehicle. They are pulled by any number of oxen, according to the load, and though they are slow and uncomfortable, they enable you to get right into the swampy areas that would otherwise be inaccessible. So early the next morning we set off, the Indian and I on horse-back, and Jacquie squatting in a cart drawn by a couple of dreamy-eyed and stoical oxen.

Our destination proved to be farther than I had thought. I had hoped that we would reach the swamp before the sun had risen too high in the sky, but by ten o'clock the heat was intense and we were still wending our way through the thorn-scrub. The speed of our little caravan was governed entirely by the oxen; they kept going at a steady slouching walk, but, as it was only half the speed of the horses, it slowed down our progress considerably. The country we were travelling through was dry and dusty, and we were forced to ride alongside the cart; for if we rode behind we were suffocated by the clouds of dust kicked up by the oxen, and if we rode in front our horses enveloped the cart in *their* dust. The landscape was alive with birds, all filled with that early-morning liveliness and bustle which seems common to birds the world over. Flocks of guira cuckoos fed in the short growth by the side of the path, churring and giggling to each other. They would wait until the lumbering cart was within six feet of them, and then they would take wing and stream off like a flock of brown-paper darts, chattering excitedly, to land twenty yards farther on. In a group of tall *palo borracho* five toucans leapt and scuttled among the branches from which the Spanish moss hung like the faint silvery spray of a fountain. The toucans watched us knowingly over their great, gleaming beaks, uttering high-pitched, Pomeranian-like yelps to each other. On every tree-stump or other vantage point sat a little white flower, a widow tyrant, its breast shining like a star. Every now and then they would slip off their perch, dive through the air like determined snowflakes, snip a passing insect neatly in their beaks and swoop back to their perch again with a flutter of neat black wings. A seriema swept across the path, paused with one leg in the air to give us an aristocratically sneering glance, dismissed us as being of no importance, and hurried on as though late for some civic function.

Presently the forest became more broken and open, and on every side was the gleam and reflection of water. Ibis, storks, and herons strolled two by two in the luxuriant herbage, with all the dignity of monks in a cloister. In the distance ahead of us we could see the small shack that was our destination, but to reach it we had to cross a level area like a small plain, which was in reality several acres of water overgrown with plants. We entered it, and within a few yards the horses and oxen were up to their bellies in water. The oxen, with their short, stubby, and very strong legs, came off better here, for the entangling underwater roots did not hamper them at all. They simply ploughed forward steadily at the same speed they had used on dry land, the thick herbage being crushed and pushed out of the way. The horses, on the other hand, were constantly getting a long lily-root entwined round their legs and stumbling. We reached the other side, and the horses hauled themselves free of the web of plants with obvious relief, while the oxen marched ashore wearing decorative swathes of lily-roots and leaves round their legs.

When we reached the hut, the Indian's wife insisted on our having a short rest and the inevitable cup of *mate*, and after the hot ride we were glad enough to sit in the shade for ten minutes. Jacquie and I were offered cups to drink from, but the rest of them shared the pot and the pipe. A small girl stood near the group, solemnly handing it from person to person as each sucked up a mouthful of the *mate* through the pipe. Presently, feeling rested and refreshed, we thanked our guide's wife for her hospitality and continued on our hunt. If we had thought that the worst of the ride was over we were sadly disappointed, for the next hour or so was sheer hell. We made our way across a large swamp surrounded on all sides by forest, so that not a breath of wind came to relieve the fierce heat of the sun. The water was deep – up to the axles of the cart-wheels – and was so overgrown with weeds and lilies that even the oxen found it heavy going. This patch of water must have been a sort of gigantic hatching ground for mosquitoes of all shapes and sizes. They rose in front of us so thickly that it was like looking through a gauzy curtain of shimmering wings; they fell on us with shrill whines of joy, and clung to us in great scab-like crusts, half drowned by our sweat but hanging on grimly, sucking with ferocious eagerness at our blood. After the first few minutes of wild irritated swiping, you sank into a sort of hypnotic trance and let them drink their fill, for if we killed a hundred with one slap there were five million others to take their places. After a while, through the shifting veil of mosquitoes, I saw that we were approaching an island in the swamp, a hillock about two hundred feet square that raised itself above the flat carpet of plants and water. It was thickly wooded and shaded, and it looked a wonderful place for a rest.

Apparently, our guide was of the same mind, for he turned in his saddle, wiping the insects away from his face with a careless hand, and pointed at the island.

'*Señor, bueno, eh?*'

'*Si, si, muy lindo,*' I agreed, and turning my horse I floundered back to where the cart was following, trailing a wide train of uprooted plants from its wheels. Jacquie was squatting in the back, an enormous straw hat perched on her head and her face invisible under a tightly wound scarf.

'Feel like a rest?' I asked.

One eye regarded me balefully from the depths of the scarf. Then she unwrapped it, displaying a face that was red and swollen with mosquito bites.

'I would like a rest,' she said bitterly, 'I would also like a cold shower, an iced drink, and about four hundred tons of D.D.T., but I don't expect for a minute I'll get them.'

'Well, you'll get the rest, anyway. There's a little island ahead and we can sit there for a bit.'

'Where is this blasted snake?'

'I don't know, but our guide seems quite confident.'

'I suppose one of us has to be.'

Our caravan hauled itself wearily out of the swamp and into the blessed shade of the trees, and while Jacquie and I sat and scratched moodily, our two Indians had a long conversation. Then the guide approached and explained that the snake should, according to his reckoning, be somewhere about here, but it had obviously gone farther than he had thought. He suggested that we should wait there for him while he rode ahead and reconnoitred. I commended the idea, gave him a cigarette, and watched him splash off into the swamp again, wearing a cloud of mosquitoes round his head and shoulders. After a doze and a cigarette I felt my spirits revive, and started to potter about among the thorn-bushes to see if I could find any reptile life. Presently I was roused by a loud cry of anguish from Jacquie.

'What's the matter?' I inquired.

'Come here quickly and get it off,' she called.

'Get what off?' I asked, hurrying through the bushes towards her.

I found her with the leg of her trousers rolled up, and there on her shin was hanging an enormous leech, like an elongated fig, its body swollen with blood.

'Good Lord!' I said; 'it's a leech.'

'I know it's a leech . . . Get it off.'

'It looks like a sort of horse-leech,' I said, kneeling down and peering at it.

'I don't want to know what damn species it is; get it off,' said Jacquie furiously; 'get it off my leg – you know I can't stand them.'

I lit a cigarette and drew on it until the end was glowing red; then I applied it to the creature's swollen posterior. It curved itself into the most violent contortions for a minute, and then released its hold and dropped to the ground, where I put my foot on it. It burst like a balloon, and a splash of scarlet blood stained the ground. Jacquie shuddered.

'Have a look and see if there are any more on me.'

But careful examination revealed no more leeches on her anatomy.

'I can't think where you got it from,' I said – 'none of us got any.'

'I don't know ... perhaps it came from the trees,' she said, and gazed up into the branches above as though expecting to see an enormous flock of leeches perched on the branches, waiting to leap on us. Then suddenly she froze.

'Gerry, look up there, quickly.'

I peered up and saw that our little scene with the leech had been witnessed by another inhabitant of the island. Half-way up the trunk of the tree we had been sitting under there was a small hole, and from its dark depths was glaring a tiny feathered face the size of a half-crown in which were two huge golden eyes. It observed us in shocked silence for a minute and then disappeared.

'What on earth was it?' asked Jacquie.

'It's one of those pigmy owls. Quick, go and get the driver's machete ... only for heaven's sake be quick and quiet about it.'

While Jacquie crept away, I circled round the tree to see if there was an exit hole, but I could see none. Then Jacquie returned with the machete; I hastily cut a long slender sapling, and then took off my shirt.

'What on earth are you doing?'

'We've got to block that hole somehow until I can climb up there,' I explained, hastily tying my shirt in a bundle at the

138

end of the stick. I approached the tree carefully with my improvised plug, and when I had manoeuvred the stick into position I suddenly jammed the shirt over the mouth of the hole.

'Hold this in place while I climb up,' I said, and, when Jacquie had taken over the stick, I shinned my way up the bark of the tree until I was perched precariously on a branch stump near the place where my shirt was decorating the trunk. Very carefully I edged my hand under it and into the hole behind. To my relief, I found that the cavity was quite shallow, and groping round I soon felt the flutter of soft wings against my fingers; I grabbed quickly and got the owl's body in my hand, but it felt so small that I wondered for the moment if I had caught the right bird. Then a small curved beak dug itself painfully into my thumb, and I knew I was not mistaken. I pulled my hand out of the hole with the ruffled and indignant little creature glaring at me over my fingers.

'I've got him,' I called triumphantly, and at that moment the stump I was standing on snapped and the owl and I fell to the ground. Luckily, I fell on my back, with my hand holding the bird in the air, so the owl had the best of the fall. Jacquie helped me up, and then I showed her our capture.

'Is it a baby?' she asked, staring at it fascinated.

'No, it's a pigmy.'

'You mean it's fully grown?' she asked incredulously, staring at the sparrow-sized bundle of ferocity, blinking its eyes and clicking its beak at us in Lilliputian rage.

'Yes, he's fully grown. They're one of the smallest owls in the world. Let's get a box out of the cart to put him in.'

Placed in a box with a wire front, the owl drew himself up to his full height of four and a half inches and uttered a faint, wheezy, chittering noise before starting to preen his disarranged plumage. His back and head were a rich, dark chocolate colour, minutely speckled with grey, and his shirt-front was creamy grey streaked with black markings. The driver of the ox-cart was as captivated with the little bird as we were, and went to great lengths to explain to me that they were called Four-eyes. I found this a rather puzzling name, until the driver tapped on the edge of the box and the owl turned his head towards the noise. On the feathers just above the nape of his neck were two circular patches of grey, showing up well against the chocolate-coloured feathers, and making it look as though he really had eyes in the back of his head.

While we were still gloating over the owl, our guide reappeared in a great flurry of water and mosquitoes, to tell us, excitedly, that he had found the snake. It was apparently about half a mile away, lying on the mat of water-plants on the surface of the swamp, quite close to the edge. He explained that we should have to take it by surprise, for it was so close to the trees that it might take cover there, and once in the thorny thickets it would be difficult, if not impossible, to find. We set off, and when we reached a spot that the guide said was close to the reptile we sent the cart off to a suitable vantage-point on the right, while we ploughed steadily forward. The water here at the edge of the swamp was fairly shallow, and not nearly so overgrown, but the bottom was uneven, and the horses kept stumbling. I realized that if the snake ran for it I could not follow on horse-back: to try to make one's horse canter in that swamp was suicidal. I should have to follow it on foot, and I began to wonder for the first time if the snake was perhaps as big as our guide had described.

The Four-eyed Bird and the Anaconda

Unfortunately, the snake saw us before we saw him. The guide suddenly uttered a sharp exclamation and pointed ahead. About fifty feet away, in a clear patch of water between two great rafts of weeds, I could see a V-shaped ripple heading rapidly towards the forest edge. Uttering a brief prayer that the snake would be of a suitable size for one person to handle, I flung the reins of my horse to the guide, grabbed a sack and leapt down into the lukewarm water. Running in water up to your knees is an exhausting pastime on any occasion, but to do it when the temperatures are in the hundreds is the sort of stupid action only a collector would contemplate. I struggled on, the sweat pouring down my face in such quantities that even the mosquitoes had no chance to settle, while ahead I could see the arrow-head of ripples rapidly approaching dry land. I was some thirty feet away when the anaconda hauled his glossy yellow and black body out of the water and started to glide into the tall grass. As I rushed forward in a desperate spurt, I tripped and fell flat on my face in the water. When I got to my feet the anaconda had vanished. I waded ashore, cursing bitterly, and walked into the tall grass where he had disappeared, to see if I could follow his trail. I had only walked about six feet when a blunt head with open mouth struck at me from a small bush, making me leap like a startled rocket. Under the bush lay the anaconda, his gleaming coils with their pattern merging into the speckled shadows so beautifully that I had not noticed him. Apparently, being full of chicken, he had found progress through the swamp just as exhausting as I had, and on reaching the tall grass had decided to rest. As I had stumbled upon him, he felt he must fight for it.

In nearly every book written about South America the author at some point or other (in some books once every other chapter) stumbles upon an anaconda. These generally measure anything from forty to a hundred and fifty feet, according to the description, in spite of the fact that the largest anaconda ever officially measured was a mere thirty feet. Inevitably, the monster attacks, and for three or four pages the author wrestles in its mighty coils until either he manages to shoot it with his trusty revolver, or it is speared by one of his trusty Indians. Now, at the risk of being described either as a charlatan or a man of immense modesty, I must describe my own joust with the anaconda.

The reptile struck at me in a very half-hearted manner, to begin with. He was not really interested in giving me good copy for a fight to the death. He merely lunged forward with open mouth, in the faint hope that I would become scared and leave him in peace, so that his digestive juices could resume their work on his chicken. Having made the gesture, and upheld his tribe's reputation for ferocity and unprovoked attack, he curled up into a tight knot under his bush and lay there, hissing gently and rather plaintively to himself. I realized that a stick of some sort would have been very useful, but the nearest clump of bushes was some distance away, and I did not dare leave him. I flipped my sack at him several times in the hope that he would bite at it and get his teeth caught in the cloth, a method which I have found useful on more than one occasion. However, he merely ducked his head under his coils and hissed a bit louder. I decided that I would have to have some assistance to distract the beast's attention, so, turning round, I waved frantically to our guide, who was ensconced with the horses in the middle of the swamp. At first, being reluctant to come any closer, he just waved back amicably, but when he saw I was getting annoyed, he urged the horse forward and splashed through the water towards me. I turned round and was just in time to see the tail of the vicious, awe-inspiring, and deadly anaconda disappearing hurriedly among the grass-stalks. There was only one thing to do. I stepped forward, grabbed the end of his tail and hauled him back into the open again.

Now what the anaconda should have done was immediately to envelop me in coil after coil of his muscular body. What he actually did was to curl up into a knot again and give a faint, frustrated hiss. I dropped the sack over his head quickly and then grabbed him behind the neck. And that, really, was that. He lay quite still, giving an occasional twitch to his tail and a faint hiss, until the guide arrived. In fact I had more trouble with the human than the reptile, for the guide was not at all keen to help me, and one is hampered in an argument when forced to embrace large quantities of snake. At last I managed

to persuade the guide that I would not let the snake harm him, and he very gingerly held the sack open while I hoisted the reptile up and put it inside.

'Did you get some good shots?' I asked Jacquie when we got back to the cart.

'I think so,' she said, 'although it was all filmed through a haze of mosquitoes. Did the snake give much trouble?'

'No; he behaved better than our guide did.'

'How big is it? It looked enormous in the view-finder. I began to wonder if you could handle it.'

'He's not terribly big. A fairly average size. I should say about eight feet, but he may not be as long as that.'

The cart and horse lurched tiredly through the swamp, where the leaves of the water-plants were touched with a pink glow from the sunset. Overhead, immense flocks of black-headed conures filled the sky, infected with the hysteria that always seems to appear in parrots towards roosting time. In great tattered formations they swept to and fro over us, chattering and screaming, while the sun sank into a lemon-coloured blur among the backs of cloud. Tired, itchy, and glowing from the sun, we reached our house at eight o'clock. After a shower and a meal we felt more human. The pigmy owl ate four fat frogs, pouncing on them with his curious tiny cry of delight, like the gentle stridulation of a baby cricket. The anaconda, now in a sort of digestive stupor, made no objection to being measured. Stretched out, he came to exactly nine feet three inches.

CHAPTER NINE

SARAH HUGGERSACK

NEXT to the parakeets in the collection – who were shrill little friends – probably the noisiest and most cheeky of our birds were the two pileated jays. These birds are similar to the English jay in shape, though smaller and of a slighter build. Here, however, the resemblance ends, for pileated jays have long, magpie-like tails of black and white, dark velvet backs, and pale primrose-yellow shirt-fronts. The colouring on the head is extraordinary. To begin with, the feathers on the forehead were black, short, and plushy, and stuck up straight, so the bird looked as though it had just had a crew cut. Behind this, on the nape, the feathers were smooth, and formed a sort of bluish-white marking which resembled a bald patch. Above each bright and roguish bronze eye was a thick 'eyebrow' of feathers of the brightest delphinium-blue.

The effect of this peculiar decoration was to give the birds a permanent appearance of surprise.

The jays were inveterate hoarders. Their motto was obviously 'waste not, want not'. Any other bird given more minced meat than it could eat would have wastefully scattered it about the cage, but not so the jays; all those bits which they could not manage were carefully collected and stored in, of all places, their water-pot. For some reason they had decided the water-pot was the best place in which to keep their supply of food, and nothing we could do would make them alter their opinion. I tried giving them two water-pots, so that they could store their meat in one and drink out of the other. The jays were delighted with the idea and promptly divided up their meat and stored it in both water-pots. They would also store peanuts, of which they were inordinately fond. There were several cracks and holes in their cage, which were admirably suited for nut-storing, except that the nuts were too big to fit in; so the jays would pick up the nuts one at a time and hop on to their perches, then by some remarkably clever juggling they would insert the peanut under the toes of their feet and proceed to deal it several hefty blows with their beaks until it was split up. Then they would pick up the pieces and try them for size; if they were too big, the same performance would be repeated. They did the same thing when eating the peanuts, except that when the nut was broken up they would put all the pieces carefully in one of their water-pots for ten minutes or so, so that they were softened and easier to eat.

One of the nicest things about the jays was their incessant chattering, for it was always subdued in tone. They would spend hours on their perches, facing each other with raised eyebrows, carrying on the most involved conversations in a series of squawks, wheezes, trills, chuckles, and yaps, managing to get the most astonishing variety of expression into these sounds. They were great mimics, and in a few days had added the barking of the village dogs to their repertoire, together with the squawk of triumph of a laying hen, cockerels crowing, Pooh the crab-eating raccoon's yarring cries, and even the metallic tapping of Julius Caesar Centurian's hammer. Just after the jays had finished their breakfast and settled down to a good gossip, the variety of sounds that came from their cage was amazing, and you would have thought the cage contained an assortment of twenty or thirty different species of birds, instead of the solitary pair. Before we had kept them long, they had mastered the cries of nearly every creature in the collection and were becoming very cocky about it. But with the arrival of Sarah Huggersack a new noise was added to the camp chorus, and it was one that the jays found impossible to master.

Paula appeared in the living-room one day bearing the luncheon tray in her brawny arms at double her normal speed. Almost inundating me with hot soup, she asked if I would please go out to the kitchen, as an Indian had brought a *bicho*, an animal of enormous stature and indescribable ferocity. No, she didn't know what sort of *bicho* it was – it was inside a sack and she hadn't seen it, but it was tearing the sack to pieces and she feared for her life. Outside the back door I found a young Indian boy squatting on his haunches, chewing a straw, and watching a small sack which was busily shuffling round in vague circles and snuffling at intervals. My only clue to the contents of the sack was a very large, curved claw sticking through at one place, but even this did not help me, for I could not, offhand, think of an animal small enough to fit in the sack, and yet at the same time big enough to possess such a claw. I surveyed the youth, who grinned back at me and bobbed his head, so that his long, straight, soot-black hair rippled.

'*Buenos días, señor.*'

'*Buenos días. Tiene un bicho?*' I asked, pointing at the waltzing sack.

'*Si, si, señor, un bicho muy lindo,*' he replied earnestly.

I decided the best thing to do was to open the sack and see the creature, but first I wanted to know what it was. I did not want to take any chances with such a claw.

'*Es bravo?*' I asked.

'No, no señor,' said the Indian, smiling, '*es manso – es chiquitito – muy manso.*'

I didn't feel my command of Spanish was sufficient for me to point out that because a creature was young it need not necessarily be very tame. Some of the most impressive scars

I possess are legacies from baby animals that didn't look capable of killing a cockroach. Hoping for the best, and trying to remember where the penicillin ointment was, I grabbed the gyrating sack and undid the mouth. There was a pause, and then from between the folds of sacking appeared a long, curved, icicle-shaped head and snout, with small, neat, furry ears, and, embedded in the ash-grey fur, two bleary little eyes that looked like soaked currants. There was another pause and then the tiny, prim mouth at the extreme end of the snout opened, and about eight inches of slender greyish-pink tongue curved out gracefully. It slid back inside again, the mouth opened a bit wider and from it came a sound that defies description. It was midway between the growl of a dog and the raucous bellow of a calf, with just the faintest suggestion of a ship's foghorn suffering from laryngitis. The sound was so powerful that Jacquie came out on to the veranda, looking startled. By this time the head had retired into the sack, except for the end of the snout. Jacquie frowned at it.

'What in the world's *that* thing,' she asked.

'That,' I said happily, 'is the end of a baby giant ant-eater's snout.'

'Is it responsible for that ghastly noise?'

'Yes, it was just greeting me in ant-eater fashion.'

Jacquie sighed lugubriously. 'It isn't enough to have the jays and parrots deafening us all day long, now we've got to add a sort of bassoon to it,' she said.

'Oh, it will be quiet enough when it's settled down,' I said airily, and the creature thrust its head out of the sack, as if in response to my remark, and let forth another bassoon solo.

I opened the sack further and peered down into it. I was astonished that such a small creature could produce such a volume of sound, for from the tip of its curved snout to the end of its tail the ant-eater measured two and a half feet.

'Why, she's minute,' I said in amazement; 'she couldn't be more than a week or so old.'

Jacquie moved over, looked into the sack, and was lost.

'Oh, isn't she adorable?' she crooned, taking it for granted

148

that it was a female. 'Poor little thing ... Here, you pay, and I'll take her inside.'

She picked up the sack and carried it gently into the house, leaving me to argue with the Indian.

When I re-entered the house, I tried to get the creature out of the sack, but this was not an easy task, for the long, curved claws on the front paws clung to the sacking with a vice-like grip. In the end it took the combined efforts of Jacquie and myself to remove her. She was the first really young giant ant-eater I had seen, and I was surprised to find that she was, in almost every way, a miniature replica of the adult. The chief difference was that her fur was short, and she had no mane of long hair on her back, but merely a ridge of bristles. Her tail, too, gave no indication of the enormous shaggy plume it was to become; it looked just like the blade of a canoe-paddle covered with hair. To my consternation, I found that the central great claw on her left foot had been ripped away and was hanging by a thread. We had to cut this away carefully and put disinfectant on the raw toe, an operation which seemed to cause her no discomfort, for she lay across my lap, clasping a large section of my trouser leg with one claw, while we doctored the other. I thought she was doomed to go through life with only one large claw, but I was mistaken, for it eventually grew again.

In the sack and on my knee she had behaved with great self-assurance and aplomb, but as soon as she was placed on the floor, she staggered round in vague circles, bellowing wildly, until she discovered Jacquie's leg, and with an inarticulate bray of delight clutched it and endeavoured to shin up it. As the trousers Jacquie was wearing were thin, the effect of the little animals' claws was considerable, and it took us some time to unhook her. During this process she attached herself to my arm, like a leech, and before I could stop her she had shinned up and arranged herself across my shoulders like a fox fur, digging her claws into my neck and back to prevent herself slipping, her long snout on one side of my face and her tail on the other. Any attempt to remove her from this perch was received with indignant snorts and a fiercer tightening of her grip, and this was so painful that I was forced to leave her where she was while we ate our lunch. She dozed intermittently while I drank my lukewarm soup, and I found that my gestures had to be very slow and deliberate, or she would suddenly awake in a panic and dig her grappling irons in, almost decapitating me. Things were complicated by Paula, who refused to come into the room. I was in no position to argue, for any incautious movement of my head put my jugular vein in grave danger. Fortified by food, we made another attempt to remove the ant-eater from my shoulders, but after my shirt had been ripped in five places and my neck in three, we abandoned the project. The difficulty was that as soon as Jacquie had prised one set of claws loose and turned to the next lot the first set would regain the ground they had lost. I began to feel like Sindbad during his association with the Old Man of the Sea. Eventually an idea struck me:

'Get a sack full of grass, darling, and when you've got one paw loose, let her take hold of the sack.'

This simple stratagem worked perfectly, and we lowered the stuffed sack to the floor, with the ant-eater clasping it desperately, a blissful expression on her face.

'What are we going to call her?' asked Jacquie, as she dealt with my honourable wounds.

'How about Sarah?' I suggested; 'she looks like a Sarah, somehow ... I know – let's call her Sarah Huggersack.'

So, Sarah Huggersack entered our lives, and a more charming and lovable personality I have rarely encountered. Up to the time I had met Sarah, I had had a fair amount of experience with giant ant-eaters, for I had captured some adults on another collecting trip to British Guiana, but I had never considered them to be beasts that were overburdened with intelligence or scintillating qualities. Sarah, however, converted me.

To begin with, she was tremendously vocal, and would not hesitate to blare her head off if she could not get her own way, whereas adult ant-eaters rarely make any sound louder than a hiss. Keep her waiting for her food, or refuse to cuddle her when she demanded affection, and Sarah battered you into submission by sheer lung-power. Although I could not have resisted buying her, I had qualms about it, for ant-eaters, having such a restricted diet in the wild state, are not the easiest things to establish on a substitute diet in captivity, even when adult. To take on the job of hand-rearing a week-old baby, therefore, was a very doubtful proposition, to say the least. Right from the start we had trouble over her bottle: the teats we had were too large for Sarah to hold comfortably in her tiny mouth. Paula made a frantic search which resulted in a very battered teat being found in some village house. This was the same size as ours, but had been used, and so was soft, and Sarah approved of it. She grew so attached to this teat, in fact, that even when we once again had a variety to offer her, she refused to drink from them and clung obstinately to the old one, sucking it so vigorously that it changed from scarlet to pink, and then to white; it became so limp that it was difficult to get it to stay on the bottle, and the hole enlarged to such an extent that, instead of a gentle stream, a positive flood of milk used to pour down Sarah's eager throat.

It was fascinating to have caught Sarah so young, for I could watch her develop day by day, and she taught me a great deal about her family. The use of her claws was an example. The front feet of an ant-eater are so designed that the animal walks on its knuckles, the two large claws thus pointing inwards and upwards. The claws, of course, are primarily used for breaking open the tough ant nests, to obtain food. I have also seen the adults using their claws as a comb for their fur. In Sarah's case, in her early stages, her claws were used solely to grip with, for the female ant-eater carries her young perched on her back. An adult, with its claw bent back against the palms like the blade of a penknife, can of course get a tremendous grip in this way, and so I was not surprised to find that Sarah, once she had fastened on to something, was extremely difficult to dislodge. As I have said, the slightest movement on the part of the thing to which she was clinging would cause her to tighten her grip convulsively. Thus, carrying her baby on her back must be an extremely painful undertaking for the female ant-eater.

Sarah also used her claws when feeding. She liked to grip a finger with one claw and keep the other raised in a sort of salute as she sucked at her bottle. Periodically, about once every fifteen seconds, she would use this claw to squeeze the teat. The teat suffered in consequence, and I was always expecting her claw to go right through it; but I couldn't break her of the habit. The female ant-eater has, therefore, to put up with the grip on the back when carrying her young, and then submit to what must be a painful assault at feeding time. Some indication of Sarah's grip can be gathered from the fact that I once placed an empty matchbox in the palm of her front paw, and when she tightened her grip – but not to the full extent – her claw went straight through the box. Then she put on full pressure and the box was flattened. The extraordinary thing was that I had placed the box *edgewise* on, and not flat, so there was quite considerable resistance.

The most worrying time with any baby wild animal is the first week, for, although it may be feeding well, you cannot tell if the milk you are giving it agrees with it. So for the first seven days or so its bowel motions become of absorbing interest to you, and you have to check them, to see that they are neither too hard nor too soft, and that the consistency is more or less normal. Diarrhoea or constipation indicates that the food is too rich or perhaps does not contain enough nourishment, and you have to vary the food accordingly. Sarah, during her first week, nearly drove us mad. To begin with, her motions were small and of a putty-like consistency, but what was more worrying still was that she only relieved herself once in two days. Thinking that she was not perhaps getting enough nourishment from her milk, I increased the vitamin content, but this made no difference at all. I thought it might help to feed her more often, and so we increased the number of feeds per day, but she still stuck rigidly to her forty-eight-hour routine. The constipation might be due to insufficient exercising, though a young ant-eater carried on its mother's back would receive little in the way of direct exercise, but might obtain a certain amount when the mother moved around. So, for half an hour every day Jacquie and I would walk slowly to and fro, while Sarah, honking indignantly, would shuffle behind, trying to climb up our legs. But this enforced exercise made no difference, and she so obviously and heartily disapproved of it that we gave it up. So she would spend all day lying in her box, clutching her sackful of straw and dozing, while her stomach grew more and more bloated. Then would come the great moment, she would relieve herself, her stomach would assume normal proportions, and for a few hours – until the next feed – she would have a slim and sylph-like figure. As this rather curious biological functioning appeared to do her no harm, I eventually ceased to worry about it. I came to the conclusion that all baby ant-eaters, when they are young, do this. I believe this must be so, for when Sarah was a little older and started to sleep without her sack, her bowels started working normally.

Sarah's one delight in life was to be hugged, and to hug in return. If I held her to my chest and supported her with one arm, I found that she clung with less painful tenacity; but her favourite perch was always across my shoulders, and no matter where she started off, she slowly crept upwards, a few inches at a time, hoping that I would not notice, until she was lying across my shoulders. At first she could not bear to be put on the ground and would bellow forlornly. When you picked her up, you could feel her heart beating like a trip hammer, and she would clutch you frantically. She did not object to being on the ground providing she could hang on to some part of you, even your foot, for it gave her a feeling of security.

When she was about a month old, she grew less scared of being on the ground, but she liked to feel that Jacquie or I was near. Her sight, like that of all ant-eaters, was very bad and if you moved more than five feet away from her, she could not see you, even if you moved. Only by smell, or by hearing you call, could she locate you. Stand still and silent, and Sarah would revolve like a top, her long snout pointing frantically in all directions, trying to find you.

The older she grew, the more skittish she became. Gone now were the days when you lifted her out of the cage, lying like some Roman potentate on her sack, to give her food. The moment the door of her cage was opened she would rush out like a tornado, breathing deeply with excitement, and clutch at her bottle so eagerly you would have thought it was the first food she had seen for weeks. She was always most lively in the evenings, and it was after her pint of supper that she felt most energetic. Her stomach bulging like a hairy balloon, you would have to work her into the mood for one of her boxing matches by pulling her tail gently. She would peer at you short-sightedly over her shoulder, and one hefty fore-paw would be brought slowly up until it was raised above her head; then, with amazing speed, she would whirl round and try to clout you. If you showed no further interest in her, she would shuffle past you several times with a preoccupied air, trailing her tail temptingly near. Grab it, and pull a second time, and Sarah would change her tactics: this time she would whirl round, stand on her hind legs, with arms raised above her head as though about to dive, and then fall flat on her face, in the hope that your hand would be underneath her. These exchanges would continue for some time until Sarah had worked off all her surplus energy, and then another stage in the game would be reached. You were supposed to lay her on her back and tickle her ribs, while she, in ecstasy, would pluck at her tummy with her long claws. When we were exhausted, we would proclaim her the winner, by picking her up and holding her under the arms, whereupon she would put both paws straight up in the air and interlock the claws over her head in the usual champ manner. She grew to like these evening romps so much that if for some reason we were forced to forgo them one evening, Sarah would sulk all next day.

The other animals, Cai, Foxey, and Pooh, were inclined to look upon Sarah with jealous eyes, for we made such a fuss of her. One day, pottering aimlessly about the camp, she wandered towards the spot where Pooh was tied. Cai and Foxey watched Sarah blundering along to what they thought was going to be the fright of her life. Pooh sat stolidly on his haunches, like a Buddha, patting his stomach with pink paws and watching Sarah's approach with a thoughtful eye. Being full of low cunning, he waited until she had ambled past, and then, leaning forward, he grabbed a large section of her trailing tail and tried to bite it. Now Sarah looks slow and stupid, but I knew from our nightly games that she could move with great speed when she wanted to. She whirled round, reared up, and bashed Pooh

on the head with great force and precision; Pooh, grunting with astonishment, scuttled off and hid in his box. Sarah, however, had tasted blood, and was not going to let her enemy off that easily; fur bristling, she wheeled about, nose in the air, trying to find out where Pooh had gone. Catching a dim glimpse of the box, she proceeded to give it a severe beating, while Pooh cowered inside. Foxey saw her heading in his direction and hastily retreated behind a bush. Cai sat smugly on top of her post, chattering softly to herself. Sarah, as she passed, caught sight of the post and, still being in a bad temper, decided to teach it a lesson. She leapt at it and delivered several uppercuts, and, while the pole swayed wildly, Cai clung to the top, screaming for help. Not until the post was leaning over drunkenly, and Cai was almost hysterical, did Sarah decide that she was the victor and wander off in search of someone to hug. It was the last time any of them tried tricks with Sarah.

The birds were quite unanimous in their dislike of the little ant-eater. I think that her long, slender snout had a faint resemblance to a snake, and this they disapproved of. I once heard the most terrible commotion in the bird section, and on going to investigate, I discovered that Sarah had somehow escaped from her cage and had her nose stuck through the wire of the seriemas' cage, to whom she had taken a fancy; the seriemas did not share her friendly attitude, and were screaming shrilly for assistance. As soon as she heard me call, however, she lost interest in the seriemas and came galloping lopsidedly towards me and shinned up my legs as far as my waist, where she settled down with a happy sigh.

Sarah had been with us some weeks when the first rains of the Chaco winter started. Now was the time when we should have to start thinking about travelling back the thousand odd miles to Buenos Aires to catch our ship. There was still one big job to accomplish before we left, and that was to make our film. I had decided that we would refrain from filming the animals in the collection until the very last moment, for then we should have a larger cast of stars. I had therefore reserved the last three weeks of our stay in the Chaco purely for filming. When this was completed, we would travel down the river to Asunción. That was our plan, but then the blow fell.

Paula brought in the tea one morning in a state of great excitement, and was so incoherent that it was some time before I could make out what she was talking about. When at last I understood, I laughed long and heartily.

Jacquie, in a semi-conscious early-morning condition, wanted to know what was amusing me.

'Paula says that there's a revolution in Asunción,' I said, chuckling.

'No, really?' said Jacquie, joining in my mirth; 'well, I must say Paraguay's living up to its reputation.'

'It's a wonder to me they know who's in power half the time, they liquidate them so rapidly,' I said, with the jovial and unctuous manner of one whose country is too cold-blooded to waste bullets or blood on politics.

'I suppose it won't affect us in any way, will it?' suggested Jacquie, sipping her tea thoughtfully.

'Good Lord, no! It'll probably all be over in a few hours – you know what it is. Instead of football, they have revolutions as the national game here – a few shots fired and everyone's happy,' I said. 'Anyway, I shall go down and find out if the radio station has any news.'

Puerto Casado boasted the astonishing luxury of a minute radio station which was in contact with the capital. By this means, lists of supplies were broadcast to Asunción and sent up on the next river steamer.

'I'll go down after breakfast,' I said, 'but I shouldn't be surprised to find it all over by now.'

I only wish I had been right.

CHAPTER TEN

RATTLESNAKES AND REVOLUTION

WHEN I arrived at the radio station after breakfast I asked the
radio operator if he had heard which side had scored the winning
goal in the revolution. Eyes flashing, arms waving he gave me the
latest information, and I suddenly realized that the situation was
far from funny. To begin with, Asunción appeared to be in a
complete uproar, with indiscriminate street-fighting all over the
place. The main centre of the battle was near the police headquarters and the military college, where the Government forces
were being besieged by the rebels. Far more serious was the fact
that the rebels had also gained control of the airfield, and had put
all the planes out of action by removing various vital parts. But,
from our point of view, the worst piece of news was that the rebels
had commandeered the river shipping, and so there would be no
more river steamers of any description until after the revolution
was over. This item of news really shook me, for the only way we
could get our collection out of the country and down to Buenos
Aires was by river transport. The radio operator went on to say
that the last time he had tried to contact Asunción there had been
no reply, so he presumed that either everyone was in hiding, or
else dead.

I returned to our little house in a much more sober frame of

,mind and told Jacquie the news. It was a situation with which we were totally unprepared to cope. Quite apart from anything else, our passports and most of our money were down in the capital, and we could do little without them. We sat drinking tea and discussing our plight, while Paula hovered round us commiseratingly, occasionally interjecting a remark which, though obviously kindly meant, generally had a depressing effect on us. When I tried to look on the bright side and suggested that within a few days either the Government forces or the rebels would have won, thus making things easier, Paula proudly informed us that Paraguay had never had such a short revolution; the last one had taken six months to die down. This time perhaps, she suggested kindly, we would have to spend six months in the Chaco. It would, she pointed out, give us plenty of opportunity to increase our collection. Ignoring this, I said that, providing the fighting was over fairly soon, everything would resume its normal course, and we could then get a river steamer down to Buenos Aires. Interrupting this flight of fancy, Paula remarked that she thought this unlikely, as during the last revolution the rebels had, for some obscure tactical reason of their own, promptly sunk all the river craft, thereby disorganizing not only the Government forces but their own as well.

In desperation I adopted Paula's attitude of looking on the darkest possible side of the picture, saying that if the worst came to the worst we could make our way across the river into Brazil, and thence overland to the coast. This idea was immediately quashed by both Jacquie and Paula: Jacquie pointed out that we were hardly in a position to undertake a thousand-mile journey through Brazil without passports or money, while Paula said that, during the *last* revolution, Brazil had armed guards posted on the river-banks, in order to repel any of the rebel forces who attempted to flee from justice. It was quite likely, she added gloomily, that if we attempted to get across the river the Brazilians might mistake us for leaders of the revolution trying to escape. I pointed out, rather acidly, that the leader of a revolution would hardly attempt to flee from justice together with his wife, a baby anteater, several dozen species of birds, snakes, and mammals, and equipment ranging from recording machines to ciné-cameras, but

Paula insisted that, on the whole, the Brazilians were not *'simpáticos'* and that this aspect would probably not occur to the guards.

After this brisk exchange, we sat in mournful silence for a bit. Then, suddenly, Jacquie had a bright idea. There was an American, a laconic, long-limbed individual, who bore a strong resemblance to Gary Cooper and owned a ranch some forty odd miles higher up the river. He had dropped in one day and had told us that if at any time we required any assistance we were not to hesitate to get in touch with him by radio. As he had spent a good many years in Paraguay, Jacquie suggested that we contact him, explain our predicament, and ask for his advice. Once again I hurried down to the radio station and persuaded the operator to put in a call to the American's ranch.

Presently his soft drawl came over the loudspeaker, slightly distorted by the roars, crackles, and wheeps of the atmospherics. Hastily I explained why I was worrying him, and asked his advice. His advice was simple and straightforward: get out of the country at the first available opportunity.

'But how can we?' I protested; 'there aren't any river steamers to take the animals on.'

'Son, you'll just have to leave your animals behind.'

'Well, supposing we did that?' I asked, a sinking feeling in the pit of my stomach, 'how do we get out then?'

'I've got a plane ... only a small one, a four-seater ... Soon as there's a suitable break I'll send her over, and then you can beat it. They generally have a parley some time during these revolutions, and it's my guess they'll be having one any day now. So be ready; I'll try and give you some warning, but I may not be able to.'

'Thanks ... thanks a lot,' I said, my thoughts whirling.

'That's O.K. Happy landings,' said the voice, and then with a series of loud crackles the loudspeaker went dead.

I thanked the radio operator absent-mindedly, and walked back to the house in the grip of one of the blackest moods of depression I can ever remember. To have worked so hard for so many months and to have assembled such a lovely collection, and then to be told at the end of it that you had to let the whole lot go, simply because some obscure Paraguayan wanted to become President by force, is not the sort of thing calculated to make you feel on top of the world. Jacquie, on being told the news, shared my view, and together we spent half an hour dealing with the ancestry, physical deformation, and purely personal habits of the leaders of the rebels – a sheer waste of time, not helping our position in any way, but it certainly relieved our feelings.

'Well,' said Jacquie when we had run out of adjectives, 'which ones are we going to let go?'

'He said to let all of them go,' I pointed out.

'But we can't,' Jacquie protested, ' – we can't let them *all* go. Some of them wouldn't last two minutes in the wilds. We'll have to take some with us, even if it means leaving most of our clothing behind.'

'Look, even if we travel naked we can't take more than three or four of the smaller things.'

'Well, that's better than nothing.'

I sighed.

'All right, have it your own way. But that brings us back to the question : which ones do we let go and which ones do we keep?'

We sat and thought about it for a bit.

'We must take Sarah, anyway,' said Jacquie at length. 'After all, she's only a baby, and she couldn't possibly fend for herself.'

'Yes, we must take her . . . but she's damned heavy, remember.'

'Then there's Cai,' continued Jacquie, warming to her rescue work : 'we can't leave her behind . . . and Pooh, poor little chap. If we let them go, they're so tame they'd go up to the first person they met, and probably get their heads blown off.'

'I must take a pair of orange armadillos, they're too rare to leave,' I said brightening, 'oh, yes, and the horned toads and those curious black ones.'

'And then there are the cuckoos,' agreed Jacquie, 'and the jays . . . They're far too tame to let go.'

'Wait a minute,' I said, coming suddenly down to earth, 'if we go on like this we'll be taking the whole damn collection, and there won't be room for us on the plane.'

'I'm sure just those few wouldn't weigh much,' said Jacquie

convincingly, 'and you could make them some light travelling cages, couldn't you?'

'Yes, I think I could. I might be able to construct something entirely out of wire.'

Greatly heartened by the thought that we would be able at least to save a few specimens from our collection, we set to work to prepare for our escape. Jacquie packed busily, dividing our belongings into two groups – those things that we simply had to take with us, such as recording machine, films, and so on, and those things that could conveniently be left behind, such as clothing, towels, nets, traps, and so forth. Meanwhile, armed with a pair of shears, a coil of wire, and a roll of small-mesh wire-netting I set to work to try and make some very light yet strong travelling cages that would hold the creatures until we reached Buenos Aires. It was no easy job, for the netting had to be bent into shape, 'sewn' up with wire, and then any sharp points had to be felt for and bent over. At the end of two hours I had made one cage large enough to hold Sarah, and my fingers and hands were scratched and torn.

'How are you getting on?' asked Jacquie, appearing with a most welcome cup of tea.

'Fine,' I said, surveying my bleeding fingers. 'I feel as though I'm doing a life sentence in Dartmoor. But I bet picking oakum is child's play to this.'

So while I continued to lacerate my hands, Jacquie took each cage as it was finished and covered it with a 'skin' of sacking sewn on with a large darning-needle. So, by ten o'clock that night we had enough cages to house those animals we intended to take with us. The cages were feather light, being only sacking and wire-netting, warm and fairly strong. They were, of course, not roomy, but for twenty-four hours the animals would come to no harm in them. The heaviest of the lot was Pooh's cage, for, knowing his burglar-like ability to break in or out of a cage, I had been forced to use wood in the construction. Tired and depressed, we crawled into bed.

'I'll start letting the other stuff go tomorrow,' I said as I switched off the light, and knew, as I said it, that it was not going to be a job I relished.

The next morning I put off the liberation duty for as long as I could, but eventually I could think of no more excuses for delaying it. The tiger bittern was the first one to be released; his wing had healed perfectly by now, and this, combined with his bad temper, gave me no qualms as to his ability to look after himself. I hauled him, protesting loudly, from his cage, carried him over to the edge of the small swamp that bordered our domain and perched him in a convenient tree. He sat on the branch, swaying drunkenly to and fro, and uttering loud and rather surprised honks. Dracula, the bare-faced ibis, was next on the list. As I carried him over to the swamp he twittered excitedly, but as soon as I placed him in the long grass and walked away he gave a squeak of alarm and scuttled after me. I picked him up and returned him to the swamp and hurried away, while he uttered hysterical squeaks for help.

I next turned my attention to the parrots and parakeets, and had the greatest difficulty in persuading them to leave their cages. When I eventually got them out, they perched in a tree nearby and refused to move, screaming loudly at intervals. Just at that moment I heard a shrill and triumphant titter and, turning round, I saw Dracula running into the camp clearing, having found his way back. I caught him and again carried him to the swamp, only to discover that the tiger bittern was rapidly approaching camp, flying heavily from tree to tree with a determined expression on his face. Having shooed them both back to the swamp, I set about letting the black-faced ibis and the seriemas go. In my melancholy mood I committed a *faux pas* by letting both species of seriemas go at once, and before I knew what was happening I was surrounded by a whirling merry-go-round of feathers, and the air was quivering with indignant screams as each seriema tried to prove its superiority over the others. I managed to separate them with the aid of a broom, and hustled them off into the undergrowth in different directions. Feeling hot, flustered, and not a little indignant that I was receiving so little cooperation from the specimens in my distasteful task, I suddenly discovered that the parrots had seized the opportunity to descend from their trees, and were now sitting in a row on top of their cages, regarding me with pensive eyes,

obviously waiting for the doors to be opened so that they could return.

I felt that I had better ignore the birds for the moment, so I started on the mammals and reptiles. Keeping only the pair we were going to take with us, I rolled all the other armadillos off into the undergrowth. The other species I arranged in a circle round the camp, their noses pointing out in the direction of the great open spaces, and hoped that they would be all right. The reptiles, to my relief, behaved perfectly and showed no inclination to stay, wriggling off into the swamp with gratifying rapidity. Feeling that I had done a good morning's work (considered from the animals' point of view alone), I went in to have some food.

Lunch was a gloomy affair, and as soon as it was over we went

outside to attend to the rest of our charges. The sight that met our eyes would have been extremely funny if it had not been so depressing.

In one corner of the camp Dracula, the tiger bittern, and the black-faced ibis were squabbling over a piece of fat that Pooh had discarded. Round the pile of unwashed pots the three-banded armadillos foraged, like a troupe of animated cannon-balls. The seriemas paced like sentries round the empty cages, and Flap-arse was pacing to and fro in an agitated manner, looking like a schoolmaster whose entire class has played truant. The parrots and parrakeets still sat in a hopeful row on top of their cages, with the exception of two who, obviously tired of waiting

165

for me to let them in again, had taken the law into their own hands, gnawed through the wire-netting front, and gained access to the cage that way. They sat on their perch glowering at us hungrily and giving those curious asthmatic grunts that some Amazon parrots use to show their indignation. Jacquie and I sat down on a box and surveyed them hopelessly.

'What are we doing to *do* with them?' she asked at length.

'I haven't the faintest idea. We can't leave them wandering around here, or they'll all be killed the moment our backs are turned.'

'Have you tried shooing them away?'

'I've tried everything short of hitting them over the head with a stick. They just won't go.'

Dracula had now left the contest over the piece of fat to the bittern and the ibis, and was busily trying to get back into his cage by trying to climb through the wire mesh which would have been a tight fit for a humming-bird.

'I wish,' I said viciously, 'we had one of those twee individuals here to see this.'

'What twee individuals?'

'Those knowledgeable sentimentalists who are forever telling me that it's cruel to lock up the poor wild creatures in little wooden boxes. I'd just like them to see how eagerly our furred and feathered brothers rush back to the wilds as soon as they're given the opportunity.'

One of the seriemas approached us and started to peck hopefully at my shoe-lace, evidently hoping it would turn out to be a worm of gigantic proportions. Dracula had eventually given up the attempt to get back into his own cage, and had compromised by squeezing through the bars of the ibis cage. He now sat inside it, peering at us with misty eyes, twittering delightedly.

'Well,' I said at length, 'I suppose if we just ignore them they'll get so hungry that they'll go off in search of food, and that will solve the problem. By tomorrow they should have disappeared.'

The rest of that day was a nightmare. Feeling that the animals should not be fed in any circumstance, we went about the task of feeding the ones we were keeping while the hungry horde of birds and animals hooted, whistled, tittered, and honked at us hungrily,

rushing to cluster round our feet whenever they saw us carrying
a dish, perching in rows on the food-table and watching us hopefully. The impulse to feed them was almost irresistible, but we had
to harden our hearts and ignore them. The only thing that kept
us going was the knowledge that by the next day hunger would
have driven them back into the wilds.

But the next morning when we went out to feed our charges we
found the animals and birds still assembled around the camp,
looking slightly more irritable and dejected than the day before.
They greeted us with such manifestations of delight that we
almost broke down and fed them. But we hardened our hearts
and pretended to ignore them, even when they clustered round
our feet and we were in grave danger of stepping on them. In the
middle of this uproar an Indian stalked into camp carrying an
old soap-box, and placed it reverently in the middle of the camp
site. Then he stepped back, tripped over a seriema who happened
to be walking past, recovered himself, and doffed his straw hat.

'*Buenos días, señor,*' he said, 'a fine *bicho* for you.'

'Oh, Lord,' groaned Jacquie; 'this *would* happen.'

'You're too late, my friend,' I said sadly. 'I do not want any
more *bichos.*'

The Indian regarded me, frowning.

'But, señor, you said you would buy *bichos,*' he said.

'I know, but that was before the revolution. Now I cannot buy,
for I cannot take my *bichos* with me ... There are no boats.' I
pointed to the mass of fauna wandering round the camp site;
'you see, I have had to let all these other *bichos* go.'

The Indian looked around him, bewildered.

'But they have not gone,' he pointed out.

'I realize that. But they will go. I am very sorry, but I cannot
buy any more.'

The Indian regarded me fixedly. He seemed to be fully aware
that I was dying to look inside the soap-box and see what the
bicho was.

'It is a good *bicho,*' he said at last in a cajoling tone, 'a very
fine *bicho* ... *muy bravo, muy venenoso* ... I had much trouble to
catch it.'

'What sort of *bicho* is it?' I asked, weakening.

He became animated.

'A *bicho* of great rarity, señor, and *muy, muy venenoso*,' he said, his black eyes sparkling, 'a *cascabel*, señor, of proportions so immense that it is impossible to describe. When he is angry he makes a noise like a thousand horses.'

I touched the box cautiously with the toe of my shoe, and immediately from inside rose the weird sound with which a rattlesnake informs the world of his presence, bad temper, and evil intentions. It is certainly one of the most extraordinary sounds made by any reptile, this curious rustling crackle that starts like a whisper and ends like the crackle of toy musketry. It is far more frightening than the ordinary hissing of a snake, for it seems to have a sort of vibrating malevolence about it, a bubbling viciousness like the simmering of a witch's brew.

'Nevertheless,' I said sadly, 'I cannot buy it, my friend.'

The Indian looked crestfallen.

'Not even for ten *guaranies*?' he asked.

I shook my head.

'Eight *guaranies*, señor?'

'No, I'm sorry, but I cannot buy it.'

The Indian sighed, knowing that I meant what I said.

'Well, señor, I will leave it with you, for it is of no use to me,' he said, and, accepting the packet of cigarettes I gave him, he picked his way through the motley crew of birds and departed, leaving us with a rattlesnake on our hands.

'And what are we going to do with that?' asked Jacquie.

'We'll record his rattle and then let him go,' I said: 'he's got a very fine rattle. I should think he's quite a big one.'

For a variety of reasons we could not get around to recording the rattlesnake that day. The next morning our released collection was still with us, but an hour's chasing eventually convinced at least some of them that we were not going to feed them, and they started to drift away. Then we got the recording machine and rigged it up near the rattlesnake's box, placed the microphone in an advantageous position, and tapped on the box hopefully. There was not a sound from within. I tapped again. Silence. I thumped on the box vigorously, with no result.

'D'you think he's dead?' asked Jacquie.

'No, it's the usual thing. These damned animals make a hell of a row until you get a recording machine anywhere near them, and then they make as much noise as a dead giraffe.'

I tipped the box gently, and felt the weight of the snake slide from one end to the other. This had the desired effect, he rattled viciously, and the green needle on the recorder swung and quivered, registering an astonishing volume of sound. Three times I tipped the box, and three times the snake responded with increasing fury. At last we had enough tape, but by this time the snake was so annoyed that he was producing a steady rattle like a machine-gun.

'Now let him go,' I said, seizing a machete.

'You aren't going to let him go here, are you?' inquired Jacquie in alarm.

'Yes, he'll be all right. I'll give him a prod and he'll whisk off into the swamp.'

'He sounds very bad-tempered. Make sure he *does* whisk off into the swamp.'

'Now stop fussing and go and stand over there,' I said, with doubtless irritating unctuousness.

Jacquie retreated to a safe place, and I proceeded to try and remove the lid of the rattlesnake's prison. This was not so easy, for the Indian had nailed it on with large and rusty nails in incredible quantities. At last I managed to force the tip of my machete blade into the crack and with a stupendous heave a large section of the lid flew off. I gave a sigh of relief and then did a very foolish thing: I bent down and peered into the box to see if the snake was all right. To say that he was furious would be an understatement. He was positively bubbling with rage, and as my face appeared in the sky above him he lunged upwards with open mouth.

Now I had always been under the impression that a rattlesnake could not lunge *upwards* at his victim, but that he had to lunge forward like any other snake. So it was with fright not unmixed with surprise that I saw the blunt head, carunculated like a pineapple, flying upwards to meet my descending face. The mouth was wide open, pink and moist, and the fangs hung down at the ready and appeared, to my startled gaze, to be about the size of a tiger's claws. I flung myself backwards in a leap that could only have been emulated but not bettered by a wallaby in the prime of life and in full control of its faculties. Unfortunately, I rather spoilt the athletic effect by tripping over my machete and sitting down heavily. The snake crawled out of the box and coiled himself up like a watch-spring, with head raised and his rattle vibrating so rapidly that it was a mere blur hanging round the end of his tail.

'Just give him a prod and he will whisk off into the swamp,' said Jacquie sarcastically.

I was in no mood to exchange saucy badinage. I went and cut myself a long stick and again approached the rattlesnake, in the hope of being able to pin him down and pick him up. However, the reptile had other ideas on the subject. He struck twice at the descending stick and then wriggled towards me rapidly with such obvious menace that I had once again to repeat my ballerina-like leap. The snake by now was in the worst possible temper and, what was more annoying, stubbornly refused to be frightened or cajoled into leaving the camp site. We tried throwing clods of earth at him, but he just coiled up and rattled. Then I threw a bucket of water over him. This worsened his obviously already high blood-pressure, and he uncoiled and wriggled towards me. The irritating part of the whole business was that we could not just leave him there to make off in his own time. There was work to be done, and one's work is rather apt to suffer by continually having to look over one's shoulder to make sure a four-foot rattlesnake isn't there to be stepped on. Also Pooh and Cai were out on their leads, and I was worried in case the reptile went up and perhaps bit one of them. Very reluctantly, I decided that the only thing to be done was to despatch the infuriated snake as quickly and as painlessly as possible, so, while Jacquie attracted his attention with the aid of the stick, I approached him cautiously from behind, manoeuvred into position and sliced off his head with the machete. His jaws kept on snapping for a full minute after his head had been severed from his body, and half an hour later you could still see slight muscular contraction if you touched his ribs with the stick. The extraordinary thing about this snake was that rattlesnakes normally cannot strike unless they are coiled up –

so as a rule, however angry one gets, they will always stay coiled up in one position ready to bite – this one, on the other hand, seemed to have no hesitation in uncoiling and coming straight for you. Whether he could have bitten us successfully with his body stretched out was rather a moot point, but it was not the sort of experiment that I cared to make.

By the following day a great number of our specimens had disappeared, though there were still one or two hanging around the camp. At midday a messenger arrived from the radio station, to say that the American had got through to inform them that there was a lull in the fighting in Asunción, and that he was sending the plane over for us in the afternoon. Frantically we bustled about packing the rest of our things and endeavouring to console Paula, who followed us from room to room, giving long, shuddering, heart-strangled sobs at the thought of our imminent departure. Having packed, we made a hurried lunch, and then set about the job of putting the animals into their travelling boxes. All of them went in without demur except Pooh, who seemed to imagine that it was some new and refined form of torture that we had invented. First we tried to lure him by throwing bananas into the cage, but with the aid of his long, artistic fingers he managed to hook them out and eat them complacently without venturing inside. Eventually, as time was growing short, I had to grab him by the scruff of his neck and the loose skin of his large behind, and bundle him head-first into his box, while he screamed like a soul in torment and clutched madly at everything with all four feet. Once inside, we gave him an egg, and he settled down quite philosophically to suck it and gave no further trouble.

Paula had now been joined by her girls and they all stood around in forlorn groups, looking rather like mourners at a funeral. The tears trickled steadily and in ever-increasing quantities down Paula's face, making havoc with her make-up, but as she appeared to derive much satisfaction from her grief, I presumed that this did not matter. Suddenly she startled us all by uttering a loud groan that would have done credit to Hamlet's father's ghost, and then crying in a sepulchral voice: 'It has come!' before plunging into another Niagara of grief. Very faintly echoing through the blue sky we could hear the pulsating throb

171

of an aeroplane engine, and at that moment the lorry drew up outside the house. While I loaded the luggage and animals on to it, Jacquie was embraced by each of Paula's girls and then eventually clutched to Paula's moist and magnificently palpitating bosom. When my turn came, I was relieved to find Paula's girls had no intention of embracing me, but merely shook my hand and gave a little dipping curtsy, making me feel like some obscure species of royalty. Paula clasped my hand in both hers and clutched it to her stomach, then she raised her tear-stained face to me.

'*Adiós, señor*,' she said, large fat tears trickling out of her black eyes. 'Good journey to you and your señora. If God wills it, you will return to the Chaco.'

Then the lorry was bouncing down the dusty rutted road and we were waving from the window to Paula and her girls, who looked like a cluster of brilliant tropical birds as they stood waving frantically, their shrill voices shouting '*Adiós*'.

We arrived at the airfield just as the plane, like a glittering silver dragon-fly, swooped down. It made an extremely bad landing and then taxied towards us.

'Ah,' said the driver of the lorry, 'you have got the mad one.'

'Mad one,' I said, puzzled; 'what mad one?'

'This pilot,' he said scornfully, jerking his thumb at the approaching plane. 'They say he is mad. Certainly he never seems to land the plane without making it jump like a deer.'

The pilot, when he scrambled down out of the machine, turned out to be a short, stocky Pole with silvery hair and the vague, gentle expression of the White Knight in *Alice through the Looking Glass*. With the aid of a small hand-weighing machine we weighed our luggage and discovered to our consternation that we were several kilos over the maximum weight that the plane was allowed to take.

'Never mind,' said the pilot, beaming at us. 'I think she will do it.'

So we proceeded to wedge our suitcases into the plane, and then we scrambled in ourselves, while the lorry driver piled my lap head-high with the assortment of animal life that we were taking with us, Sarah, who had refused her bottle half an hour before, now decided that she was hungry, and honked dismally at the front of her cage until I was forced to take her out and put her on Jacquie's lap to keep her quiet.

The pilot fiddled with the controls, then gave a smile of child-like pleasure when the engine roared into life. 'Very difficult,' he said, and laughed merrily. We taxied about in all directions for some five minutes before we found a dry enough patch to allow us to take off. The pilot let her out and the plane roared across the grass, jumping and lurching. We left the ground at the last possible moment and, zooming some six inches over the tops of the trees that bordered the airfield, the pilot wiped his forehead.

'Now she is up,' he yelled at me. 'All we have to worry about now is to get her down again.'

Below us the great flat plain stretched, blurred with heat-haze. The plane banked and then straightened out, and we were flying over the great molten curves of the river that coiled and wound away into the shimmering obscurity of the horizon towards Asunción.

INTERLUDE

I HAVE never liked cities particularly, and I never thought that I should be glad to see one. But the relief and pleasure we felt were extraordinary when we looked out of the plane and saw Buenos Aires beneath the wing, like a vast geometrical pattern of sequins glittering in the dusk. At the airport I made my inevitable pilgrimage to the nearest phone booth and dialled Bebita's number.

'Ah, child, I am so glad you are safe. Ah, you have no idea how we worried about you. Where are you now? At the airport? Well, come to dinner.'

'It's the animals again,' I said gloomily. 'We've got to find somewhere to put them. It's bitterly cold here, and they'll get pneumonia if we don't get them into the warm soon.'

'Ah, of course, the animals,' said Bebita. 'I have fixed a little house for them B-B-Belgrano.'

'A *house*?'

'Yes, only a little one, of course. It has, I think, two rooms. It has running water, but I do not think it is heated. B-b-but that does not matter – you can call here and I will lend you a stove.'

'I can only suppose that this house belongs to a friend of yours?'

'B-b-but naturally. You will have to return the stove soon, though, b-b-because it b-b-belongs to Monono, and he will simply die without it.'

Interlude

Bebita's 'little house' turned out to be two good-sized rooms leading out into a little courtyard surrounded by a high wall. Leading off this was another small building which contained a large sink. With the aid of the stove, surreptitiously removed from Bebita's husband's room, we got the temperature nice and high, and all the animals started to look better. A phone call to Rafael had brought him scurrying round, spectacles gleaming, armed with fruit, meat, and bread removed from his mother's larder. When I protested that his mother would probably take exception to this, he pointed out that the only alternative was for the animals to go hungry, for all the shops were shut. My indignation at this rape of his mother's larder was then forgotten, and we gave ourselves up to the pleasure of stuffing our animals with delicacies which they had never had before – such things as grapes, pears, apples, and cherries. Then, leaving them warm and full, we went to Bebita's, where we sat down to the first civilized meal we had eaten in months. At last, as replete as our animals, we sank into chairs and sipped our coffee.

'And what will you do now?' asked Bebita.

'Well, we've got a few days left before the ship sails. We'll just have to try and get as much stuff in that time as we can.'

'You will want to go out into the *campo*?' she asked.

'If it's possible.'

'I will ask Maria Mercedes if she will let you go down to her *estancia*.'

'D'you think she would?'

'But naturally,' began Bebita, 'she's . . .'

'I know . . . she's a friend of yours.'

So it was arranged that we take the train from Buenos Aires out to Monasterio, some forty miles away. Near here lay Secunda, the *estancia* of the De Sotos. Here Rafael and his brother Carlos would be waiting to help us.

CHAPTER ELEVEN

THE RHEA HUNT

THE village of Monasterio lay some forty miles from Buenos Aires, and we travelled there by train. Once we had left the last straggling houses of the capital behind, the pampa stretched on either side of the track, limitless and frosted with dew. Along the edge of the track grew a wide swathe of convolvulus, the flowers a brilliant electric blue, growing so thickly that they all but obscured the heart-shaped leaves.

Monasterio turned out to be a small village that looked like a Hollywood film-set for a Western film. A straggle of square houses lined a street that was muddy, deeply lined with wheel-ruts and the marks of horses' hooves. On the corner stood the village store and tavern, its shelves lined with an incredible quantity of merchandise, from cigarettes to gin, from rat-traps to khaki drill. Outside this store several horses were tethered to a fence, while inside their owners drank and gossiped. They were on the whole short, rather stocky men with brown faces, sun-crinkled, eyes as black as jet, and large rather Victorian moustaches stained with nicotine. They were wearing the typical peon's outfit: wrinkled, black half-boots with small spurs; *bombachas,* the baggy trousers that hang down over the top of the boot like plus-fours; blouse-like shirts with a brightly coloured handkerchief knotted round the throat, and perched on their heads were the small, black pork-pie hats with narrow brims turned up in front, held on to the head by an elastic band round the back of the head. Their broad leather belts were studded with silver crowns, stars, and other decorations, and from each hung a short but serviceable knife.

As we entered the store they turned to stare at us, not rudely, but with interest. In reply to our greeting in bad Spanish, they grinned broadly and replied courteously. I bought some cigarettes, and we hung around the store, waiting for Carlos and Rafael to appear. Presently there was a jingling of harness, the clop of hooves and the scrunch of wheels, and a small dog-cart came lurching down the road; and in it was our erstwhile interpreter and his brother Carlos. Rafael greeted us with overwhelming enthusiasm, his spectacles flashing like a lighthouse, and introduced us to his brother. Carlos was taller than Rafael, and gave the erroneous impression of being portly. His pale, calm face had a faintly Asiatic look about it, with small dark eyes and glossy black hair. While Rafael hopped about like an excited crow, talking fast and almost incomprehensibly, Carlos quietly and methodically loaded our bags into the cart and then sat patiently waiting for us to climb in. When we were installed he slapped the horses' rumps with the reins, clucked at them affectionately, and the cart trundled down the road. We drove for about half an hour, the road lying as straight as a wand across the vast expanse of grass. Here and there a herd of some hundred head of cattle grazed slowly, knee-deep in the pasture, and over them wheeled the spur-winged plovers on black-and-white wings. In the ditches at the roadside, filled with water and lush plants, ducks fed in small flocks, and rose with a clap of wings as we passed. Presently, Carlos pointed ahead to where a wood of dark trees lay – a black reef across the green of the pampa.

'That is Secunda,' he said, smiling at us, 'ten minutes we'll arrive there.'

'I hope we'll like it,' I said jokingly.

Rafael turned to me, his eyes wide with shocked expression behind his glasses.

'Migosh!' he said, aghast at such a thought, 'of course you will like, Gerry. Secunda is *our estancia*.'

Secunda was a long, low, whitewashed house squatting elegantly between the huge lake on one hand and a thick wood of eucalyptus and cedar of Lebanon on the other. From the back windows you looked out over the placid grey waters of the lake with its faint green rim of pampa; and from the front you looked out at a formal Victorian garden, the clipped box hedges lining the weed-grown path, the small well, its mouth nearly choked with ferns and moss. In odd corners, among the geometrical flower-beds littered with a glowing mass of fallen oranges, the pale statues glimmered in the shade of the cedars. On the lake the black-necked swans swam in droves, like drifting ice-packs on the steel-grey surface, and groups of spoonbills fed among the reed-beds, like heaps of roses among the green. In the cool garden humming-birds hung purring over the well, and among the orange trees and on the path strutted the oven-birds, with inflated chests; and on the flower-beds minute grey doves with mauve eyes fed hurriedly and secretively. There was a silence and peace here of a lost and forgotten world, a silence broken only by the staccato cry of the oven-birds, or the soft stammer of wings as the tiny doves flew up into the eucalyptus.

After we had settled in and unpacked our things, we assembled in the living-room for a conference about our plan of campaign. The first thing I wanted to do was to try to film the rhea, the South American equivalent of the African ostrich. Secunda was one of the few *estancias* within easy reach of Buenos Aires which still had wild flocks of these great birds. I had mentioned this to Rafael in Buenos Aires, and now I asked him what chance there was of locating a flock and filming it.

'Do not worry,' said Rafael complacently. 'Carlos and I have fix everything.'

'Yes,' said Carlos, 'we go look for the *ñandu* this afternoon.'

'Also, I think maybe you like to film the way the peons catch the *ñandu*, no?' asked Rafael.

'How do they catch them?'

'The old way, with the *boleadoras* ... you know, the three balls on a string.'

'Good Lord! yes,' I said enthusiastically. 'I'd love to film that.'

'It is all arrange,' said Carlos. 'This afternoon we go in the cart, the peons go on horses. We find *ñandu*, the peons catch them, you film them. It is good?'

'Wonderful,' I said; 'and if we don't get them today, can we try tomorrow?'

'Of course,' said Rafael.

'We will try and try until we find them,' said Carlos, and the two brothers beamed at each other.

After lunch the small cart appeared, its wheels scrunching softly on the damp gravel. Carlos was driving, slapping the grey horses' buttocks gently with the reins. He pulled up opposite the veranda, jumped to the ground, and walked towards me; the big, fat greys stood with drooping heads, champing thoughtfully on their bits.

'You ready, Gerry?' inquired Carlos.

'Yes, I'm ready. Have the others gone on?'

'Yes, they and Rafael have taken horses ... I get six peons. Is that good?'

'Fine ... All we want now is my wife,' I said, gazing round hopefully.

Carlos sat down on the wall and lit a cigarette.

'Always we wait for womans,' he said philosophically.

A large yellow butterfly drifted over the grey's heads, pausing by their ears as if struck with the thought that they might turn out to be a variety of hairy arum. The greys nodded their heads vigorously, and the butterfly flew off in its drunken, zig-zag way. A humming-bird sped the dark cedars, stopped suddenly in its own length, flew backwards for six inches, turned, and dived at a low swinging cedar branch, where it captured a spider with a minute squeak of triumph, and then shot off between the orange trees. Jacquie appeared on the veranda.

'Hullo!' she said brightly. 'Are you ready?'

'Yes,' said Carlos and I in unison.

'Now, are you sure you've got everything? The ciné, the Rollei, film, exposure meter, lens hood, tripod?'

'Yes, everything,' I said smugly; 'nothing left out, nothing forgotten.'

'What about the umbrella?' she inquired.

'Damn, no. I forgot the umbrella.' I turned to Carlos. 'You haven't got an umbrella I could borrow, have you?'

'Umbrella?' echoed Carlos, mystified.

'Yes, an umbrella.'

'What is this umbrella?' asked Carlos.

It's extremely difficult to think of a good description of an umbrella at a moment's notice.

'It's one of those things you use when it's raining,' I said.

'It folds up,' said Jacquie.

'You open it out again when it rains.'

'It's like a mushroom.'

'Ah!' said Carlos, his face clearing; 'I know.'

'Have you got one?'

Carlos gave me a reproachful look.

'Of course ... I tell you we have everything.'

He disappeared into the house, and returned carrying a Japanese paper parasol decked out in gay colours, with a circumference about half that of a bicycle wheel.

'It is good?' he asked, twirling it proudly so that the colours ran together.

'You haven't got anything bigger, have you?'

'Bigger? No, no bigger. What you want this for, Gerry?'

'To cover the camera, so that the sun doesn't make the film too hot.'

'Ah!' said Carlos. 'Well, this will be good. I will hold it.'

We climbed into the little cart, and Carlos slapped the massive grey rumps with the flat of the reins and chirruped. The greys sighed deeply and sorrowfully and lurched forward. The drive was lined with giant eucalyptus trees, with their bark peeling off in huge twisted strips, showing the gleaming white trunk beneath. In the branches were massive structures, huge matted haystack-like collections of twigs, the tenement nests of the Quaker parrakeets. These slender grass-green birds flew chittering and screaming through the branches as we passed below, and swooped, glittering in the sunshine, into the entrance holes of their enormous communal nests. 'Eeee-hup! eeee-hup!' sang Carlos falsetto, and the greys broke into a shambling trot, snorting affrontedly. We reached the end of the long, tree-lined drive, and there before us lay the pampa, glistening and golden in the afternoon sun. The greys pulled the cart over the dew-soaked grass, weaving in and out among the giant thistles, each standing stiffly, as tall as a man on horseback, like spiky and weird candelabra with the bright purple flame of the flower on each branch. A burrowing owl, like a little grey ghost, did a dance above the mouth of its burrow as we passed: two steps one way, two steps the other; pause, to stare with golden eyes; shake the head from side to side, bob up and down rapidly; then a leap off the ground and a swift circling flight on wings as soft and silent as a cloud.

The cart rumbled and staggered on and, ahead, the pampa stretched to the horizon, a flat, placid sea of golden grass, shadowed in places where the thistles grew more thickly. Here and there, like a small dark wave on that smooth expanse, a small copse of wind-tangled trees gave shade to the cattle. The sky was early morning blue, and great puffy cumulus-clouds moved across it with the speed and dignity of albino snails on a pale window-pane. The thistles grew thicker, and the horses had to weave more and more, to avoid bumping into them and retaining a bellyful of spikes. The wheels crushed the brittle plants down with a noise like miniature musketry. A hare leapt from under the greys' thudding hooves and loped off in a curving run before freezing again and melting into the brownish haze of thistles. Far ahead we could see tiny dark shapes spotted with bright colours... the peons on horseback on the horizon.

They were waiting for me, bunched together in the long grass. Their horses moved restlessly, heads tossing and feet mincing. The peons laughed and chattered together, their brown faces alight with excitement, and, as they swayed and turned on their waltzing horses, the silver medallions that studded their broad leather belts glittered in the sun. Carlos drove our cart into their midst and the greys stopped, heads drooping, emitting loud sighs as of exhaustion. Carlos and the peons worked out our plan of campaign: the peons would split up into two groups, riding spread out into a long line, with the cart at the centre. As soon as the rheas broke cover, they would try to encircle the birds and drive them back to the cart, so that I could get the ciné-camera working.

When the babel had died down a bit: 'D'you think we'll find some *ñandu*, Carlos?'

Carlos shrugged. 'I think so. Rafael say he see them here yesterday. If they not here they will be in the next *potrero*.'

He chirruped to the horses, and they roused themselves from their trance and the cart moved on through the crackling thistle plants. We had not travelled more than fifty feet when one of the outriders let out a long-drawn whoop and waved excitedly at us, pointing ahead at a particularly thick patch of thistles into which the cart was just about to plunge. Carlos pulled the greys up sharply, and we stood on the seat to peer over the thistles, a mist of purple flowers. For a minute we could see nothing, and then Carlos grasped my arm and pointed.

'There, Gerry, see? *ñandu* . . .'

In the maze of thistles with their grey-and-white stalks I could distinguish a bulky form dodging and twisting. The peons had started to close in, when suddenly one of them stood up in his stirrups and waved his hand and shouted.

'What's he saying, Carlos?' I asked.

'He says it *ñandu* with babies,' said Carlos, and, pulling the greys round, he slapped them into a canter, so that the cart bounced and rattled along the side of the thistle-patch. Where the thistles ended and the grass began he pulled up.

'Watch, Gerry, watch; they will come this way,' he said.

We sat watching the tall wall of thistles, listening to the scrunching as the peons' horses forced their way through. Then, suddenly, a tall thistle swayed, cracked, and fell to the ground, and over its prickly carcase a rhea leapt out on to the green grass, with the grace and lightness of a ballet-dancer making an entrance. It was a large male, and he paused for one brief moment after his appearance, so that we could see him. He looked like a small, grey ostrich, with black markings on his face and throat. But his neck and head were not bald and ugly, like the ostrich's, but neatly feathered; his eyes had not the oafish expression of the ostrich, but were large, liquid, and intelligent. He paused for that one brief moment, getting his bearings, and then he saw us. He twirled like a top and was off across the pampa, taking great strides, with his head and neck stretched out in front of him and his great feet almost touching his chin with every step. He seemed to bounce more than run, as though his legs were giant springs causing him to rebound from the earth. Standing upright, he had been some five and a half feet high, but now, running with the speed of a galloping horse, his whole being – body, legs, and neck – was stretched out and streamlined. As he ran, one of the peons crashed through the barrier of thistles and cantered out on to the grass within twenty feet of the flying bird, and we were treated to the sight of a rhea's evasive tactics. As soon as he saw the horse and rider, his head came up, and he seemed to stop dead in the middle of one of his prodigious bounds, twist round in mid-air, and set off in the opposite direction, without any appreciable loss of speed. This time he ran in a zig-zag pattern, each bound taking him six feet to the right, and then six feet to the left, so that from the rear he looked like a gigantic feathered frog.

Just as Carlos was about to urge the greys forward again, the second rhea broke cover. It was a smaller bird, and of a lighter shade of grey, and it bounded through the gap in the thistles that the first one had created, and then skidded to a halt on the grass.

'This one is womans,' whispered Carlos. 'See, she is small.'

The female rhea could see us, but she did not sprint off as the male had done: instead, she stood there, shifting uneasily from one leg to the other, and watching us with large, timid eyes. Suddenly we realized the reason for her delayed flight, for through the thistles scuttled her brood – eleven baby rheas that could not have been much more than a few days old. Their round, fluffy bodies were about half the size of a football, mounted on thick, stumpy legs ending in great splay feet. Their baby down was a light creamy fawn, with neat slate-grey stripes, and they stood about a foot high. They waddled out of the forest of thistles and gathered round their mother's enormous feet, their eyes bright and unafraid, squeaking shrilly to each other. The mother glanced down at them, but it was obviously impossible for her to know by looking at the milling, wasp-striped swarm whether they were all there or not, so she turned and set off across the grass. She ran, as it were, in slow motion, her head up, her big feet thumping the turf with each stride. The babies followed, running as their mother ran, but strung out in a line behind her: the effect was rather ludicrous, for the mother looked like an elderly, rather arty, spinster running for a bus with all the dignity she could muster, trailing behind her a striped feather boa that bobbed and twisted through the grass.

When the rhea family had vanished from view, and Jacquie had finished uttering crooning noises over the appearance of the babies, Carlos started the cart once more and we crackled onwards through the thistles.

'Soon we will see more, the big ones,' said Carlos, and the words were hardly out of his mouth when we saw Rafael galloping towards us, waving his hat, his scarlet scarf trailing out behind. He crashed through the thistles and pulled up alongside the cart, spouting a flood of Spanish and gesturing wildly. Carlos turned to us, his eyes gleaming.

'Rafael say that many *ñandúes* are sitting over there. He says we take this cart and go over there, then Rafael and the other mens will make the *ñandúes* run near us.'

Rafael galloped off to instruct the other horsemen in their part in the plan, while Carlos urged the reluctant greys through the prickly thistles at a gallop. We burst out on to the pampa and thundered across it, the cart swaying so much that I thought it would overturn at any minute. Carlos crouched on the seat, slapping the swaying bottoms of the horses with the reins and uttering shrill nasal cries of encouragement. A pair of spur-wing plover, black and white as two dominos against the green, watched our lurching approach and then ran six feet and leapt lightly into the air, where they flew around on their piebald wings, screaming 'Tero ... tero ... tero ...' as they swooped over us,

warning the creatures of the pampa of our approach. Leaning
precariously out of the swaying cart, I caught a glimpse of the
horsemen about half a mile away, strung out in a line, waiting
for us to reach the right position. The heat from the sun was now
terrific, and the grey's flanks were striped darkly with sweat: the
horizon was blurred and heat-shimmered, as though you looked
at it through a misted glass. Carlos suddenly pulled on the reins
and brought the cart to a standstill.

'Here is good, Gerry. We will take the camera over there,' he
said, pointing. 'The *ñandu* will run this way.'

We scrambled down from the cart, I carrying the camera
and tripod, while Carlos strode ahead armed with the tiny
paper parasol. Jacquie remained in the cart, field-glasses glued
to her eyes, ready to warn us when the rheas broke cover.
Carlos and I walked some fifty yards away from the cart to
a spot where we could command a clear view of a wide
'avenue' of grass between two great thistle patches, and there
I set up the camera, took light readings, and focused, while
Carlos held the ridiculous parasol over me to keep the camera
cool.

'All right,' I said at last, wiping the sweat from my face.

Carlos raised the vivid parasol and waved it from side to
side, and in the distance we could faintly hear the shrill cries of
the peons as they urged their horses into the thistle jungle.
Then there was silence. Since we remained without movement,
the two plovers circled round several times and then landed
near us, where they took sudden darting runs from side to side,
and paused while they bobbed up and down suspiciously.
Jacquie sat immobile in the cart, her hat pushed on to the
back of her head, the glasses to her eyes. The greys stood with
drooping heads, occasionally shifting their weight from one
haunch to the other, like elderly barmaids towards closing
time. I could feel the sweat trickling down my face and back,
and my shirt stuck unpleasantly to me. Suddenly Jacquie
raised her hat and waved it wildly from side to side, at the
same time emitting ear-splitting and incomprehensible instructions to us. At the same moment the two plovers leapt
from the ground and circled round wildly, screaming loudly,

and we could hear the distant cracking of the thistles, the thunder of the horses' hooves and the excited cries of the peons. Then from the thistle-bed appeared the rheas.

I never would have believed that a ground bird could move with the speed and grace of a bird in flight, but I learnt otherwise that morning. There were eight rheas, spread out in roughly a V-formation, and they seemed to be running as fast as they could. Their long legs were moving with such speed that they were blurred, being only clearly defined on the downward stroke when the foot touched the ground and lifted the bird forward. Their necks were stretched out almost straight, and their wings were held away from their bodies and hanging down slightly. Clearly above the noisy screams of the plovers we could hear the rapid and rhythmic thudding of their feet on the iron-hard ground. If it had not been for this, you could have imagined they were on wheels, so swift and effortless was their movement. As I say, they appeared to be running as fast as they were able, but suddenly two peons galloped out of the thistles, uttering shrill whoops, and an amazing thing happened. Each rhea tucked his tail in as though fearing a slap on the rump, and they all accelerated to twice their previous speed in what appeared to be three enormous, splay-footed leaps. Certainly they dwindled into the distance with astonishing rapidity. The peons galloped after them, and I could see one of them loosening the *boleadoras* that hung from his belt.

'Surely they're not going to catch them right over there, Carlos; I can't possibly film them at that distance.'

'No, no,' said Carlos soothingly; 'they will go round them and bring them back. Let us go back to the cart ... there is most shade there.'

'How long will they be rounding them up?'

'Oh, five minutes, maybe.'

We walked back to the cart, where Jacquie in her grandstand seat was bouncing up and down, field-glasses to her eyes, giving onomatopoeic cries of encouragement to the distant hunt. I set the camera up in the small patch of shade cast by the cart, and climbed up beside her.

'What's happening?' I asked, for by now the peons and the quarry were distant specks on the horizon.

'Isn't this exciting?' she cried, retaining a firm hold on the glasses as I tried to take them from her; 'it's terribly exciting. Did you see them run? I didn't know they could run so fast.'

'Let's have a look.'

'All right, all right, in a minute. I just want to see ... Oh, oh, no, no, look out ...'

'What's happened?'

'They tried to break back, but Rafael saw them in time ... Oh, just look at that one running ... Did you ever see anything like it?'

'No,' I said truthfully; 'so what about letting me have a look?'

I prised the glasses from her reluctant grasp and trained them on the distant scene. I could see the rheas dodging and twisting among the thistles with an ease and grace that would have been the envy and despair of a professional footballer. The peons were galloping hither and thither, endeavouring to keep the birds in a fairly tight bunch and drive them back. All the peons now had their *boleadoras* out, and I could see the balls gleaming on the ends of the long strings as they whirled them round and round their heads. The rheas turned in a bunch and ran towards us, and with cries of triumph the peons wheeled their horses and followed. I handed the glasses back to Jacquie and scrambled down to set up the camera. I had scarcely focused when the rheas appeared, running in a tight bunch, straight towards us. At about seventy yards they saw us, and all swerved at right angles at the same moment and with such precision that the move might have been carefully rehearsed. Hot on their heels came the peons, the horses' hooves kicking up lumps of black earth, the *boleadoras* whirling round their heads in a blurred glinting pattern emitting a shrill whistling sound.

The shrill cries, the vibrating thud of the hooves, the whine of the *boleadoras*, and then they were all past, and the noises faded in the distance. Only the plovers flew round and round above us, hysterically calling. Jacquie kept up a running commentary from the cart above.

'Rafael's going to the right with Eduardo ... they're still running ... ah! ... one's broken away to the right and Eduardo after it ... oh, now the whole bunch have scattered ... they're all over the place ... they'll never round them up now ... one of them's going to throw his *boleadoras* ... oh, he's missed ... you should have seen that rhea's swerve ... what on earth's that one doing? ... it's turned right round ... it's coming back ... Rafael's after it ... it's coming back ... it's coming back ...'

I had just lit a cigarette, but had to throw it down and leap for the camera as the rhea came crashing through the thistles. I had thought that there would be a pause of at least a quarter of an hour before the peons succeeded in rounding up the birds, and so, although the camera was wound up, it was not focused, nor had I taken a light reading. But there was no time to remedy the defect, for the bird was bearing down upon us at a speed of twenty miles an hour. I slewed the camera round on the tripod, got the rheas framed in the view-finder and pressed the button, wondering, as I did so, whether anything would come out at all. The rhea was about a hundred and fifty feet away when I started to film, with Rafael fairly close behind. His proximity obviously worried the bird, for it did not seem to notice either the cart or the camera, through which I could see it running straight towards me. It came nearer and nearer, gradually filling the view-finder; I could hear muffled squeaks from Jacquie above me. The rhea kept on coming towards me until the whole of the view-finder was filled. I began to get worried, for the bird did not seem to notice either me or the camera, and I had no particular desire to be hit amidships by a couple of hundred pounds of speeding rhea; uttering a brief prayer, I kept my finger down on the button. The rhea suddenly seemed to notice me for the first time, a ludicrously horrified look came into its eyes and its muscles contracted as it made a sudden wild swerve to the left and disappeared from my vision. I stood up and wiped my forehead.

Jacquie and Carlos were regarding me owlishly from the safety of the cart.

'How close did it get?' I asked, for it was difficult to tell whilst filming.

'It swerved when it got to that tuft of grass there,' said Jacquie.

I paced from the tripod to the tuft of grass. It was just under six feet.

The rhea's wild swerve was its undoing, for Rafael was so close behind that even that slight deviation lost it several yards of its lead. Rafael, urging his sweat-stained horse to a terrific effort, overhauled the flying bird and turned it back towards the camera. The rhea came scudding back, and this time I was ready. I could hear the whine of the *boleadoras* reach a crescendo ending in a sort of long-drawn 'wheep'. The cord and the balls flew flailing through the air, wound themselves with octopus-like skill round the legs and neck of the flying bird. It ran for two more steps, then the cord tightened and it fell to the ground, legs and wings thrashing. Rafael, uttering a long-drawn cry of triumph, pulled up alongside it and was down in a second, grasping the kicking legs that could easily have disembowelled him if his grip had loosened. The rhea struggled briefly and then lay still. Carlos, dancing triumphantly on the seat of the cart, whooped long and loud to tell the other peons we had been successful, and when they galloped up we all gathered round our quarry.

It was a large bird, with great muscular thighs like a ballerina's. In contrast, the wing-bones were fragile and soft, for they could be bent like a green twig. The eyes were enormous, almost covering the side of the skull, fringed with thick, film-star-like eyelashes. The large feet with their four toes were thick and powerful. The centre toe was the longest, and it was armed with a long, curved claw. Whether the bird kicked from the back or the front, this claw met its adversary first, and acted with the slashing, tearing qualities of a sharp knife. The feathers, which were quite long, looked more like elongated fronds of grey fern. When I had examined the bird, and taken some close-ups of it, we unwound the *boleadoras* from its legs and neck. It lay for a moment in the grass, and then suddenly

190

its strong legs shot it to its feet, and it bounced off through the thistles, gathering speed as it ran.

We turned the cart round and started back towards Secunda and a meal. The peons, laughing and chattering, rode close around us, their belts glittering in the sun, their bits and bridles jangling musically. The horses were black with sweat, but though they must obviously have been tired, their step was jaunty and light, and they bickered and snapped skittishly at each other. The greys, who had done little but stand between the shafts all afternoon, plodded onwards as though at the end of their strength. Behind us the pampa stretched, limitless, golden, and quiet. In the distance two black-and-white specks rose above the grass briefly, and very faintly I could hear the voice of the pampa, the shrill warning to all the living creatures that lived there, the cry of the ever-watchful plovers: 'Tero ... tero ... tero ... teroterotero ...'

ADIOS!

IT was nearing the day of departure. With the utmost reluctance
we had to leave the *estancia* Secunda, taking with us the animals
we had caught: armadillos, opossums, and a handful of nice
birds. We travelled back to Buenos Aires in the train, the
animals accompanying us in the luggage van. With these new
additions our collection began to look *more* like a collection and
less like the remnants from a pet-shop sale. But we still had very
few birds, and, as I knew that Argentina contains some extremely
interesting species, this gap in our collection irritated me.

Then, the day before we sailed, I remembered something that
Bebita had told me, so I phoned her up.

'Bebita, didn't you say you knew of a bird shop somewhere
in Buenos Aires?'

'A b-b-bird shop? Ahhh, yes, there is one I have seen. It is
somewhere near the station.'

'Will you take me and show me?'

'B-b-but naturally. Come to lunch, and we will go afterwards.'

After a prolonged lunch, Bebita, Jacquie, and I climbed into
a taxi and sped through the wide streets in search of the bird

shop. We ran it to earth, eventually, on one side of an enormous square which was lined with hundreds of tiny stalls, selling
meat, vegetables, and other produce. The shop was large, and,
to our delight, contained an extensive and varied stock. Slowly
we walked round staring avidly into cages that pulsated with
birds of all shapes, sizes, and colours. The proprietor, who
looked like an unsuccessful all-in-wrestler, followed us around
with a predatory gleam in his black eyes.

'Have you decided what you want?' inquired Bebita.

'Yes, I know what I want, but it's a question of price. The
owner does not look as though he's going to be reasonable.'

Bebita, tall, elegantly clad, turned her amused gaze on to
the squat owner of the store. Taking off her gloves, she placed
them carefully on a sack of bird seed, and then smiled dazzlingly
at the man. He blushed and ducked his head in salute. Bebita
turned to me.

'He looks so *sweet*,' she said, and really meant it.

Still unused to Bebita's ability to see something divine in
people who looked to me as though they would cheerfully
deliver their own mothers to the knackers' yard for half a
crown, I just gaped at the villainous pet-shop owner.

'Well,' I said at last, 'he doesn't look sweet to *me*.'

'B-b-but I'm sure he is an angel,' said Bebita firmly; 'now,
you just show me the b-b-birds you want and I will talk with
him.'

Feeling that this was quite the wrong way to start a bargain,
I led her round the cages again and pointed out the specimens,
some of which were so unusual that they made my mouth
water just to look at them. Bebita then asked me how much I
was prepared to pay for them, and I named a price which I
thought was fair without being exorbitant. Bebita floated over to
the owner, turned him scarlet again with another smile, and in a
gentle voice – the sort of voice which you use for talking with
angels – she started to discuss the purchase of the birds. As her
voice went on, punctuated now and then by an eager '*Si, si,
señora*' from the owner, Jacquie and I wandered round the
darker and less accessible parts of the shop. Eventually, some
twenty minutes later, we drifted back. Bebita still stood among

the dirty cages like a visiting goddess, while the proprietor had seated himself on a sack of seed and was mopping his face. His '*Si, si, señora,*' which still accompanied Bebita's discourse, had lost its first enthusiasm, and was now more doubtful. Suddenly he shrugged, threw out his hands and smiled up at her. Bebita looked at him fondly as though he had been her only son.

'*B-b-bueno,*' she said, '*muchísimas gracias, señor.*'

'*De nada, señora,*' he replied.

Bebita turned to me.

'I have b-b-bought them for you,' she said.

'Good. What's the damage?'

Bebita then named a price which was a quarter of what I said I was willing to pay.

'But Bebita, that's highway robbery,' I said incredulously.

'No, no, child,' she said earnestly; 'all these b-b-birds are very common here, so it's silly for you to pay too much. B-b-besides, the man is, as I said, an angel, and he likes reducing his price for me.'

'I give up,' I said resignedly. 'Would you like to come on my next trip with me? You'd save me pounds.'

'Silly, silly, silly,' said Bebita, chuckling, 'I didn't save you pounds; it was this man that you said looked so awful.'

I glared at her, and then made a dignified retreat to choose my birds and cage them. When this was done, a mountainous pile of cages done up in brown paper stood on the counter. Having paid the man, amid the usual exchange of '*gracias*', I then asked him, through Bebita, whether he ever had any waterfowl for sale.

Not waterfowl, he replied, but he had some other, similar birds, which the señor might be interested in. He led us through a door at the back of the shop out to a tiny lavatory. Throwing open the door, he pointed, and I only just managed to stifle the exclamation of delight that rose to my lips, for there, crouched on either side of the lavatory, were two dirty, exhausted, but still beautiful black-necked swans. Trying to appear unconcerned, I examined them. They were both very thin, and seemed to have reached the stage of weakness which is characterized by complete apathy and lack of fear. In any other circumstances I would not have dreamt of buying such decrepit birds, but I knew that this was my last chance to obtain any of these swans. Apart from this, I felt that if they were going to die, at least they should die in comfort; to leave those lovely birds languishing by the side of a lavatory pan was more than I was able to do. Bebita therefore went into battle again, and after some stiff bargaining the swans were mine. Then came a problem, for the owner had no cages big enough to transport them. At length we unearthed two sacks, and the swans were encased in them, with their heads sticking out. Then, collecting up our purchases, we were bowed out of the shop by the owner. Once outside, a sudden thought came to me.

'And how are we going to get to Belgrano?' I asked.

'We will get a taxi,' said Bebita.

I had a swan under each arm, and felt rather as Alice must have felt when she took part in the famous croquet match with the flamingoes.

'We won't get in a taxi with this lot,' I said; 'they're not allowed to carry livestock . . . We've had this trouble before.'

'Wait here and I will find a taxi,' said Bebita, and she floated across the road to the rank, picked out the car with the most unsympathetic and unsavoury-looking driver, and brought him round to where we were standing.

For one startled moment he stared at the sacks under my arm, from which the swans' heads protruded like albino pythons, then he turned to Bebita.

'These are *bichos*,' he said; 'we are forbidden to carry *bichos*.' Bebita smiled at him.

'But if you did not *know* we had *b-b-bichos* you would not be to b-b-blame,' she explained.

The taxi-driver reeled under the smile, but was not quite convinced.

'But one can see they are *bichos*,' he protested.

'Only these,' said Bebita, pointing at the swans, 'and if they were in the b-b-boot you would not see them.'

The taxi-man grunted sceptically.

'All right, but I haven't seen anything, remember. If they stop us I shall deny all knowledge.'

So, with the swans in the boot and the front seat piled high with cages from which came a chorus of flutterings and twitterings which the taxi-man endeavoured to ignore, we drove towards Belgrano.

'How d'you manage to get these taxi-men to do what you want?' I asked. 'I can't even get them to carry *me* sometimes, let alone a menagerie.'

'But they are so sweet,' said Bebita, regarding with affection the fat neck of our driver; 'they will always try and help.'

I sighed; Bebita had a magic touch which no one else could attempt to emulate. The irritating part was that, when she made the obviously ludicrous statement that some person who looked like a fugitive from a chain gang was an angel, he then proceeded to act just like one. It was all very puzzling.

This load of last-minute specimens created several difficulties for us. Before we could get on the ship the following afternoon, we had to have them all caged properly, and this was no easy job. A frantic phone call brought Carlos and Rafael scurrying to Belgrano, bringing with them their cousin Enrique. We rushed out in a body to the local wood-yard, and while I drew designs of the sort of cages I wanted, the carpenter worked his circular saw frantically, cutting out pieces of plywood to the correct dimensions. Then, staggering under the weight, we carried the wood back to the house in Belgrano and set about nailing it into cages. By half past eleven that night we had succeeded in caging a quarter of the birds. Seeing that it was going to be an all-night job, we sent Jacquie back to the hotel, so that in the morning, when we would feel terrible, she would feel rested and refreshed and able to cope with feeding the animals. Carlos made a rapid pilgrimage to a nearby café and returned with hot coffee, rolls, and a bottle of gin. Consuming these supplies, we carried on with our cage-making. At ten to twelve there came a knock on the outside door.

'This,' I said to Carlos, 'is the first outraged neighbour wanting to know what the hell we're hammering at this hour of night ... You'd better go; that gin hasn't done my Spanish any good.'

Carlos returned soon, and with him was a thin bespectacled man with a marked American accent who introduced himself as

Adios!

Mr Hahn, the Buenos Aires correspondent of the *Daily Mirror* – of all things.

'I heard that you all escaped from the Paraguayan revolution by the skin of your teeth, and I wondered if you'd care to give me the story,' he explained.

'Certainly,' I said, hospitably pulling up a cage for him to sit on, and pouring him a cupful of gin. 'What would you like to know?'

He smelt the gin suspiciously, glanced into the cage before seating himself, and took out a notebook.

'Everything,' he said firmly.

So I started to relate the story of our Paraguayan journey, my highly coloured account being interrupted by bursts of hammering, sawing, and even louder bursts of Spanish oaths from Carlos, Rafael, and Enrique. At length, Mr Hahn put his notebook away.

'I think,' he said, taking off his coat and rolling up his shirt sleeves – '*I think* I could concentrate better on your story if I had some more gin and joined in this woodcutters' ball.'

So throughout the night, fortified by gin, coffee, rolls, and bursts of song, Carlos, Rafael, Enrique, myself, and the Buenos Aires correspondent of the *Daily Mirror* laboured to finish the cages. By the time the first coffee-shops opened at five-thirty we had finished. After a quick coffee, I crawled back to the hotel and flung myself on the bed to try to get some rest before starting for the docks.

Our lorry, with Carlos and Rafael perched on top and Jacquie and I in the cab, rolled on to the docks alongside the ship at two-thirty. By four o'clock nearly everyone in the place, including several interested bystanders, had examined our export permits. At four-thirty they told us we could carry the stuff on board. It was then that something occurred which might not only have put paid to the trip entirely, but finished me off as well. They were loading enormous bales of skins, which, for some obscure reason, were being swung on to the ship over the gangway up which we had to carry our animals. I descended from the lorry, took the cage containing Cai, the monkey, in my arms, and was just about to tell Carlos to carry Sarah himself, when something that felt

197

like a howitzer shell caught me across the back and thighs, lifted me into the air and hurled me flat on my face some twenty feet from where I had been standing. The shock of this was indescribable. As I soared through the air, I could not even imagine what it was that had delivered such a blow. Then I hit the ground and rolled over. My back was numb, my left thigh was aching savagely, so that I was sure it was broken, and I was shaking so much with the shock that I could not even stand when a horrified Carlos tried to get me to my feet. It was five minutes before I could stand upright and discover to my relief that my leg was not broken. Even then my hands were shaking so much that I could not hold a cigarette, and Carlos had to do it for me. While I sat and tried to control my nerves, Carlos explained what had happened. A crane-driver had swung a bale of skins off the dock, but had kept them too low. Instead of clearing the heavy wooden gangway, they had struck it amidships, and then the bale of skins and the gangway had swept along the docks and hit me. Luckily, this murderous missile had almost reached the end of its swing when it struck me, or else I should have been split in half like a soft banana.

'I must say,' I pointed out shakily to Carlos, 'it's not the sort of farewell I expected of Argentina.'

Eventually the animals were safely stowed on deck, with tarpaulins over them, and we could go down to the smoking-room, where all our friends were gathered. We drank and talked with them in the usual bright and rather inane way that one does when one knows that parting is imminent. Then, at last, the time came when they had to go ashore. We stood by the rail and watched our string of friends go down the gangway and then assemble in a crowd on the docks. We could just see them in the fast-gathering dusk: Carlos's moon face and the flash of his wife's dark hair; Rafael and Enrique with their gaucho hats tilted on the backs of their heads; Marie Rene and Mercedes waving handkerchiefs; Marie Mercedes looking more like a Dresden shepherdess than ever in the dim light; and Bebita, tall, beautiful, and calm. Her voice came to us clearly as the ship drew away.

'Good journey, children; b-b-but don't forget to come back.'

Adios!

We waved and nodded and then, as our friends started to disappear into the fast-gathering dusk, the air was full of the most mournful sound in the world: the deep, lugubrious roar of the siren, the sound of a ship saying good-bye.

ACKNOWLEDGEMENTS

BRITAIN

Our trip would have had little hope of maturing had it not been for the enthusiasm and kindness of Dr Derisi, the former Argentine Ambassador in London, who gave the whole plan his official blessing and helped in a variety of ways. Mr Peter Newborn, of the Argentine Embassy, was most helpful and gave us much valuable advice on complicated matters of currency and custom permits.

At the Foreign Office, Mr Hiller gave us much valuable help and advice.

Mr Peter Scott and the Severn Wildfowl Trust also gave us much assistance and provided us with numerous introductions.

At the B.B.C. the following people gave us help and advice on sound-recording equipment, and also supplied us with letters of introduction: Mrs Nesta Pain, Mr Laurence Gilliam, Mr Leonard Cottrell, and Mr W. O. Galbraith.

Miss Rosemary Clifford of the Latin-American Department of the Central Office of Information did a great deal towards smoothing our path on arrival in Buenos Aires.

Mr Norman Zimmern gave us many valuable introductions in South America.

Messrs A. P. Manners Ltd of Bournemouth were most courteous and helpful in advising us on photographic equipment and in developing our films.

To Joseph Gundry & Co of Bridport go our thanks for making a number of flight-nets in record time, all of which were excellent.

ARGENTINA

We should like to express our gratitude to Señor Apold and Señor Vasquez of the Ministry of Information.

At the Ministry of Agriculture the following people gave us help without which we could have achieved very little: Señor Hogan, the Minister of Agriculture; Dr Lago, Secretary General, and Dr Godoy, who was in charge of the Department of Animal Conservation, and who was so efficient and helpful over our collecting permits.

We met with nothing but courtesy and efficiency from all officials during our stay in Argentina, and we should like to thank all those members of the Airport, Docks, and Customs with whom we came in contact.

The Drunken Forest

The Head of the Aduana was extremely kind in granting us import and export licences for our weird assortment of equipment.

At the British Embassy our thanks go to the former Ambassador, Sir Henry Bradshaw Mack, K.C.M.G.; Mr Allan, First Secretary; Mr Stephen Lockhart, Head of Chancery; Mr King, the Consul-General; Mr Leadbitter, First Secretary of Information. Our very special thanks go to Mr George Gibbs, assuredly the most long-suffering Assistant Secretary for Information that any Embassy has ever had. He managed to cope successfully with problems so far removed from his job as the best way to bottle-feed an ant-eater while on an aerodrome, and the cheapest place to buy wire-netting. He was throughout our stay a tower of strength, and we are for ever in his debt. Also of the Embassy we should like to thank Mr Kelly, Mr Roquet, who sorted out our photographic problems, and Mr O'Brien, who arranged all our baggage difficulties.

We should also like to thank the Blue Star Line for allowing us to bring our animals back on one of their ships. Mr Wilson, the Manager, and Mr Fraser, the Passenger Manager, at their Buenos Aires office did everything they could to help us. Captain Horne and the whole crew of the *Uruguay Star* went out of their way to make our return voyage as pleasant as possible.

In Argentina we had so much help and kindness shown to us that the list is necessarily a long one. We should like to thank the following:

Mrs Lassie Greenslet, who so kindly put her delightful Buenos Aires flat at our disposal, in which we stayed for so long she must have wondered if she was ever going to get rid of us. Her sister, Mrs Puleston, was most kind to us, and we are indebted to their niece, Miss Ada Osborn, for some nice specimens she collected for us.

Mr Ian Gibson for acting as our guide and assistant. Mr and Mrs Boote and their family for allowing us to stay on their delightful *estancia* and for displaying such enthusiasm in helping us with our work. Mr Donald McIver, who gave us a lot of very valuable assistance in collecting and putting transport at our disposal. Mr William Partridge of the Natural History Museum, who supplied us with much information on bird distribution and who put at our disposal the magnificent series of skins he had collected from various parts of Argentina. Mr Carr-Vernon of Western Union, who gave us many facilities.

Marie Mercedes De Soto Acebal, her husband, and family showed us such kindness during our stay in Argentina that it is impossible for us to thank them adequately. The youngest son, Rafael, accompanied us to Paraguay, and without his help we would have achieved very little. When in Buenos Aires, and also when staying on their *estancia,*

Acknowledgements

the rest of the family readily devoted their time and energies to help us with our work, and we could not have wished for more delightful assistants and friends.

Bebita Fanny de Llambi de Campbell de Ferreyra, her husband, and their family were wonderful to us during our stay. We practically lived at their flat, and Bebita herself did more than any other one person towards making our stay in Argentina such a happy one. I have repaid her very uncharitably by portraying her in the preceding pages. Her brother, Boy de Llambi de Campbell, and his wife, Bebe, were also charming to us, and without their assistance on our Paraguayan venture we would not have obtained some of our best specimens.

The President and the ladies of the Twentieth Century Club of Buenos Aires showed us lavish hospitality and much courage in inviting me to address them.

I should like to make a special point of thanking all those peons and other workers on the *estancias*, Los Ingleses and Secunda, for the generous way in which they gave up their spare time to helping us.

PARAGUAY

In Paraguay we should like to thank Captain Sarmaniego and Señor Axxolini, who both showed us much kindness and assisted us in many ways.

We should also like to thank Braniff Airways, who took over so competently the last stage of our retreat from Paraguay.

Last but not least I should like to thank Sophie, my secretary, who did so much of the donkey work in the preparation of the manuscript without being able to share in the pleasures of the trip.

FOR THE BEST IN PAPERBACKS, LOOK FOR THE 🐧

In every corner of the world, on every subject under the sun, Penguin represents quality and variety – the very best in publishing today.

For complete information about books available from Penguin – including Puffins, Penguin Classics and Arkana – and how to order them, write to us at the appropriate address below. Please note that for copyright reasons the selection of books varies from country to country.

In the United Kingdom: Please write to *Dept E.P., Penguin Books Ltd, Harmondsworth, Middlesex, UB7 0DA.*

If you have any difficulty in obtaining a title, please send your order with the correct money, plus ten per cent for postage and packaging, to *PO Box No 11, West Drayton, Middlesex*

In the United States: Please write to *Dept BA, Penguin, 299 Murray Hill Parkway, East Rutherford, New Jersey 07073*

In Canada: Please write to *Penguin Books Canada Ltd, 2801 John Street, Markham, Ontario L3R 1B4*

In Australia: Please write to the *Marketing Department, Penguin Books Australia Ltd, P.O. Box 257, Ringwood, Victoria 3134*

In New Zealand: Please write to the *Marketing Department, Penguin Books (NZ) Ltd, Private Bag, Takapuna, Auckland 9*

In India: Please write to *Penguin Overseas Ltd, 706 Eros Apartments, 56 Nehru Place, New Delhi, 110019*

In the Netherlands: Please write to *Penguin Books Nederland B.V., Postbus 195, NL–1380AD Weesp*

In West Germany: Please write to *Penguin Books Ltd, Friedrichstrasse 10–12, D–6000 Frankfurt/Main 1*

In Spain: Please write to *Longman Penguin España, Calle San Nicolas 15, E–28013 Madrid*

In Italy: Please write to *Penguin Italia s.r.l., Via Como 4, I-20096 Pioltello (Milano)*

In France: Please write to *Penguin Books Ltd, 39 Rue de Montmorency, F-75003 Paris*

In Japan: Please write to *Longman Penguin Japan Co Ltd, Yamaguchi Building, 2–12–9 Kanda Jimbocho, Chiyoda-Ku, Tokyo 101*

JERSEY WILDLIFE PRESERVATION TRUST

Gerald Durrell writes:

Have you enjoyed this Book?

If you have, it is the animals that have made this possible; and these animals are not just characters in a book: They *really* exist. But many of them will not exist for much longer unless they have your help.

All over the world the wildlife that I write about is in grave danger. It is being exterminated by what we call the progress of civilization. A great number of creatures will become extinct in a very short time if something is not done, and done swiftly.

Some time ago I created on the Island of Jersey a zoological park which is now the headquarters of the Jersey Wildlife Preservation Trust. Our aim is to create a sanctuary in which we can establish breeding colonies of these threatened species, so that, even if they become extinct in the wild state, they will not vanish forever.

To do this work money is required.

Therefore we need as many members as possible to join the Trust. It will cost you little, but you will be helping a cause that is of the utmost importance and urgency. I say 'urgency' advisedly, because, as you read this, yet another species is added to the danger list.

If the animals I write about have given you pleasure, please join the Trust. The animals will be greatly indebted for every subscription received.

Full particulars can be obtained from:

The Secretary,
Jersey Wildlife Preservation Trust,
Les Augres Manor,
JERSEY, Channel Islands.

BY THE SAME AUTHOR

Three Singles to Adventure

Takes the reader to South America, where Durrell meets the sacki-winki and the green sloth, hears the horrifying sound of the piranha fish on the rampage, and learns how to lasso a galloping ant-eater. 'Stuffed with exquisitely ridiculous situations' – *Spectator*

The Whispering Land

Patagonia this time, where penguins and elephant seals make way for an absurd family of foxes who dance gracefully with a roll of lavatory paper, and Durrell baits a trap for a vampire bat with his own toes.

A Zoo in my Luggage

The author and his wife, back from the Cameroons, face a problem when they find themselves back at home with Cholmondely the chimpanzee, Bug-eye the bush-baby, and other equally exotic creatures, and nowhere to put them.

Other titles published

THE BAFUT BEAGLES
MY FAMILY AND OTHER ANIMALS
ENCOUNTERS WITH ANIMALS
MENAGERIE MANOR